The Second Face of Valor

The Second Face of Valor

By Ray Grant Toepfer

CHILTON BOOKS
A Division of Chilton Company
Publishers
Philadelphia and New York

To Edie, with love

Contents

Contents

The Second Face of Valor

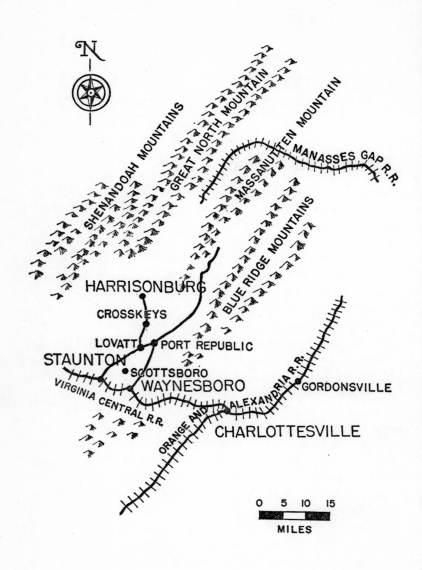

CHAPTER 1

The Last Snow of the Winter

OUTSIDE Grandfather Hauser's window, the snow was falling in huge, unreal clots. Already the day was darkening, and when sixteen-year-old Thomas Tanner stole a glance at the French clock on the mantel, it lacked but ten minutes to five, the hour at which his lesson would end. The hour had been set after much discussion between his father, who insisted that Tom be properly washed and brushed before supper, and his grandfather, who maintained that two hours a day was all too little time to devote to the study of the classics.

The arrangement, whereby Tom studied with his grandfather, had begun during vacation periods from the academy, in order to prepare him for college and the study of law. When the war had broken out two years ago, in the spring of '61, the custom had been extended to include the study of law in the early afternoon, so that Tom would not lose too much time before he went to the army.

With a stately, yet graceful pattern of chimes, the clock announced the end of the study period. The door opened and Grandfather Hauser walked in. As though mistrustful of the clock, he fished in his pocket for the big gold repeater he had carried since his graduation from Harvard College, forty-five years before. A large, heavy man, he was no longer an active practitioner of law. He took a case now and then to keep his hand in, as he put it,

1

but his chief income derived from the rental of farm lands which he had shrewdly acquired over the years.

"How did it go today, Thomas?"

"Pretty well, sir. What happened when Troy fell?"

Grandfather Hauser chuckled. "Read it and find out."

"Why did it fall?"

"The Greeks sent in a wooden horse filled with soldiers. You read about that."

"Yes, sir. Could that happen to us?"

"What do you mean?"

"Well, if the Yankees sent in people who pretended to be Confederates, couldn't they beat us?"

Grandfather Hauser drew himself up to full height. "We won't let them. We've already had a few spies, and we've caught them and dealt with them in the proper fashion."

Tom smothered a grin. It was typical of Grandfather Hauser to turn to rhetoric over some great, but impersonal issue. Yet he was invariably calm when some crisis arose within the family.

"You forget about spies and run on home, boy. It's getting dark. I'll check your translation tonight."

Tom entered another world as soon as he opened the door to the outside. The snow was falling heavily out of a gray Virginia sky, and the tiny lights of lamps or candles were already starring the windows of other houses in the village. Winter was a lonely time, and this winter had been lonelier than usual. His elder brother Ambrose—Sandy for short—was away with the Confederate Army; Will, the eldest of the three, had been killed at First Manassas a year and a half ago. Will had been a ministerial student. Sandy had been in his last year at William and Mary when he joined the army; when the war was over, he intended to become a doctor, like his father. Long ago Tom had decided to be a lawyer.

2

The village of Lovatt looked particularly defenseless in the snow. It would be an easy matter for Federal cavalry to take the town. For that matter, even a band of outlaws could ride in and loot and murder and burn with impunity. The town had no defense worthy of the name.

In the first year of the war, they had all been confident that sixty days would see the newborn Confederacy firmly established, with an army capable of protecting its territory. Instead, the war had dragged on for an intolerable time; it would be two years in April since the first gun had been fired at Sumter.

The last light of the village faded in the gloom behind Tom to the north, and for a moment he was alone with the trees and the snow, and the fields haphazardly marked by erratic stone fences.

Lovatt was a small hamlet that had grown around the tavern which had been built at the intersection of the Shenandoah Valley Pike and the Port Republic road shortly after the War of Independence. Flanking or facing the tavern were upward of a dozen homes or shops, all of neat frame construction, painted white, and faded or stained to varying shades of gray or even yellow, according to the original quality of their paint and their angle of exposure to the winds that howled down from Great North Mountain, only five miles to the west.

Grandfather Hauser's house was a hundred yards north of McNair's tavern and just across the road from the timber yard, which was north of Mrs. Ryan's bake shop. The bake shop was just north of the tavern and on the same side of the road. Still further north on the Pike, which connected Staunton on the south with Harrisonburg on the north, were the residence of Reverend Harmon and the Methodist church.

Beyond them stood the Barnes house, a red brick box of indeterminate age and no particular grace. Sally Lou Barnes was Sandy's best girl.

3

It was just about a mile from Grandpa's house south to Center Creek; Tom had often heard his father say as much in the course of the many and interminable arguments concerning distance, boundaries, and how long it should take a man to walk a mile that Doctor Tanner enjoyed with his father-in-law. Tom's home was just about halfway between Grandpa's and the creek.

He passed a tree on his left, and suddenly the house loomed solid and tangible in the eddying snow. Originally, the house had been built foursquare, but Doctor Tanner had added a one-story ell at the rear which housed the pantry, the summer kitchen, and the laundry. Downstairs were the dining room, the front and rear parlors, and Doctor Tanner's office and consultation room. The second floor was occupied by four bed chambers and a connecting hallway. The rooms bore a striking similarity, one to another; all were square, all had corner fireplaces, due to the location of the two main chimneys, which had served all of the rooms in the original house.

The building had been erected some sixty years before by the youngest son of a Tidewater planter who had attempted to farm. In the course of time, it had fallen into disuse until Tom's Grandfather Hauser had acquired it and given it to Tom's parents as a wedding present. In the twenty-two years that the Tanners had owned it, the house had received semiannual coats of whitewash, designed to mitigate the harsh rose color of the brick walls. The whitewash never remained for long; soon after each application, rain would wash off enough of it to expose a blurred, pink ghost of the original color.

Now the front door opened, spilling yellow lamplight across the snow-covered steps, and Tom saw his mother peering out into the gloom. She was something like the house, he thought; never changing, always dependable.

She leaned forward now, cupping her hand to shield

4

the chimney of the lamp she held. "What're you doing out there, Tom? We're waiting supper for you."

Small boned and still slender, she held the door open for him. Her heavy black hair was gathered in a simple and unfashionable knot at the back of her head. Humor crinkled the corners of her mouth. "Pa give you a good lesson?"

He kissed her cheek. "I think so. He didn't throw any books at me."

"That's a good sign," she smiled. "Now you get washed. Your father is hungry, and he won't eat without you."

As Tom passed the head of the stairs, he saw that the door of William's room was ajar. The light from his candle reflected from a clean counterpane and gleamed on the spotless floor. Although Will had been dead well over a year, Mama saw to it that Betsy cleaned the room as often and as thoroughly as she did the other rooms. It was eerie in a way; the room was kept just as Will had left it on his last visit home. It was as if Mama expected him to return at any moment.

He put down the candlestick beside the mirror on the washstand and splashed icy water from his pitcher into the basin. As he soaped his hands with the yellow sliver from the dish, he could hear the pad of Betsy's footsteps carrying hot dishes from the kitchen to the dining room. From the rear parlor came the rumble of his father's voice reading something aloud.

For a moment he sputtered as the water burned his face, and then he toweled vigorously to send the blood racing back into circulation. He dampened his hairbrush slightly with the soapy water and turned to the mirror.

Presently a pleasant-faced young man looked back at him from the mirror. Somewhat curly chestnut hair surmounted a sallow face with high cheekbones and a determined chin. If only I were older, he thought despair-

5

ingly. Sandy was a captain already, and he was—still a schoolboy!

If he were eighteen, he could join the army without Pa's permission. He would never get it, he knew; both his parents had forbidden discussion of the subject since Will's death. "We'll talk about it when you're eighteen," Pa had said. But he dreamed of it. In his imagination he was in Sandy's battery, perhaps an officer directing the fire of the guns under Sandy's watchful eye. His uniform was of fine, gray cadet cloth, and he wore a scarlet sash under his swordbelt . . .

"Thomas!" His father's voice boomed from the floor below. "We're hungry, boy!"

His parents were already seated when he came into the dining room. He took his place on the side of the table, opposite the green-shaded, cut-glass lamp that rested in the exact center of the linen cloth.

"Bless us, O Lord," Pa began, and he folded his hands.

Betsy stood in the shadows near the kitchen door, her dark face bent, her hands trembling slightly with barely-suppressed excitement. Prayers were the most important part of Betsy's life. Each day was marked by prayers and the periods of work that lay between them. In her youth, Betsy had been owned by a devout Presbyterian who had successfully indoctrinated her with the tenets of his denomination. She remained somewhat scornful of the Tanners' Methodism, considering it too lax by comparison with the faith of her former owner.

Betsy had been with the Tanners since their marriage, twenty-two years before. Mr. Hauser had bought her as a gift for Tom's mother, and Doctor Tanner had promptly manumitted her, declaring that he had never owned a slave and that he would not begin now.

Betsy stood her ground. She had heard how the white folks in big cities rounded up all the free Negroes who

6

couldn't find work and put them in jail and made them work for nothing. It was better to work for a kind master. An agreement was reached whereby Betsy stayed on to help with the children and do the cooking and the housework in return for her food, shelter, clothing, and twenty dollars a year. It was a satisfactory arrangement on all sides.

"Amen," Doctor Tanner said, as he reached for the carving knife. "Well, Tom. How did it go today?"

"Pretty well, sir."

"Splendid. Your grandfather is an excellent mentor. You may count yourself fortunate."

"I'm sure Tom does," his mother said smoothly. "Even if Father is a little overbearing at times."

Doctor Tanner grinned. "Now that you mention it, my dear, I'm inclined toward the same opinion. Just this morning he stopped me on my way to set a broken leg. I couldn't get away for a good ten minutes."

"Perhaps you answered him, sir," Tom said solemnly. "That generally seems to give him a fresh start."

"Don't be disrespectful, boy," Doctor Tanner said mildly. "But you may have a point. I did offer an objection or two when he gave his opinion that the war might last another two years."

"And you don't think so, dear?" Tom's mother asked.

Doctor Tanner's attention was successfully diverted from his father-in-law. His favorite subject was the war. One of its most pleasant subdivisions was the impossibility of the opponents carrying on a senseless slaughter longer than the end of the next summer. By that time, he thought, both sides would have had enough. They would be willing to sit down and resolve their differences over a conference table.

"It isn't slavery, for most of us," he was saying. "We don't deny the moral injustice of the institution, here in

7

the Valley. It's a question of coercion. We cannot let those people in the North dictate to us."

Doctor Tanner had been opposed to slavery for a long time. The youngest of five brothers, he had been raised on an impoverished Carolina plantation. He had seen at first hand the wasteful misuse of land coupled with economic decay that the system involved. He could remember the lavish days when the plantation was new and compare his memories with the worn-out land going back to slash pine. If you were big enough, it didn't matter. You moved on to virgin fields and began the process all over again. You maintained the original holding as a showplace, out of sheer sentiment. Tobacco land worn out in Virginia? Set up in Georgia. Cotton does right well in Georgia. Mighty good money in Louisiana, should you fancy sugar. But you needed slaves, cheap labor. And if anyone said cheap was dear, you paid him no mind. You just had to keep growing; that was the secret. If you stopped growing, the system didn't work.

The Tanners had not grown. The land produced less and less tobacco, and the quality deteriorated as well. The slaves still had to be fed and clothed, the aged and infirm as well as the able-bodied. It was an oft-repeated tale to which there could be but one ending. The ending occurred in the summer of 1830, with the death of Joseph Tanner's father.

Daniel, the eldest brother, sold the estate. It was his to sell or retain, as he pleased. He divided the proceeds of the sale equally among the others. As for himself, he was going west, he said. A man could pick up land for a song out in Tennessee. John, Matthew, and Henry pooled their funds to invest in a Mississippi land company. And Joseph went to medical school.

Joseph Tanner did not have the illusion of his older brothers that a fortune could be recouped by speculation.

8

He was too young to have sampled the easy nectar of adult life on a prosperous plantation. He only knew that what had been was no more, and that there was no security beyond that which a man could make with his own hands.

If he had needed an additional reason for preferring to place his future in his own capable hands rather than those of a bevy of slaves, he found it in his religion. He had become converted to Methodism early in his study of medicine. Since he had been in the North at that time, he followed the teaching of that branch of the persuasion, which held that human bondage was immoral.

But Tom thought that Pa's arguments against slavery or against the probability of a long war never seemed to ring true. They were arguments and nothing more. For a thing to be true, you had to believe in it with all your heart. You couldn't simply give it lip service.

Sometimes Pa wasn't consistent. For instance, he always said that it was right for the white man to expand his borders, even though he took his land from the Indians. Yet Pa was the first to cry shame at a strong boy preying upon a weaker, or a grown man abusing a child or an animal.

On occasion, Tom had been cautioned to spare Betsy's feelings by being silent when he hadn't liked something she had prepared for a meal. But if it was wrong to oppress a weaker person, why was it right for a large nation like the United States to oppress the Indians? Why was it wrong to tease Betsy, but right to ask her to work for them for twenty dollars a year and found? Of course she was not technically a slave; but that was little more than a polite fiction: she would not be able to leave them, even if she wished to do so.

"Now they're talking about forming a militia company

here in Lovatt," Tom's father was saying. "We need one about as much as Alabama needs more cotton."

"What's that about a company, Pa?"

"Your grandfather and Jeems McNair have been talking about asking the able-bodied men to form a militia company for the protection of the town. In my opinion, it's the most brilliant scheme yet devised for wasting the time of sensible men."

"I don't know, sir," Tom interjected. "It seemed to me as I came home tonight that the town looked mighty helpless. There are no troops nearer than Staunton, and even if the Yankees are up along the Rappahannock, there's always the chance that they might send a detachment up the Valley."

"Supposing they did?" the doctor demanded. "What good would twenty or thirty militiamen do? Let alone the fact that the war'll be over by next year. Mark my words; moderation will win the day."

"Militia might not stop the Yankees, sir, but it would be might useful against guerrillas. Grandpa was telling me just yesterday about a gang of deserters that looted a town on the other side of Great North Mountain last week. They burned and stole food and clothing and left the people with nothing."

"Well, there may be something to that," Pa conceded. "But another thing is this: how many of our able townspeople would stand and fight if there were a raid? Precious few, I suspect."

"We won't know until we try, Pa."

His father grinned disarmingly. "You're right about that, Tom. I suppose it will at least keep people out of mischief, and it might even be valuable. Perhaps I was too hasty."

Tom pressed his advantage. "Would you object to my joining the company, Pa?"

10

"You? You're only sixteen."

"I can ride and shoot as well as anyone. In another year I'll be old enough . . ."

"We're not going to discuss that, Tom."

"Perhaps we should," Mama said from the foot of the table. "Tom will take his place beside Will and Sandy one day."

Pa sat motionless as if he refused to believe what he had heard. Tom's mind raced backwards in time, remembering the allusions his mother had made to Will as if he were alive, as if somehow a miracle would happen that would restore the lost son to his neatly furbished room upstairs, where his clothing and his papers and his books waited for him.

"We must face it, Joseph," Mama continued. "There is a possibility that the war may last longer than we think. If it does, Tom should have some sort of experience to prepare him for the army."

"Of course, my dear," Pa said. His eyes sought Tom's, implored silence. "Shall we discuss it some other time?"

From the doorway Betsy cleared her throat. "Can I take away the dishes now, Miss Mary?"

"Yes, Betsy."

As his parents preceded him into the back parlor, Tom remained behind. "Getting pretty close to my birthday, Betsy," he hinted. "I'm going to be seventeen."

"Everybody knows that," Betsy said scornfully.

"I sure wish I knew what I was getting."

"I just bet you do."

"Do you know what it is?"

"Maybe yes and maybe no."

He coaxed. "Come on, Betsy; I'm your favorite. You wouldn't know what to do without me."

Betsy chuckled. "Oh, yes I do! I'd lead me a peaceful life without so much devilment. No more sand in the sugar. No more of them crawly worms in my bed. It'd be mighty relaxing."

"Remember when you were sick, Betsy? And I brought your supper to you and read you parts of the Bible?"

Betsy glowered at him across the table. "The one thing ain't got nothing to do with the other, Mister Tom. I don't know what kind of present they're going to give you, and I wouldn't tell you if I did."

"You'll be sorry."

Betsy pointedly ignored him. She stacked the dishes and walked out to the kitchen. He began to whistle, just to show Betsy how little he cared.

A comfortable wood fire was burning in the fireplace of the rear parlor. Mama was already busy with her needle and darning egg and the basket of torn stockings that never seemed to empty, no matter how hard she worked.

"Want to play checkers, Tom?" Pa asked.

"I'd like to, sir. Unless you'd rather read."

"No. The news is very depressing."

The checker-board was kept in the drawer of the secretary that stood in the corner diagonally opposite the fireplace. It had been given to Sandy and William by their Grandmother Hauser shortly before her death ten years before. The original pieces had been lost long ago, but Will had fashioned replacements by cross-sectioning a willow branch with Pa's bone saw. Half the pieces had been dyed with butternuts, dipped into Betsy's caldron of brown dye when her attention had been distracted. The choice of black or red, therefore, was purely an academic one. Actually, the pieces were either the natural yellowish white of willow, or a deep brown.

Doctor Tanner positioned his men on the scuffed squares and examined his watch. "I should have heard

12

from the Lacy girl before this," he offered by way of explanation. "First babies are always hard. But even so. Your move, Thomas."

He moved his right-hand checker to the right diagonal. It would be safe from attack there; possibly he could ambush one of the white pieces with it.

Pa thrust boldly from the center and precipitated a series of jumps. "Clears the board for maneuvering," he said. Already he had emptied his king row, massing his remaining men to Tom's left.

Tom cautiously advanced his original checker. His father forced a jump and crowned a king. Suddenly the game was limited to three whites blocking four butternuts, and the sole butternut king was chased into an untenable side position by two white kings.

"Concede?"

"Yes, sir."

"Poor butternut brown," Pa smiled. "You relied too heavily on defense, Tom. The only defense worth having is that gained by offense."

Tom chuckled. "I'll remember that for our next game."

"I'd like to give you a return game, but I have to look in on the Lacy girl. Would you saddle Brutus for me, please? And bring him around to the front door."

"Saddle him, sir?"

"Yes. The snow might get too deep for the buggy. If it continues, I don't know how we'll get supplies."

As Tom left the room to get his jacket, he glanced back. His parents were embracing, standing before the fire, and it came to him that when he went to the war they would be alone. He was leaving his boyhood behind him, even now. It had been a lovely time, but it was almost over.

Out in the stable, his mingled feelings of relief at being almost grown and of regret at leaving the familiar

13

and the well loved persisted. He wanted to be a man, and to be a man in this year was to be a soldier. But the old, carefree time was still compelling, still urging him to linger.

He put down the old tin lantern he had brought from the house and removed the worn saddle from its peg. Brutus struggled to his feet and stood patiently, while Tom spread the saddle blanket and positioned the saddle.

"Poor old Brutus," he soothed the gelding. "It's cold out there. I hope they give you a feed." He tightened the girths, waited until Brutus expelled his breath, and then retightened them. It was the one trick that Brutus knew, holding his air so that the girths would be comfortably loose. If you didn't retighten them, it was possible to find the saddle slipping to Brutus' underside and you along with it.

He led Brutus out into the night. The snow had stopped, and a cold wind keened down from Great North Mountain, laying the high spots bare. The stars burned fiercely in the black sky.

Pa was waiting at the front door, muffled to the ears in a heavy greatcoat, his shabby black satchel in his right hand.

"I hope this is the last snow of the winter," he said. "It's pretty nearly March."

"Yes, sir!" Tom said, thinking of his impending birthday.

Pa smiled. "That's right; you've got a birthday coming up, haven't you? Seventeen is pretty near old enough to know what you want to do, I reckon." He held the bag in his left hand, gripped the pommel of the saddle, and swung himself easily into place. From his new perch he looked down at Tom. "If you're so all-fired set on it, you can join the militia company, if they get one started."

"Thank you, Pa!"

14

"Mind you, I still think it's an abysmal waste of time."

Tom grinned to himself as Pa jogged off down the drive. It was like Pa to put up a good fight and then let you do what you wanted to do afterwards, as long as it didn't hurt you. He guessed that that was part of being a man.

This would probably be the last snow of the winter, he thought as he looked after Pa and Brutus. Soon the warm winds of spring would come to melt it into a memory. And soon he would be a member of the Lovatt company. It would take him a long time before he could take his place beside Sandy, as Mama had put it, but the company would be a good starting place. He hoped that he would be as good a soldier as Sandy, some day.

He had to measure up to Sandy, because that was what Pa and Mama really wanted.

CHAPTER 2

A Visit From the Enemy

ALTHOUGH there was a great deal of talk in Lovatt about the desirability of forming a company, no company was formed. The Federals, apparently unaware that their reception committee had not yet been formed, didn't wait. The first of the enemy reached Lovatt at the end of March. They came down the Pike on tired horses, looking uncomfortably hot in their woolen uniforms.

Tom, looking out of Grandpa Hauser's front window, saw the first of them halt near the house. There were about sixty of them, as near as he could judge. As he watched, four riders detached themselves from the main body and raced through the town, apparently to draw fire from any Confederate troops stationed there.

"Can't ride for beans," Grandpa said scornfully. "They sit their mounts like so many sacks of meal."

In spite of the seriousness of the situation, Tom smiled. Grandpa had a war of his own with the Yankees. It was parallel to the war waged by the Confederacy, but it remained separate from it.

"The way those people mishandle horseflesh, they'll be needing replacements," Grandpa continued. "I'm not going to furnish them; take the mare and cut around the east edge of town. If your Pa is home, take Brutus and hide him and the mare in the woods along Centre Creek."

16

"Me? What about the Yankees?"

"Stuff," Grandpa said testily. "You can outrun them. Get moving, boy."

Tom ran out the rear door and sprinted across the yard to the stable. He grabbed a saddle blanket and the saddle from its peg and went to the mare's stall. Outside he could hear the clatter of hooves in the road, the murmur of voices. He wasn't going to have a lot of time. For a moment he thought bitterly of the company of militia that he was to have joined, and of how it had never come into being. And then he thought that maybe it took something like this to get things started.

He led the mare out into the yard and swung up into the saddle. If he could only get across the Port Republic road before he was spotted, he'd be in the clear. He knew the country and the enemy didn't. He could outrun them once he got in the open. The danger was being trapped here in town.

He walked the mare across the yard to the lane that led out to the road. The mare tossed her head impatiently and neighed. Tom froze. A horse and rider were coming around the corner of the house. In a lightning flash he saw the golden chevrons on the man's blouse, the heavy red beard on his face, the gleam of brass from the hilt of his saber. And then he slapped the mare with the ends of the reins, and she bolted down the lane towards the road.

Someone yelled behind him, and then there was the muffled pop of a pistol and the drone of a ball overhead. And then he was in the Port Republic road, and he could hear nothing but the pound of the mare's hooves and the rush of wind past his face.

Just short of the Dorfer house he turned south and rode across the pasture. He risked a glance behind him, but he could see nothing of the man who had fired at him. Apparently the sergeant had orders not to give chase.

17

Trees loomed ahead of him, and he bent low in the saddle to avoid the branches. He pulled on the reins, and the mare slowed obediently. He only had another mile to go, and there was no sense in wasting the mare's strength.

When he reached the house, he halted for a moment in the woods to make sure that the Yankees hadn't got there before him. It looked quiet enough, so he went on to the stable. Brutus looked out from his stall quizzically, as Tom tied the mare to a post.

In the kitchen, Betsy turned from her stove in surprise. "What are you doing home so early?" she wanted to know.

"Yankees, Betsy," he said tersely. "Where's Pa?"

"He's in his office up front," Betsy said. "Where's the Yankees?"

The door to the dining room opened, and Mama came in. She held up a warning hand. "Pa's having a nap on his couch. What's all this about Yankees?"

"They're in town, Mama. Grandpa sent me home with his mare so they wouldn't steal her."

"Good. You'd better take Brutus and go off down the creek. They won't follow you there."

"What about Pa?"

"I'll tell him. You just get moving before they get here. And don't come back until you're sure it's safe."

He felt a glow of pride. Even if Mama did sometimes talk as though Will were alive, she was always up to the occasion when there was an emergency.

Tom waited through the long afternoon in a little hollow near the creek. It was dull and tedious, and he wished he had thought of bringing a book with him to pass the time. He wondered how often Sandy had had to wait like this, not knowing what was going on, not daring

18

to move. If he were only a captain like Sandy, he wouldn't have to wait. He'd be giving orders, taking some sort of action!

Sam Dorfer joined him just before suppertime. Sam was the son of the Lovatt butcher, and he was Tom's best friend.

"They've cleared out of town," Sam reported. "I've got three horses with me. The Yankees started down the road for our place, but then they turned off the road and cut back to the Pike. I watched them turn into your place. It looks like they might stay there tonight."

If only he were Sandy and could do something about it!

While Doctor Tanner watched from the window of his office, a sergeant and three troopers detached themselves from the remainder and rode to the rear of the house. The remaining body swung in across the ditch, trampling across the lawn and the flowerbeds. The young officer who was apparently in charge dismounted and walked up the steps. A moment later his knock rang through the hall.

He was very young, no older than Sandy. Doctor Tanner suppressed an impulse to smile at the formal manner that accentuated rather than concealed the obvious reluctance of the boy.

"Sir, we have orders to search for Rebel soldiers."

"There are no Confederate soldiers here."

The boy smiled. "I regret that I must search the house despite your reassurance."

Doctor Tanner stood aside.

The search was perfunctory. Even Doctor Tanner had to admit that any clever Rebel with his wits about him could have successfully concealed himself. Mary was in the kitchen with Betsy; she did not even look up when they

19

entered. She was like a small child, pretending that the bogyman was not there. If she pretended hard enough, perhaps he would go away.

In Will's room, the lieutenant glanced at the ambrotype that Mary had placed on the mantel. "Your son, sir?"

"My son." He was overcome by a sudden impulse to tell the boy about Will. "He was a divinity student. We lost him at First Manasses."

"I'm sorry." The boy paused. "I didn't join up until last September."

"Yes." He was tired. It had been a mistake to mention Will to the boy. "And this room across the hall belongs to my son Ambrose. He is with the army at present."

The lieutenant only nodded.

That night, the troop bivouacked in the old orchard. They were not like the traditional wooden nutmeg sellers or the peddlers of clocks that refused to run. Some of them were laughing and joking among themselves, and you would have found it hard to tell them apart from a group of Southern boys, if it hadn't been for their hard, unmusical speech and their blue uniforms. One or two of them even asked permission to draw water from the well, just as Southern boys would have done.

But the chickens suffered. After dark, the Federals built a great fire, using most of Betsy's firewood in the process. Several of them entered the henhouse. Doctor Tanner watched from the window of the upstairs hall with compressed lips. If he went down and spoke to the officer about it, he might be able to prevent further depredations. But he hadn't fallen so low that he had to ask favors of a Federal officer. The chickens were not that important.

He wondered whether Tom had witnessed the theft of the chickens. Probably. Tom and the Dorfer boy would be watching everything that went on. He hoped that the boys would do nothing rash.

Before he retired for the night, he made the rounds of the lower floor, locking the windows and bolting the doors. It was something he had never done—at least not in years. Valley folk didn't have to lock doors against anyone except a horde of Union rascals who stole a person's chickens and burned up all his firewood to roast them with!

In the kitchen he discovered Betsy stretched out on the table, using a pile of soiled linen as a mattress, with one clean sheet over the whole.

"Excuse me, Betsy. I didn't know you were sleeping in here."

Betsy nodded vigorously. "Yes, sir! I ain't going to sleep out there in my house with all that trash running around loose. A person could get murdered!"

"Quite right. You stay here as long as you like."

No matter how you tried, you couldn't avoid the war. It came to you in a scarcity of drugs, in higher prices for the things you had to buy. It killed your son, and it wasted years of everyone's time. It set a band of vandals upon your doorstep and scared the daylights out of your servant. It was there, and you couldn't do a thing about it.

The preliminary stutters of the bugle woke Tom in the gray half-light of dawn. He listened for a moment, and then he rolled over and shook Sam awake.

"What's the matter?" Sam said sleepily.

"They're waking up. I'm going to get over there and see what's going on. You stay with the horses, will you?"

Sam nodded sleepily. "Don't get caught."

The trees were dripping with the moisture of early dawn as he made his way through the woods back of the

21

house. There was a path that he and Sam had used as boys, but he stayed away from it now. The Yankees would be bound to have a sentry posted somewhere along it. They would probably have sentries stationed around the yard, too. It wouldn't do to get too close to the house.

He found a place about fifty yards behind Betsy's house. There were a few trees, but for the most part low underbrush covered the area. He got down on his belly and wriggled to the edge of the brush patch until he could see the yard by parting the bushes slightly.

From his vantage point he could see the back of the house, faintly pink and luminous in the early morning light, the stable, and the picket line to which were tethered the horses of the command. There were twenty horses, so that meant that the original group of yesterday had split.

The men were lounging around small cooking fires that they had lighted on the grass. They had apparently finished their hardtack and bacon and were drinking their coffee before they moved out. One of the men stood to one side with the bugler. The first man was apparently the commander of the troop, judging from the gold braid on his shoulder straps.

The bugler turned away, saluted smartly, and raised his bugle to his lips. As Tom watched fascinated, the men gulped down the rest of their coffee and kicked dirt over the fires. They moved quickly by ones and twos to the picket line and began to saddle their mounts.

The bugle sounded again, and the men mounted in a tight, compact formation. A red beard blazed over the blue tunic of a burly sergeant, and Tom recognized him as the man who had chased him in the lane yesterday. The officer took his place in front of the line and gave an order. The troop pivoted and moved down the lane in a column of twos, the sergeant riding last. As Tom watched,

22

the sergeant suddenly wheeled and rode back to the stable. He bent low and rode inside while the column jingled off down the lane to the Pike.

A moment later the man reappeared, still mounted. He slapped the flank of his horse with the ends of the reins and cantered off after the troop.

Satisfied that the Yankees were gone, Tom crawled back through the brush to the shelter of the woods. It was time to get the horses.

Betsy opened the door of the washroom. It was a wonderful morning! Now that the soldiers had gone, anyhow. She walked out towards her little house, humming as she went. If you had a little music, no matter what kind, you never got scared the way you did otherwise. She opened the door cautiously. Didn't look like anybody had come in. Couldn't tell, though. She peered through the doorway, to either side. Then she looked under the bed. Nobody. Her Bible was still on the deal table where she had left it.

Sometimes she wished she could read. It would be a comfort to read about the olden times, especially like now when there was a war going on. If you could read how other people had gone through things like this, it made them easier for you to take. But she did know some of it by heart, anyhow. Even if she couldn't read it, she still had the place where all the fine sounding words were kept.

No time to be wasted, though! It was time to be making breakfast. Doctor would want his coffee, directly; else he'd get grumpy and fidgety-like. And Mister Tom ought to be home soon. He could probably eat a horse after sleeping out all night. She turned back to the door.

An inquisitive tongue of flame was running up the doorway of the barn. As nearly as she could make out, the

23

inside was filled with smoke. Oh, Lord, she prayed. Don't let the buggy burn! She ran to the well and hauled up the bucket. Swinging it free of the chain, she trotted across the yard and heaved the water at the flames nearest her. The fire spat and sizzled as the water struck it, but a moment later it was burning as brightly as ever.

"Fire!"

She ran back to the well and hitched the bucket to the chain. Why didn't they hear her? She slapped the rope and the bucket heeled over and began to fill.

"Fire! You all come on!"

Swiftly she hauled up the dripping bucket, unhitched it, and began to run across the yard. The rear door flew open, and the doctor sprinted towards her with an agility she hadn't thought he still possessed.

"Good work, Betsy. Give me this, and you go inside and drag out the washtubs and the spare pails."

She nodded. Doctor could haul up the water from the washtubs and throw it on the fire. She would fill the tubs from the well. Doctor, he thought of pretty nearly everything.

In the washroom she seized a wooden tub and began to drag it across the stone floor.

"Whatever are you doing, Betsy? What was all the shouting about?"

"Yankees, Miss Mary. They done set a fire in the barn."

Miss Mary turned pale with rage. "Is there no limit to what those ruffians will do? I'll get the other one, Betsy."

When she got out to the well, Doctor was breathing hard. He had made one trip of his own, in addition to completing the one she had begun. Steam was mixed with the smoke now, and the fire on the doorpost was out, but it was crackling away inside. She sank another bucket, and then she and Miss Mary began to pull it up.

It was the first of many.

24

Once the doctor got the hay thoroughly wetted down, the fire was out. Although the post was charred, it was still solid. A great patch of siding had burned away, exposing the studs and cross beams underneath, but the latter seemed solid, too. Tom and Sam Dorfer rode up just in time to give a hand with the last few buckets.

"It was sheer spite," the doctor said. "And I can't see why. I said nothing to them, even when they stole the chickens."

Tom frowned, remembering the sergeant. "I think he was the one who tried to chase me over at Grandpa's yesterday. Maybe he was mad because of that." He thought about it for a moment. "I should have gone to the barn after he left to see what he was doing in there."

"You can't always think of everything," the doctor said. "I wish Sandy had been here, though."

Tom winced, but the doctor paid little attention. He was making a mental estimate of the amount of siding that would be needed to repair the stable, and he was balancing its probable cost against the sum owed him by Matt Hunnicut down at the timber yard for treatment of a broken ankle, two years ago come September.

CHAPTER 3

The Lovatt Company

A MONTH after the Federal incursion into
Lovatt, Tom and Sam Dorfer were busily
engaged in cutting saplings. It was hot and humid, and
there was no breeze to speak of.

Tom put down his hatchet and wiped his face. "Hot
going, ain't it?" Sam said. They were in the woods just
back of the Dorfer place, and it was too far from the
creek to be cool.

"I sure wish we'd started cutting down by the creek."

"We'd have further to tote them," Sam said shortly.
"Your grandpa know where you are?"

"He knows I'm with you. He doesn't know what we're
doing. He wouldn't mind, though."

"Will Kinyard said not to tell until we got organized
and had our first drill and all. Otherwise, somebody
might blab to the Yankees." Sam paused to spit dramati-
cally. "He's the captain, you know. Whatever he says, we
got to do it."

Privately, Tom thought that this might be a little too
much authority to be delegated to a nineteen-year-old
whose sole claim to command was a year of service in the
army and the loss of his right arm. Will had come back to
Lovatt a wiser young man than he had left, although not
necessarily a sadder one. His obvious relish for recounting
his adventures left no doubt in anyone's mind that he had

26

enjoyed his army experiences, with the exception of his wound.

He had enjoyed the army so much that he set about organizing the militia company that was to defend Lovatt. Until the advent of the Federal cavalry patrol a month ago, no one had worried about the safety of Lovatt, except Jeems McNair and Andrew Hauser. Will, therefore, had been that classic model of success: the right man in the right place at the right time. He had immediately set about his "recruiting." A few oldsters joined because Will had "fit in the war." Sam and Tom had joined because they had once dreamed of forming their own company.

Will appointed himself captain. That was probably what he would have done in Will's place, Tom admitted to himself, but he wouldn't have given so many orders. Will insisted on being obeyed in everything, no matter how small. Sam and Tom had been the least rebellious of the lot, and for that reason Will had appointed Sam as lieutenant and Tom as sergeant.

This morning, the lieutenant and the sergeant were cutting poles to make pikes for drill. Mr. Smith was furnishing sheet iron for the blades, Joe Ryan was going to cut them and sharpen them, and the boys were then going to attach them to the poles by sawing a lengthwise slot, inserting the blade, and binding it in place with wire.

Sam jerked upright and put his hands to his sides. "Detail! Attention!"

Tom glanced around. It was not until he saw Will Kinyard bearing down on them that he realized he was the detail. He hastily assumed the awkward posture Will had taught them.

"Hat ease, men," Will said, graciously returning Sam's salute with his left hand. "Hat ease. How's it going?"

"Pretty good, Will. We got ten poles trimmed."

"How you doing, Tom?"

27

"We're getting there."

"I was talking to Joe Ryan just now. He's got that there iron all shaped. All he's got to do is sharpen the points and then he'll be done. You reckon you fellows could set them in the poles this afternoon? We could have us a sure-enough drill before it gets dark."

"I don't know," Tom said. "Grandpa's expecting me."

"It surely would be fine, if we could get started," Will said wistfully. "Of course if we cain't do her, that's all there is to it."

With sudden intuition, Tom realized why Will was so anxious to begin drilling. A poor farmer's son, he had not amounted to a great deal before the war. His year of army service had made him feel important for the first time in his life. Now that he was back, he probably felt more useless than before he had gone away. There was very little that a one-armed man could do as ably as a whole man, especially on a farm. Take away Will's company, and you had taken away half of Will's reason for living.

"My father might need me, too," Sam said.

"Sure, that's all right. We'll do her when there's more time," Will said. His lank, tow-colored hair flopped over his face as he raised his hat to scratch his head.

"Wait a minute," Tom said. "I'll tell Grandpa. If I explain, I'm pretty sure he'll let me have the afternoon off."

"Well, now," Will considered. "That would surely be fine. I reckon I could cut them slots, if I put the poles in a vise."

"I'll ask Pa," Sam said abruptly.

The three boys smiled at each other. Everything was all right again.

The drill that evening was an unqualified success, thanks to the moral and practical backing of Mr. Hauser

28

and Jeems McNair. At first, Jeems had taken a dim view of the proceedings. "What good is it going to do if the Yankees have guns and they don't?" he wanted to know.

"You're missing the point, Jeems," Mr. Hauser said. "The point is that they want to do something. They're too young or too old to serve in the army, or they've got too many ties. But the Yankees can come down here and raid with hardly a thing to stop them."

"You're forgetting the Laurel brigade. Even if Ashby is dead, the brigade is still working."

Mr. Hauser shook his head. "The Laurel brigade can't help us. They're part of the army, now. Besides, no band of irregular cavalry ever won a war. These boys need the older men to give them dignity. They need to feel they're doing something important so that they'll take it seriously. Then maybe they'll learn a few things that will help them when they go into the army."

"What if the Yankees come?"

"Maybe we'll get rifles by then. If not, are we any worse off than we were before?" Mr. Hauser grinned. "Besides, Jeems, the company will have you and me as members. How can it lose?"

"Me?"

"You. Think of how mad John Dorfer'll be when he hears we're in it and he can't be because of his heart condition."

Jeems chuckled. "I never thought of that. All right, you talked me into it. We'll join up tonight."

Often the success or failure of a venture is determined by some small incident, unobtrusive, and by itself quite insignificant. In the case of the Lovatt company, Mr. Hauser and Jeems McNair provided the incident. The idlers who came to scoff at one-armed Will Kinyard's collection of boys and decrepit old men were silenced by the sight of Mr. Hauser's faithful attention to the unfamiliar orders, by Jeems McNair's surprising stamina, even after the quick-time twice around Hunnicut's timber yard.

Will Kinyard was in his glory. Before he had dismissed the company, he had already had an inspiration: if the company shaped up the way it looked like it would, maybe he could take it to the army. They might even confirm him in his self-appointed rank.

Everyone agreed that the company needed muskets. That was a serious flaw. The pikes would only be useful at close quarters. Of course, now that the Yankees had gone running back towards Washington for a third time, following Chancellorsville, there probably wouldn't be any need for the company in the near future. Still, it didn't cost anything, and it provided a good excuse for visiting town in the middle of the week.

"It surely would look more like a company of militia if we had muskets," Jeems said as he and Andrew Hauser prepared to go home through the gathering dusk.

Grandpa Hauser nodded. "This ought to stimulate trade for you, Jeems, muskets or no. A man can raise quite a thirst strutting around playing soldier."

Jeems grinned. "To tell you the truth, I figured it that way, too."

Tom and Sam Dorfer walked towards them, in company with Will Kinyard. Will's face was scarlet from pride or exertion.

"Well, boys," Grandpa Hauser said. "It looks like we've got a company."

"I reckon we got about the finest company I ever did see," Will said proudly. "I never figured they'd do half as good as they done. If we had us some rifles, you couldn't tell us from regular soldiers."

"Yes, sir. That's all we need," Sam chimed in.

Grandpa Hauser winked at Tom. "It seems to me Congressman Boteler ought to remember me. I was thinking maybe the government could get us some muskets. They

30

have enough captured Yankee rifles to replace some of the muskets the troops have been using. I could write to the Congressman and ask him." He paused. "I don't think we could get rifles, but maybe muskets would do. For a starter, anyway."

"That would be right fine," Will said. "That would be right kind of you, sir."

"I'll do it tonight, Captain. The pleasure will be mine. Jeems? I'll accompany you. Goodnight, boys."

Amid a chorus of "Goodnight, sir," the two gentlemen moved off in the direction of McNair's ordinary. It was pleasant to stroll through the soft, enfolding dusk of the Valley. Some light yet lingered over Great North Mountain, and here and there oil lamps glowed yellow through the dark-hued windows.

Jeems removed his makeshift sign, "Closed for Drill," from the door and put it in his pocket. "Got to save paper," he said by way of apology. "It's getting scarce as hen's teeth."

"So are a lot of things. Joseph was saying just yesterday that he'd have to gather herbs and concoct his own drugs. Half the things he ordered from Richmond didn't arrive and those that did were three times their usual price.

"Horace!" Jeems called. "Bring some lights!"

A light-colored Negro appeared from the nether regions that housed the kitchen and the storeroom. He carried a glowing lamp in one hand, a splinter in the other. With the splinter, lighted from the lamp in his hand, he passed behind the bar, touching the splinter momentarily to each of the two lamps there. Then he pulled down the two ceiling lamps and lighted them in turn.

"Getting low on oil, Mister Jeems," he said.

"It hasn't come; I've ordered a barrel." Jeems went behind the bar. "How about a drink before the crowd arrives, Andrew?"

"Delighted, Jeems. I wonder they aren't here already."

Jeems grinned. "They don't know I'm back. I said I was going to stop off at John Dorfer's for a moment before I opened." He became serious. "I wanted to talk to you about a matter that's been on my mind before I broached it to anyone else."

"Your servant, Jeems. Fire away."

The younger man hesitated for a moment. "It's about young Kinyard. He's not well off."

"Financially? Or otherwise?"

"I was thinking in financial terms. The lad has no income whatsoever. Now, supposing we were to suggest that the town hire him as a drillmaster and lookout? I'd put in fifty cents a week and his dinner."

"Done, Jeems. You can count me in, and I'll take up a collection. What would he do as a lookout, though?"

"He could get a pretty good view of things from the church steeple," Jeems said. "Maybe he could stay up there from noon until dusk and warn us of raiders. We could have another boy get up there in the morning." He unlocked a cupboard beneath the bar and drew out a squat bottle from which he poured two drinks. "The last of the French brandy," he explained.

Grandpa Hauser raised his glass. "To a good cause and a better friendship, Jeems."

Tom dozed while Grandpa rambled on. He was content. Ever since Sally Lou Barnes, Sandy's best girl, had said that his prowess on the drill field was a credit to Sandy, he had felt that the world held little more to be desired. Mama had sewn blue chevrons on the jacket of his old suit to emphasize his new standing as sergeant of the Lovatt company. The chevrons were bright, and they stood out handsomely against the black broadcloth. If they had been on the gray jacket of Sandy's old suit which he now wore to church, he would have looked more like a

32

real soldier; but Mama had nipped that in the bud. If he drilled in his best clothes, she said, in no time at all he'd have nothing to wear.

And it really didn't matter what he wore. He didn't have to go around play-acting. He was a real soldier, in a way, just by belonging to the militia. The Yankees had come once; it was conceivable that they would come again. If they did, he'd have a man's part to play, as Grandpa had said. And if that didn't make him a soldier, he didn't know what would.

"Perhaps you find the study of law fatiguing this afternoon?" Grandpa Hauser asked with mock courtesy.

All at once his reverie was at an end. He was back in the hot, dusty parlor with the gilt French clock casting off the minutes. Grandpa had been lecturing him on real estate. "No, sir," he denied. "I was just thinking about something."

"That was obvious," Grandpa said drily. He shuffled his papers together. "I suppose there are more interesting things to occupy one's mind. Especially when one is a sergeant."

Tom grinned. "To tell the truth, sir, some such thoughts were occupying my mind."

"You wouldn't be human if they didn't. Go ahead and enjoy it while you can. If you have the intelligence I think you have, you'll realize that after a while even soldiering becomes boring."

"Yes, Grandpa."

"You're too young to realize it, but the appalling thing about war is its waste. Waste of time, waste of money, and—most of all—waste of lives. How many men who might have become good lawyers or doctors or poets have been killed already, God alone knows." Grandpa rapped his pipe sharply on the edge of the hearth. "Have you heard from your cousin Alison?"

33

"Nothing for quite a while, sir."

"I was wondering how they're making out. Better get on home, now. Drill coming up tonight."

As Tom closed Grandpa's front gate, he saw Jeems McNair standing on the veranda of the tavern. "Hello, Mr. McNair."

Jeems raised a freckled hand in salutation. "I have a letter for your pa, Tom. Wait a minute; I'll fetch it." In a moment, he was back with the letter, a single sheet folded in thirds and sealed with a blob of ordinary candle wax.

"Is there a charge on this, Mr. McNair?"

"Not to you, Sergeant," Jeems smiled. "Just don't be too hard on us old gaffers if we aren't as spry as we ought to be."

"No, sir. Thank you, Mr. McNair. I'll see you tonight."

He had recognized Aunt Anne's spidery hand in the superscription, and by the time he got home, his curiosity was aboil. A letter from Aunt Anne meant news of Cousin Alison, and that was always welcome news to Tom.

Anne West was not really an aunt, except by courtesy. She was a cousin of Mama's, and they had been close friends as girls. She was a cheerful, if improvident woman whose husband had been killed in the Mexican War. She lived happily, if precariously, by giving lessons in watercolor, music, and French. She had an unfortunate habit of beginning sentences that trailed off somewhere short of completion. The habit irritated Mama, and so they saw little of Aunt Anne, although she lived no more than twenty miles from Lovatt.

Cousin Alison was a year Tom's junior. He remembered her as a tall, awkward girl with yellow hair that ruffled in the wind. To his everlasting surprise, when he had last seen her, at Christmastime, she had become extremely pretty. It was a pity that they didn't live closer, he thought as Mama looked at the letter in his hand. Cousin Alison was the sort of girl who could skate as well as a boy, and she seemed to know just what you were thinking before you got around to talking about it.

Mama laid aside her mending and opened the flap of the letter. "Anne's in trouble," she said almost at once. "That woman seems to have a knack for it. Things always happen to Anne."

Pa, who was just coming through the door, winked at Tom. "Who's this, Mary?"

"Anne. Part of their house was damaged by fire. I suppose that servant of theirs is to blame, somehow. She's worse than Anne when it comes to flightiness."

"That's a shame. What are they going to do?"

"Come here, for one thing. A neighbor is going to repair the damage, but she wants to visit us for a while. It must be lonely in Scottsburg, now."

Pa nodded in agreement. "When is she coming?"

"She said any time someone could come for her. That probably means she'll be here most of the summer."

"Tom could go get them tomorrow morning. I can either borrow your father's mare or rent a nag from Joe Ryan."

"You don't mind, do you?"

"Of course not, my dear. We must be willing to share what we have with those less fortunate. I suppose they can sleep in Will's room."

"No," Mama said sharply. "They can stay in Sandy's room. Will might . . ."

"Of course," Pa said quickly. "Sandy's room it is. Tom, can you go over and get them tomorrow morning?"

"Yes, Pa."

Mama smiled. "You'll have to drive carefully, Tom. You know Aunt Anne doesn't trust careless drivers!"

"Yes, ma'am."

Pa turned to him then. "I'd like to see you in the office before supper, Tom. Just something I'd like to show you."

Mama looked at Pa and sniffed. "For men only, Joseph?"

"For men only, my dear."

Mama sniffed again. "And to think I might have had daughters!"

Pa's office was always nice and cool in the morning, because it faced west and the sun didn't get to it until well along in the afternoon. Now, however, it was just as hot as Grandpa's study had been, and that was very warm indeed.

"I don't want to worry you unnecessarily," Pa said. "But keep your eyes open tomorrow."

"Sir?"

"It's not just a question of careful driving. Brutus couldn't run away if he wanted to. And I know you pay heed to the road. It's just that you can't tell who else might be traveling that road."

"The Yankees seem to have pretty well cleared out of the Valley, haven't they?"

Pa nodded. "We won't have to worry much about them for a while. They're probably scared by the way our boys fought this spring up at Chancellorsville. No, it's not them I'm worried about. It's deserters and those who never joined the army at all. It's a lonely road to Scottsburg."

"Have you heard of any deserters around here, Pa?"

"McNair said two suspicious-looking men came through last Wednesday. Men on the run generally live by their wits. Or by their weapons. That's why I'm giving you this." Pa's hand raised from the desk to expose a small, double-barreled derringer. "It's loaded and capped. Use it if you have to."

36

"Yes, sir." He picked up the small pistol and slipped it into his pocket. And then he remembered what Pa had said about wishing Sandy had been there when the Yankees came. "Am I growing up the way you want, Pa?"

Pa smiled. "That's why I'm trusting you to go fetch your Aunt Anne."

As soon as he turned off the Pike the next morning, Tom was in another time, another place. The rutted dirt road was baked iron-hard by the June sun, and the buggy jounced along in the ridges like a thing possessed of a demon. The trees overhung the track to the point where the sun was at times obscured. Conscious of Pa's warning, he drove with the pistol tucked up his left sleeve, where he could reach it quickly.

But nothing of moment occurred; he was almost sorry to see the trees thin on either side to make room for the tiny hamlet. Still, Scottsburg itself was touched with the magic wand of adventure. In other days, it had been the fortified home of a man named Scott, who had barricaded himself on the one hand from the Indians, and on the other from the long, searching arm of the king's law. Others had come to the house for protection or for shelter from the elements on their way west. Few had stayed. It was a place that one passed through, but it was not a place to settle down in. The Indians were not a threat to peaceful settlers, now; they had long since moved westward, beyond the mountains. And the king's minions on this side of the water had long since mouldered to their finite dust. Only a mill beside a brawling mountain stream kept Scottsburg alive.

From the outskirts of the village, he could pick out Aunt Anne's house. The clapboards needed paint badly. Even from a distance, he could see areas of bare, gray-weathered boards. A large blackened patch along one corner showed where the fire had eaten through the outer walls.

He drove into the yard and stopped beside the hitching post that leaned drunkenly to one side. Brutus cast an interested eye at the long, luxuriant grass growing alongside the hedgerow. He would need a good rest and feed to prepare him for the return trip, Tom decided. For now, he could graze. A little later, he could be watered and have a bait of oats. That was one thing about living in a small town, as Pa said. Food was available at the lowest prices. And you could generally buy oats for a good horse.

Brutus stepped out of the shafts with an air. He had done well for an old horse, and he knew it. Tom unbuckled his collar and harness and slipped a hackamore around his neck. It was more of a compliment than a preventative; both he and Brutus knew that Brutus would not run away. But Brutus felt flattered at being treated like a young and fiery stallion.

Tom secured the free end of the hackamore to the iron ring on the hitching post. Satisfied that Brutus could reach the grass, he brushed off his hands and walked around to the front steps. Almost immediately the door opened, and Aunt Anne smiled a welcome.

"How nice to see you, Thomas! We were hoping you'd come one day soon."

"Thank you, ma'am. You're looking well; how is Cousin Alison?"

"Very well, thank you. Are we to go back with you, Tom?"

"I hope to have that pleasure," Tom smiled.

Aunt Anne gave him a mock curtsy. "My goodness! You're growing up, aren't you? Just as polite and all as Sandy and poor . . . it seems like yesterday we were at your house for Christmas . . ."

38

A lovely, radiant Alison came out of the gloom. "Won't you come in, Cousin Tom? Mama'll keep you talking here all day, if you let her!"

She had grown since Christmas, Tom thought. Her bright head would come above his shoulder. There was no getting around the fact that Cousin Alison was becoming a woman.

"If I could have the pleasure of seeing you, Cousin, I wouldn't mind standing here all day and all night, too."

Alison flushed. "How you do talk, Cousin!" But she stole a pleased glance at him as he followed Aunt Anne into the house.

He waited in the front room off the hall while Aunt Anne and Cousin Alison completed their packing. It was a pleasant room, although it was sadly in need of paint. Long, open shelves on either side of the fireplace contained a profusion of books; the old-fashioned furniture was plain, but it shone with the years of polishing it had received. It was the sort of room one would choose to linger in with a favorite book, or with a favorite person.

"I'm going to miss this room," Cousin Alison said from the doorway.

"It's lovely." He hesitated. "It's the sort of room you'd like to stay in."

Their eyes shared a secret.

"Are you ready, Alison?" Aunt Anne called down the stairs.

Cousin Alison smiled ruefully at him, and then she answered Aunt Anne. "All ready, Mama."

Although Tom half-hoped that some element of danger might intrude upon the return trip and give him an opportunity to prove himself a worthy guardian, none offered itself. The buggy sailed through a sea of riotous green leaves, lush with spring. It pitched and rocked over the bumps, the only voyager upon that course. Even Aunt Anne's vivid imagination could not materialize a single marauder to be vanquished by the sergeant of the Lovatt company.

Yet when he retired that night and looked back upon the day, it seemed wholly satisfying. He had ridden or driven as far as Scottsburg before; that was no novelty. The day had been lovely, almost perfect—but so had many others. What was it, then?

He closed his eyes, and immediately he was back in the front room of Aunt Anne's house, with the soft light from the north window falling kindly upon the worn furniture and the faded bindings of the books. Alison was speaking, and her low, soft voice had a soothing quality that fitted perfectly with the mood of the room. When I am old and tired, he thought, I hope I have a place like this to go to.

And then he knew why this had been so satisfying a day.

CHAPTER 4

On a Day in June

WILL KINYARD kept daily vigil in the steeple of the church. No raid had touched Lovatt so far, but stories made their way up and down the Pike, relating the fate of small towns that had been looted by strong bands of bushwhackers. As Mr. Hauser pointed out, you couldn't trust any stranger these days, no matter what color shirt he wore. Confederate deserters would be just as prone to loot Lovatt as would Federal troopers. Mr. McNair was worried, too; Will had seen a shotgun behind the bar, and that spelled trouble.

Will was getting two dollars a week, Yankee silver, just for watching up here in the church steeple and for drilling the company three nights a week. Pa took a dollar on account of things weren't going so good, but Will was saving the other dollar every week for when the war was over.

It was right pretty up in the steeple. You could see a whole piece of the Pike, clear down to where it turned, north of Mr. Barnes's pasture. You could see all the way up to the high ground beyond Centre Creek. Off to the East, Massanutten shimmered in the heat. That was sure enough a wild place. Pretty nearly nobody lived there, Pa said. Some day, maybe he'd go there and see for himself. Even with only one arm, a man could use a hatchet

41

or make a fire or shoot off a carbine. It just took a little longer than it used to, was all.

Will moved around the narrow platform to get out of the sun. It was right hot, and there wasn't more than the ghost of a breeze, even up here. His worn-out army shoe touched the plate that had held the dinner Mr. Mc-Nair's man Horace had brought him. That was a mighty nice thing for Mr. McNair to do: send him some fixings every day. Mr. McNair and Mr. Hauser, they were the finest men you'd ever want to know.

Dust swirled over near the foot of Great North Mountain. There was a kind of trail over that way. It cut through the woods and joined the Pike just south of town. That had been the way the Yankees had gone, the time they left Lovatt. This here was probably some farmer's rig.

He touched the butt of the small pocket pistol he told folks he'd taken off a Yankee. He had, in a way; but the Yankee was dead when he did it. He didn't have so many cartridges for the pistol, but it didn't matter. In a real fight, he wouldn't have time to reload. He spun the cylinder with his forefinger. All set to go. It might not be as new or as fancy as the revolvers the officers carried, but it could shoot, right enough.

The dust cloud was a great deal closer, now. Maybe it wasn't a farmer's wagon at that. It appeared to be more like a party of horsemen. And if it were following the trail, it ought to be further south. He shielded his eyes from the afternoon sun and stared intently at the break in the trees that the dust cloud was apparently headed for. A moment later they appeared. Better than a mile away, he decided. About eight or ten of them—call it ten. And they could be Yankees; it was hard to tell, what with the sun shining in his eyes and the dust and all. But if they weren't, he'd look mighty foolish ringing the bell for nothing at all.

42

For a moment he hesitated, and then he remembered what Mr. Hauser had said about not trusting any stranger. Foolish or not, he was going to ring that bell!

Tom jumped in his chair when he heard the first boom of the bell, but Grandpa only closed his book quietly and smiled. "This may prove to be an exciting afternoon," he said. "Let us prepare to meet the visitors."

Tom's throat constricted and he found himself incapable of speech. Grandpa opened the cupboard beside the fireplace and took out his rifle. Its octagonal barrel gleamed like silver from years of cleaning and use; the curly maple stock shone like glass. "A good Kentucky rifle is a better implement of war than a pike," Grandpa said with dry humor.

"I left my pike home."

Grandpa smiled reassuringly. "Never mind. I have a derringer you can use. Know how it works?"

"Yes sir. Pa gave me his to carry when I went to call for Aunt Anne."

Grandpa slung a baldric to which were fastened an old-fashioned powder horn and bullet pouch over his shoulder. "The pistol's in the drawer of the desk," he said as casually as though they were going to a Tuesday night drill. "Let's get going."

Will Kinyard was already waiting for them outside McNair's tavern. In spite of the heat, he was wearing his old army blouse, with one of the gilt buttons missing. It made a strange contrast to his dark brown pants. Jeems McNair was standing on the veranda. He had a heavy Sharps rifle cradled in the crook of his left arm. Just inside the door, Horace was examining the hammers of McNair's double-barreled shotgun.

"You going to let him use that against white men?" Will asked with disbelief.

43

"I sure am, if they try to bust in," Jeems said shortly. "Nobody walks through that door unless I say so."

Four men hurried down the road, sheepishly clutching their pikes. A fifth, Joe Ryan, carried an ancient pistol, brown with rust. "What's the fuss, Will?" he wanted to know.

"About eight or ten horsemen coming down from North Mountain. I couldn't make out who they were, but it didn't look like they was up to no good. They left the back trail."

"Is that all?" Joe spat his disgust.

"He did right, Joe," Grandpa said firmly. "You can't tell whom to trust these days."

"Waste of time, if we're going to get hauled out every time Will sees a shadow move."

"All war is a waste of time, if it comes to that," Grandpa said tersely. He filled the pan of his rifle with priming powder, closed the pan, and rubbed his thumb over the flint.

"Well," Joe Ryan said. "Now that we're here, we might as well find out what Will saw. Which way was they headed?"

"From North Mountain," Will said impatiently. "Just like I was telling you. They was coming like they was riding straight for Mr. Hunnicut's place. Come on; let's go see!"

By tacit consent, there were no commands. Will walked in front of everybody; that was the sole concession to his captaincy. Sam Dorfer came pelting up to join them as they rounded the corner of the tavern. He reported to Will.

"Couldn't get here no sooner, Captain," he panted. "I forgot where I put my pike. Where's yours, Tom?"

"I've got a derringer."

Will stopped. Ahead of them a long stretch of meadow

44

ran uphill to a patch of trees. The meadow was empty. "They must've turned off," Will said finally.

"Sure they was there in the first place?" someone jeered.

"Sure, I'm sure," Will said hotly. "They're circling around, is all. Or watching from the woods to see what we're going to do."

"What we ought to do," Joe Ryan said reflectively, "is go back to work. I've got a horse to shoe."

Jeems McNair pulled back the hammer of his Sharps with an oily click. "There's something out there, Joe. Look at the birds circling. Something scared them."

Will's face gleamed with sweat. "Tom, you run up to the church and climb the steeple. See if you can see them."

Fear rose in Tom like a wave. He had imagined that if the enemy came, they would ride up the Pike in a neat formation. The company would be waiting to receive them, lined up in the road in front of the tavern, all armed with the new muskets Grandpa had written away for. Instead of that, only half the company was here, armed with the pikes he and Sam and Will had made and a few decrepit old guns. And the enemy was out there somewhere, waiting to strike, well aware of their feeble preparations, and offering no target.

Will Kinyard was scared, too. Whoever was out there in the woods had had experience with this sort of thing before. They might stay out there until night before they made a move. Or they might circle and come in from a different direction. Either of these things was possible, and here the men were already eager to go home.

"Suppose they split up, Will?" Mr. McNair asked. "What do we do then?"

"We got to hit them before they do. If they split up, it

45

won't be until after they hit town. We'll have plenty of time to get at them."

"How many did you say there were?" Joe Ryan asked. From the tone of his voice it was obvious that he didn't believe there was anybody out there at all.

"I seen maybe ten. There could be fifty of them." He looked up at the steeple of the church. Tom's face appeared in the nearest window opening. Tom must have pretty near run up the ladder to get there so fast.

Tom waved and yelled something. He couldn't hear what it was, because they were all gabbling together behind him like a flock of geese.

"Will you all keep quiet, so's I can hear?"

Joe Ryan sniggered. Will knew just what he was thinking. The shirttail boys were playing war and wasting everybody's time. Well, Joe Ryan would find out directly!

". . . back of my grandpa's," Tom was yelling. "Five of them coming in south of Dorfer's."

Will swore under his breath. So the skunks had split up! And he only had twelve men, counting Tom. "Sam, you take everybody but Mr. McNair and Mr. Hauser and go on down to your place. I'll stay here and try to head off the ones coming this way."

He tried to think of what the captain of his old company would have done. It wasn't a good idea to split your men in the face of the enemy, he knew; but the enemy had split up, too. There wasn't anything he could do but meet them as they came. Everything was moving now, moving at a good clip, and you had to stay on your toes and not miss anything, or you were lost. He knew.

Two of the men started off down the Pike. Mr. Barnes and Todd Harper, his hired man. "Where you going, Mr. Barnes?" Will called. "You got to go help them out down at Dorfer's."

Mr. Barnes looked back. "I'm going to take care of my

46

property, if it's any of your business. If I'd stayed home, I'd have saved myself a walk."

"Men, we all got to work together!"

But it was no use. Sam and Joe Ryan were headed for the Dorfer place with Mr. Hunnicut in tow. The others were trotting off, each in the direction of his own house, his own land, and his own family. And not a single shot had yet been fired.

"Tom and I will cover the rear of my house," Mr. Hauser was saying to Mr. McNair. "If you stay in the front of the tavern, perhaps you can protect our rear."

Jeems McNair shook his head. "The boy's only got a wee pistol that wouldn't scare a mouse at twenty feet. I'll join you."

"How about the tavern?"

"Horace'll take care of it. He's got the shotgun."

The company had vanished as completely as though it never had been. Somehow, Will had lost control over the men. He had seen his own officers praise or bully their men into a reluctant obedience; now he knew how they must have felt. He had never felt so ashamed in all his life.

Tom came pelting down the road. "Where'd everybody go?"

"They all took off," Will said. "Sam took a couple down to his place, and your grandpa and McNair are in your grandpa's house waiting.

"We aren't soldiers," Tom said. "I sure am sorry, Will. I reckon we just don't know how soldiers ought to act."

"I reckon not." Tom was a good boy, sure enough. He tried mightly hard to do the right thing. When he went in the army, he'd make a right fine soldier. He would for a fact.

"What're we going to do, Captain?"

One man more had remained loyal to the Lovatt company. Will made the first of his last two decisions as captain. "You better run on home, Tom. Let your folks know what's going on. It's too late to fight together. It's got to be every man for his own self."

"Will you be all right?"

A shot boomed in the timber beyond Dorfer's. For a moment there was a pause, and then a fusilade of shots came all at once, pretty near like volley firing. "Keep to the trees on the west side of the Pike. I'll be all right."

He put his hand on Tom's shoulder in an awkward gesture. Right now he felt closer than a brother to old Tom, even if Tom was the doctor's son and he was the son of a poor dirt farmer. "Keep to them trees, and when you get there get on upstairs where you can see to shoot. Take care, now!"

"Yes, sir. You, too, Will!"

McNair's heavy Sharps boomed, followed by the flat crack of Andrew Hauser's Kentucky rifle. Will watched Tom run around the corner of a building, and then he headed for the Hauser place. If the company didn't owe him obedience, then he didn't owe it leadership. He yanked his pistol out of the holster and cocked it.

Should he go upstairs and join Mr. McNair and Mr. Hauser? If the raiders tried to burn the house down, he'd do better staying outside where he could stop them. They could come in from the north side of the house and no one the wiser, unless somebody stayed out here to watch. He slid around the corner of the house and ducked behind a rain barrel. He'd stay outside.

It was the last of his two decisions.

Behind him Tom could hear the steady crackle of rifle fire, punctuated here and there by the hollow boom of a smoothbore musket. He hoped Pa had stuck to his schedule and stayed home this afternoon.

48

Once out of the village, he ran along beside the Pike where he could take some cover from stray shots behind a low stone wall. He carried the derringer in his hand at first; then he dropped it down the front of his shirt for safekeeping. It would be useless here, anyhow; it had an extremely short range.

When he was almost home, he went back to the Pike. The raiders had apparently concentrated on the town and would not bother with the houses on the outskirts until they had finished in town. He thought fleetingly of Sally Lou Barnes. She'd be all right, he decided; he had seen Mr. Barnes and Todd Harper headed for the Barnes place. And Alison? If Pa were home, they could probably make out. Pa had his derringer and his rifle, and there was Sandy's rifle and Will's shotgun.

He pounded up the steps and opened the front door. It took a moment for his eyes to adjust to the dim interior.

"Pa?"

The silence was absolute. He bolted the front door behind him and hurried down the hall. Maybe they all had gone out to stroll under the apple trees in back. It was always a little cooler out there. He'd ask Betsy.

When he opened the door of the kitchen, Betsy was standing with her back to the stove. She almost faced him. Beside her, Pa, Mama, Aunt Anne, and Cousin Alison were lined up as though they had been waiting for him.

"Raiders in town!" he gasped. "We've got to hurry!"

A shadow moved behind him. Pa shouted "No!" As he half-turned to face the unknown, darkness crashed on his head.

He heard voices, but he kept his eyes closed. He was tired from the running, and there was this horrible pain in his head. It was like the time he had fallen out of a

49

tree, and Mama had put cloths wrung in cold water on his head. But he hadn't fallen out of a tree this time. The tree had fallen on him. He listened.

"I'm a doctor," Pa was saying. "At least let me go tend to my son."

Somebody laughed. It was a mean, ugly kind of laugh.

"Please," Mama said.

A strange voice barked. "Shut up. He's better off than you're going to be, unless I see some hard money. You get up enough, maybe nothing'll happen to you.

He opened his eyes cautiously. A burly man was standing right in front of him, so close that he could smell the leather of the man's boots. They were beautiful boots, highly polished. Except for the boots, the man was in rags. A torn, ragged pair of blue trousers, a filthy gray jacket, and a plug hat, dented in the crown, completed the costume.

"You act reasonable," the man continued, "I won't tell the others about you." His voice was all honey-sweet, now.

One of the bushwhackers, of course. An enterprising man who had tackled the house single-handed to avoid sharing whatever loot there might be with the rest of the band. He had the courage of desperation.

Tom saw a new, long-barreled revolver swinging from the bushwhacker's right hand, a gobbet of meat in the other. There was the same mixture of fascination and revulsion in Tom as if he had seen a snake.

Snakes were to be killed. You didn't have to think twice about that. He moved his right hand gingerly towards the front of his shirt. The man's legs would conceal his movement from the others. The hand with the meat moved up and out of sight, followed by a hearty sound of mastication.

Tom's hand closed around the claw-shaped butt of the derringer, and he felt for the hammers with his thumb. Which hammer controlled which trigger? Cock them

50

both. How his head ached! The bushwhacker must have hit him over the head with his pistol. He eased back the first hammer; no danger of picking the wrong barrel. Only one trigger for both barrels. Why hadn't he noticed that before?

The hammer went to cock with a faint click, and the boot nearest him scraped on the floor. The man was turning around, and it was now or not at all, even though only one hammer was cocked, and even though there'd never be time for the other. He twisted his body and pushed himself to a half-sitting position with his left elbow as the man turned his head.

The curiosity in the man's eyes turned to alarm as the derringer showed, and the pistol in his right hand jerked. Mama said "Shoot!" He knew the barrel was straight, and he pulled hard, and a long moment later there was a puff of smoke and a small noise like a bump.

He clawed for the second hammer, and then the man hinged in the middle and at the knees, and went to the floor in a heap.

"See to Anne, Mary," Pa ordered, and then he came over to Tom. "How's your head, boy?"

"It's going to stay on, sir."

Pa knelt down beside the bushwhacker. "He's dead," he muttered. "We've got to get him out of here."

"Yes, Pa," he said obediently. He had killed a man. He had earned his stripes as sergeant of the Lovatt company. Suddenly it didn't matter any more that he was sergeant. He didn't want to be anything of the sort. He wanted to be the boy who played checkers with Pa and who played legal puzzles with Cousin Alison, and who had never killed anyone.

Pa looked at him. "You did the right thing. You know that, don't you?"

He nodded. He supposed that it had been the right

thing. It was just that he wished it hadn't been him who had to do it.

"You going to be sick?"

He shook his head and the pain beat against his skull. "I don't think so."

"Do you want to stay here with the ladies?"

His head cleared, and he tucked the derringer back in his shirt. The barrel was still hot. It burned against his chest. "No, sir. I shot him; I'll bury him."

Pa nodded his approval. "You're Sandy's brother, all right. Give me the derringer. I want to give it to your mother. You can take his pistol. I'll help you load him on his horse."

They worked quickly. It was as though it were an everyday occurrence, shooting a man. Tom unstrapped the dead man's gun belt and holster. They had a common origin with the boots: the belt buckle was lettered "U.S.," and the leather holster flap was so stamped. He buckled the belt around his waist and sheathed the heavy pistol.

"Ready?" Pa asked.

He nodded. "Shall I get Brutus?"

"Get his mare and Brutus, as well. Take him out to the woods along Centre Creek and see if you can hide him. Tie up his horse and ride back on Brutus. We'll bury him and pick up his horse tonight. And hurry. I may need you."

"Yes, Pa." He went through the door into the burning sunlight.

The bushwhacker's mare stamped and whinnied when she scented blood, but once they had the dead man tied to the saddle, she quieted. Tom led Brutus out of the shed where the doctor had taken him for safety at the first sound of gunfire from town.

As he rode off through the orchard leading the mare, he

could hear firing still going on in the village. He wondered how Will Kinyard and Sam were doing. Will, Grandpa, and Mr. McNair ought to be just about a match for anything that might come along. There wasn't anything he could do to help them now, anyway. He'd do well to see to it that he didn't need any help himself.

With a sense of relief, he left the open rows of trees in the orchard for the tangled underbrush of the woods. Apparently the fighting around Dorfer's had died out; the shots sounded further away, rather than closer, although he had been heading towards the back of the Dorfer land on his way to the creek. Maybe the bushwhackers had been beaten off.

Perhaps three hundred yards inside the tangle he found what he was looking for. A shallow ravine, cut by erosion, drained the upper reaches of the wood into Centre Creek. Laurel grew along its sides in thick profusion, and the springy branches interlaced at the top to form a sort of leafy roof.

He tied the raider's mare and Brutus to one tree. Perhaps they would calm each other. Pa had tied the bushwhacker's hands to his feet under the mare's belly. The body might slip, but it couldn't fall off. Now, however, he had to get next to the frightened horse to cut or untie the rope. He began by rubbing Brutus about the ears, talking to him the while. It was a caress that never failed on Brutus. After a bit, the strange mare looked over at Brutus to see what was going on. It was Tom's chance, and he made the most of it.

The mare suffered her ears to be scratched and her flanks to be patted. Still talking, Tom reached down to untie the knot Pa had tied. The proximity to the dead man set his teeth on edge. At least the body was free; he grasped a boot in either hand and pulled. The mare screamed with terror and arched her back for a leap. The

53

body came away with a bone-crushing thud, and he drew it out of reach of the flashing hooves. The worse of it was over.

He led the horses down the slope that led to Centre Creek. A good drink of water would work wonders with them all. He could leave the mare tied up near the creek.

Behind the woods a bugle yelled stridently, and the firing was all but drowned in a wild cheer. At the moment, he didn't much care whom the bugle represented; even Yankees were better than bushwhackers.

Tom dismounted while he was still under cover of the trees in the orchard and tied Brutus there. The house looked much the same as when he had left, but he was not going to come bursting in a second time. One crack on the head was quite enough. He kept trees between himself and the house, until at last he was behind Betsy's shack. Then he sprinted across the open ground to the rear door.

The door opened as he reached for the knob. Mama stood there, holding the derringer. "Were you seen?"

"No, ma'am. I got rid of him down in the woods. I tied up his mare down by the creek."

She nodded. "You did well. Pa is at the front watching. Cousin Alison is upstairs looking out a rear window, and Betsy is in Sandy's room with Aunt Anne." She grinned triumphantly. "We have a fortress to rival Torquilstone."

"Torquilstone?"

"In *Ivanhoe*, boy," she said impatiently.

"Yes, Mama." He reached for the buckle of the gun belt to unstrap it. "I reckon I'd better give this to Pa, now."

She shook her head impatiently. "These are times when a man must carry a gun. Today, you became a man." She grasped his arm with one strong hand. "Soon you

54

will take your place with your brothers. Do you understand?"

Her eyes burned into his as though she could transfer some of her own fierce determination to his soul. He quailed before it.

"Don't fail me, boy!" she ordered.

CHAPTER 5

Tom Has a Problem

THE excitement was over. The battle of Lovatt had been fought and won with the aid of a troop of irregular cavalry and a bugle. Jeems McNair was in the best position to collect the personal accounts of the individual heroes—and everyone was a hero, of course.

"Personally, I think the bugle was worth more than the irregulars," he confided to Doctor Tanner. "The bushwhackers heard that horn, and they skedaddled."

Doctor Tanner chuckled. Leave it to Jeems to cut the self-appointed heroes down to size. "I don't know but what the irregulars are as bad as the Yankees, when it comes to foraging. They got two hams off me."

"It was a good thing some of the folks in this town found out where some of the other folks stood," Jeems continued. "Your father-in-law was madder'n a hornet when he saw Barnes go tailing off for home."

"Yes. I was right sorry to hear about Will Kinyard. He was a fine boy, and he had more courage and loyalty than a lot of grown men."

"That's for sure. I figured he'd come in Andrew's house with me, but then we saw him out by the rain barrel popping away at one of the guerrillas behind the barn. His gun was empty, and he couldn't load too fast, of course, being one-armed and all. One of them must have snuck around behind him."

"How'd Horace do?"

"Pretty good. Two of them got around to the west side of the tavern, and old Horace yanked both triggers at once. He winged one of them with buckshot and scared the daylights out of the other. He doggone near knocked his own head off with the recoil. Your boy Tom did well. The whole town's talking about it."

"We're very proud of Tom," Doctor Tanner said carefully. "He did a man's work that day."

"I wouldn't say he looks particularly happy about it," Jeems said drily.

That much was certainly true, Doctor Tanner thought as he rode Brutus up the Pike towards home and his dinner. Something was bothering Tom. He poked around as if he didn't quite know what to do with himself. He had even withdrawn from his cousin. That was a pity, for Alison was a lovely child, and she was understanding far beyond her years.

It might be a good thing for Tom if the company got started again. It would be something for him to do, and it would also give him valuable training in leadership, if he were made an officer. The way things stood now, Tom might well be elected captain, if he were to try to resuscitate the company. Jeems McNair was not the only one who spoke well of Tom; the whole town knew of his exploit and compared him with Sandy.

Thinking of Sandy made him remember the letter Jeems had just given him. As was his custom, he had not opened it, knowing that Mary would want to have him read it to her so that they could share the letter at the same time. "Get along, Brutus," he urged.

Mary Tanner was sewing with Anne and Alison in the rear parlor. It was a sad commentary on the state of the war, she thought as she contrasted the coarse muslin they were fashioning into everyday shirts for Joseph and Tom with the fine-woven Madras of three years ago.

The sound of Brutus' stately tread on the gravel outside reminded her that dinner time was at hand. Joseph had continued to ride Brutus, even though they now had the robber's horse. It was like Joseph to be contented with things as they were, to resist change. Secretly, however, she was glad that things had worked out so that Tom had a horse of his own to ride. He had earned the right to it, and Will and Sandy would certainly be proud of their brother when they learned of his deed.

"Joseph is back," Anne said, putting aside her work.

"Yes. It's getting on towards noon."

Joseph's heavy tread came down the hall, paused at the door. "We're in here," Mary called.

"Good morning, ladies," Joseph said gallantly. "Busy as bees, I see."

Alison smiled at him. She was a fine girl, Mary thought. It was so nice to have other women about! And Alison might have been her own daughter, the way she was always willing to help with things.

"We're making shirts this morning. You and Tom have been going through your old ones at a tremendous rate."

"I have a letter from Sandy," Joseph said with an apologetic cough.

"Mother?" Alison suggested tactfully.

"Yes?"

"I'm sure Uncle Joe and Aunt Mary will excuse us while we go upstairs and freshen ourselves."

Mary saw that Anne was reluctant; of course she wanted to hear Sandy's news, but she could wait. Now was for Joseph and herself.

" 'My dear parents,' " Joseph read when Anne and Alison had gone. " 'Just a line to inform you that I am well. We have been engaged in minor actions, but the losses

58

in my battery were not heavy. I hope to have some great and pleasing news to relate in my next letter. This year of 1863 promises to be the most eventful year in my entire life! God bless you and keep you well. Your loving son, Sandy.' "

Joseph folded the letter and handed it to her. "It's not a very long letter," he said ruefully.

"But he's safe and well, Joseph."

"Yes, that's the important thing. I wonder what his great and pleasing news is. He's already a captain. Have you any idea what it might be?"

"I have," she smiled, thinking of Sally Lou Barnes. "But this is woman's business; I'm not saying. Come! Let's call Anne and Alison down for dinner."

Tom walked up the path to Reverend Harmon's house. His mind was in a turmoil, and perhaps the minister could set it at ease.

He hadn't wanted to kill anyone. He knew that killing the bushwhacker had been necessary, because the war had made it so; but that didn't help. The war had made it necessary for someone to kill his gentle brother Will, two years ago. It had made it necessary for someone to deprive Will Kinyard of an arm, and finally of his life.

Necessary! His eyes burned with unshed tears as he remembered how kind and patient Will Kinyard had been. What might Will have accomplished with his life, had he been allowed to live? Was any war worth the loss of one single life? Let alone those of his brother and his friend?

Reverend Harmon indicated a straight-backed chair at the opposite end of the table from his own. The table was a fine old piece, fashioned of mahogany for another age. It was the pastor's most valuable possession.

"How may I help you, Thomas?"

Now that the moment had come, he was not certain

just how to begin. "I'm not sure, sir. I guess I don't feel at ease with myself."

"That's not a happy state of affairs, since you have to live with yourself," the pastor remarked drily. "You know, of course, that the entire town is proud of you for your act of courage. You saved several lives by your deed."

"Yes, sir. Maybe that's part of the trouble. I wanted to help, and I—did what I had to do. But anyone else would have done the same thing."

Reverend Harmon nodded. "You killed a man in self-defense. That is permitted, although we advocate non-violence. But you don't feel that you should be praised for it; is that it?"

"Part of it, sir. I guess the rest of it is that I didn't give him a chance to throw down his gun and quit. I just shot him without even thinking about it. And I didn't feel wrong while I did it. That came later."

"You were responsible for other lives, Thomas," the minister said firmly. "You had to do exactly as you did. That is why you felt no sense of wrong at the time. You are assuming blame for the action of the townsfolk who praised you. But that's not your fault."

"No, sir. But I don't think I could do it again."

"Why not wait until the time comes? There's not much sense in crossing that bridge until you come to it. You may never be faced with that decision again."

"I'll have to go in the army, sir."

"When you get to the army, Thomas, I'm sure you'll do the right thing."

Whatever consolation Tom had received from Reverend Harmon evaporated in direct proportion to the distance he placed between them. By the time he reached home, he felt the same as he had felt before he had gone. It was something he had to work out for himself, he

60

guessed. He would have to decide what he would do before the occasion arose, because otherwise he would be acting blindly, without reason. He had certainly learned the value of reason from Grandpa.

He unsaddled the mare and turned her loose to browse with Brutus in the pasture behind the barn. He wished someone would turn him out to pasture. It would be kind of pleasant not to have to think—just for a while, anyhow.

Pa would be in his office, now; Mama and Aunt Anne and Cousin Alison would probably be in the back parlor sewing. He didn't much want to see any of them. He'd take a stroll in the woods. It would be cool there. And quiet.

"Cousin Tom?"

Bad luck! Alison had spied him and come to the back door. "Yes, Cousin Alison."

She held her skirts safely above the ground and raced across the yard. "Please take me with you! It's so hot in there, and I've been cooped up sewing all the livelong day!"

"Won't Aunt Anne be wondering where you are?"

"Mama said it would be all right." Her face clouded. "Unless you don't want to take me."

"Of course I do," he lied gallantly. "It's right hot this afternoon. Much too hot to stay indoors."

"Good! Where shall we go?"

"How about down to Centre Creek?"

"Where we went skating two years ago?"

"That's a nice place. Unless there are too many insects, it should be pleasant."

It was cool down by the creek. The stream chuckled over a bevy of rocks, branches rustled in the faint breeze, and the tall grass whispered a rumor of summer.

61

"Sam Dorfer and I come here to fish, sometimes. Would you care to sit on this log, Cousin? It's quite firm, and I'll spread my handkerchief."

Alison smiled impishly and made a mock curtsy. "I'd be delighted, Cousin Tom. Would you care to join me?"

"Will Kinyard used to come down here with us," he said abruptly. "The boy who was killed. He was a rough-shod fellow, but I liked him."

Alison looked steadily at him through half-lowered eyelids. Her eyes were almost green in the light that filtered down through the overhanging branches.

"What's been bothering you, Cousin Tom?"

He shivered involuntarily, checked himself. "I don't know. I think I'm wondering whether I could bring myself to kill a man again."

"You mustn't blame yourself for what happened. There was nothing else you could have done," she said gently.

"I know. It didn't bother me at the time. I guess it was because I didn't know him. But when I heard about Will Kinyard—and remembered our Will—I realized that someone must have known that man, too. And his pistol belonged to someone else. It was a brand-new navy Colt, like the Yankee officers use. That means he killed somebody to get it. Where will it all stop? How can I go in the army and do the same thing?"

"You can't take the responsibility for all killing upon your own shoulders. That's not fair to you."

"I don't have the courage for that. All I'm thinking is that I might go to war and kill someone like Will. I couldn't live with myself if I did that."

"I know, Cousin Tom."

"I believe in our cause and in everything it stands for, except for slavery. I wish I were like Sandy and could go out and do brave things and make everyone proud of me. I'd fight for that, if for nothing else. But I keep remembering Will, and then I don't know."

62

"I wouldn't want you to be like Sandy," Alison said thoughtfully. "I like you as you are."

"That was a nice thing to say."

She smiled. "When the time comes for you to decide, I'm sure your decision will be a wise one. And I'll be on your side, whatever it is."

He felt strangely at peace. Perhaps there was no need to make up his mind right this minute. It was enough to know that someone else knew what he was thinking and why he was thinking it.

Doctor Tanner was not happy. Tom was worried about something, and he wasn't talking about it. For a time the doctor was able to forget his personal concern in the rush of news that came with July, but only for a time.

July had been an eventful month for Lovatt. The news of the battle of Gettysburg was succeeded in late July by the announcement that Ambrose Tanner had been promoted to major as a reward for extreme gallantry in action. By now, everyone was familiar with the most minute details of General Lee's determination to carry the war north. Rumor said that the battle had been bungled, that the Federals had almost destroyed the Army of Northern Virginia as the result of General Longstreet's hesitation; but that was probably just a Yankee trick to undermine people's confidence. More important to Lovatt, three more young men would not be returning to their homes. The casualty lists were long.

In the middle of the month, two riders attempted to rob McNair's tavern, but were frustrated by the appearance of Horace in their rear, armed with the shotgun Jeems had given him following his defense of the tavern against the bushwhackers a month ago.

Following the battle of McNair's, as Mr. Hauser waggishly described it, came the reading of banns, announcing the impending union of Major Ambrose Tanner and

Miss Sally Lou Barnes. It was somewhat anticlimactic; everyone had expected the engagement to be announced before fall, as Sally Lou had confided to her friends. The reading of banns meant that Sandy could be expected home soon, perhaps at the end of the month. Neither army could be expected to get back in fighting shape for a long time after the holocaust that had been Gettysburg.

The final event in July was the sudden death of Mrs. Barnes. She had been ailing during the summer, and she had called on Doctor Tanner once or twice in an attempt to find out what was wrong. Earlier in the month, she had complained of chest pains, and by the time Mr. Barnes decided to ask Doctor Tanner to call, she had a temperature of over 104 degrees and a thoroughly matured case of influenza. Doctor Tanner consoled himself with the thought that she had never been a strong woman, and that had she not succumbed to influenza, she would in all likelihood have succumbed to something else.

The worst of it was that now Sandy's marriage would have to be postponed. Sally Lou would be in mourning for at least six months.

It was a reflection of the effect the war was having on people, he decided. Before the war he would never have been so little affected by death. Now, with the endless lists of casualties (is Sandy's name on this one?) constantly before him, he could not help but be indifferent to the death of a vain, somewhat stupid woman. The newspaper he received from Staunton said that the flower of Southern manhood was dying. The doctor agreed. He wondered if people who didn't have sons in the army felt the same. Perhaps not.

And that brought him back to Tom. Soon Tom would be going into the army. Would he be able to live up to Sandy? Sandy came vividly to mind. His waving black hair, his air of alertness, his friendly grin, and his calm self-assurance had made him a natural leader. His indisputable bravery in battle had made him a legend in his own time. He was idolized for his handsome appearance and his modesty, and his reckless heroism symbolized all that was fine and good in the gray-clad armies for the people of the Valley.

The air of assurance; that was what Tom lacked. He doubted himself, the doctor decided. He wished Tom would speak out so that he could set his mind straight. But whenever he tried to talk with Tom these days, the boy found an excuse to terminate the conversation. The only person he seemed to talk to was his cousin.

Doctor Tanner had hope, though. When Sandy came home, he'd be able to get some sense out of Tom. He brightened at the thought of seeing Sandy again, and for a time he forgot his concern with Tom.

CHAPTER 6

A Furlough for Sandy

SANDY rode into the yard one rainy morning in the early part of August. Beneath his new poncho, his uniform was a gray field blazoned with blue patches. His boots were scratched and dull, and the soles were all but worn through. He had managed to acquire a severe case of diarrhea—"squitters," he called it—and his ride down Pike from Staunton had been punctuated by frequent stops. He looked gaunt. Only his smile was reminiscent of the old Sandy.

Doctor Tanner prescribed a diet that consisted mainly of cheese, and ordered the all-but-conquered hero to bed for the rest of the day. Sandy only smiled and shook his head. First he had to see Sally Lou, he said. Aided and abetted by Betsy, who cleaned his hat and boots and helped him squeeze into the gray suit that Tom generously loaned him, he got his way. Her mother had died; it was only good manners to pay his respects.

But when Sandy rode homeward from the Barnes's and Grandpa Hauser's, he was a sadder but wiser young man. He recalled Sergeant Harrison's parting words: "The home folks won't be any different, sir. You will."

Harrison had been nearly right. Mr. Barnes, for all his alleged patriotism, was merely another farmer holding his grain for the highest prices he could squeeze from an ineffective and impoverished government. For Sally Lou, the Confederacy was personified by her concept of himself, and by the songs he had seen on the pianoforte. "The Bonnie Blue Flag," "The Southern Marseillaise," and "Lorena" were more suited to the spring of 1861 than they were to the summer of 1863.

Even Grandpa had been a disappointment. His war was embodied in the glowing pages of *The Jeffersonian*, the speeches of Mr. Davis, and the admirable constitution drawn up by Mr. Stephens. His legal mind gloried in political skirmishes at Richmond and in the newest policies of the government. It did not take into account the men who straggled on the way to Gettysburg because their shoes had worn out. Neither did it consider the effects of short rations, heavy casualties, and long marches on the digestive tracts of men and horses.

Such factors were apparently only the concern of the men who wore cadet gray or butternut brown, and they were not to be weighed by civilians in their concept of the war.

In this mood he went to see Pa. The office was fragrant with the fumes of Pa's pipe, as usual. Although Sandy did not use tobacco, he liked the odor of a pipe.

Pa looked up from his pills and nodded. "How are the Barneses?"

"Fine, sir."

"It's good to be back, I imagine. Did you see your grandfather?"

"Yes, sir."

Pa poured the pills into a small brown bottle and fumbled for pen and ink. "Laudanum," he explained. "No more to be had, unless you want to pay its weight in gold. What's the matter with you?"

"I'm out of step with the regiment, Pa."

"People aren't acting the way you thought they would?"

"They aren't thinking the way I expected. Nobody

67

seems to have any idea of what the war is all about. Grandpa was talking about Mr. Davis and the new plan to print more money that won't be worth as much as the last batch was. Mr. Barnes was busy explaining how he could get rich selling his grain to civilians in Richmond instead of to the government."

"Do you think he'll succeed?" Pa asked.

"I have my doubts. He can't get his wheat to Richmond all by himself. He needs transport. And if he sells in Staunton, he'll have to sell cheap."

"I'm devastated at the thought, as I know you must be," Pa smiled. "But he's an exception, surely?"

"Thank Heaven!"

"We may not always understand you boys, but we try to. You've suffered a disappointment, having your marriage postponed. We may not know how to aim a six-pounder, but we can understand a boy coming home to get married and then not being able to."

"It's not that, Pa. It's a little different. We just don't see things from the same viewpoint."

A rap on the door was followed by Tom's head. "May I come in, too?"

"By all means," Pa said amiably. "This is our refuge from the fairer sex. We could hardly refuse you the opportunity to share in our sanctuary."

"I hear you've become quite a young warrior," Sandy said.

"I'd rather not talk about that."

Sandy felt his temper rising. Rather not talk about it, indeed! "Grandpa told me that your company and the cavalry accounted for six of them, with a loss of only one man. You should be very proud of that."

Tom's lips twitched, but he said nothing.

"How is the company?" Sandy pressed.

"It's disbanded. It didn't really function. When the

68

bushwhackers came, everybody went his own way, just as if there had never been a company."

"Tom was stunned by the outlaw, you know," Pa said. "He was knocked to the floor, and for a few moments he was quite unconscious."

"Your first big fight. You did well."

"I suppose so," Tom said indifferently. "If you'll excuse me now, I'd like to wash."

When Tom had gone, Sandy shook his head in bewilderment. "That's what I meant, Pa. I don't understand civilians."

After the initial disappointment of the delay in his wedding plans, Sandy realized that he was perhaps more relieved than otherwise. Right now, were Sally Lou to marry him, she would be marrying a stranger. In some ways she was as much a stranger to him, and that was worse. The face that peered from his shaving mirror each morning was the same, but what lay behind it was not. The war made strangers of friends and friends of strangers; it buried the familiar and exposed the weird depths of character that no one suspected. Very few people managed to remain consistent, he reflected. He had not known Sergeant Harrison or Captain Marle before the war, but he was sure that they had not changed. Colonel Hulme had not changed in the short time he had known him, either. But almost everyone else had.

Not unnaturally, he found himself anticipating his return to the familiar milieu of the battalion, the reception by the hardened, laughing young men who saw things the way he did, who laughed at the same jokes, and who followed the same demanding profession. Would he ever be able to become a doctor, as he had planned? Would he ever be suited for anything not connected with the army? Sometimes he wondered.

Of all the persons he met in the course of his visit,

69

Tom was the least understandable. He would have expected Tom to be proud of his feat, perhaps even boastful. After all, Tom had been so anxious to grow up. He could remember how proud the boy had been that day almost three years ago when he had been permitted to drive to Staunton by himself, when Sandy and Will had come home for Christmas. Surely this, too, was a part of growing up and assuming the responsibilities of manhood? But Tom was not proud; he was only tactful, avoiding the subject and Sandy, as well. All of them stood together against Tom in this—all of them, that is, save Alison. Where Mama pretended not to notice Tom's attitude, or Pa displayed his concern, Alison openly took Tom's part. No words were ever spoken; it was perhaps too serious a thing to be talked about. But whenever Tom was about, Alison was near at hand, ready to play checkers, or to discuss Mr. Thackeray's novels, or merely to chat.

Sandy spent most of his time with Sally Lou or riding to and from the Barnes house. Apparently he had silenced Mr. Barnes's fear about the propriety of such frequent visits. For his part, Tom was glad to be able to escape Sandy for most of the day. An ever widening gulf had come between them; it was as though they didn't even think alike any more. Sandy began from one viewpoint and he from another, and the further they pursued a subject, the greater was the divergence.

As a result of this, Tom spent as much time with Grandpa Hauser as the latter could afford, pursuing the law in a desultory fashion, listening to Grandpa's interminable hunting stories, and trying to pretend that the war would be at an end before he would have to go. If Grandpa was aware of his views, that ardent secessionist said nothing.

70

The perusal of Blackstone would have been a dull affair indeed, had it not been for Cousin Alison. She transformed the legal verbiage and the interminable references to cases long dead and buried into a sort of game. During the day, while Tom was away at his reading or passing time with Sam Dorfer, she would concoct legal tangles that they could work on in the evenings.

"A man named Brown has owned a piece of property for twenty years," she would begin. "His neighbor, Mr. Smith, was obliged to travel around it in order to reach the main road to town. Finally, Mr. Brown told Mr. Smith that he might cross his land to reach the road. But one day they quarreled, and Mr. Brown put up a gate to prevent Mr. Smith from crossing his land. Mr. Smith sued. What right had he to trespass upon Mr. Brown's property?"

"I'd say he had right of thorofare," Tom would answer. "Until this incident, he had crossed Mr. Brown's property so often that it became an established right."

"But Mr. Brown closed his gate one day a year."

"You didn't tell me that, Cousin!"

"You should have asked me," she would tease.

Occasionally Pa would join in the game, summoning his knowledge of legal medicine to bait the cleverly laid traps with which he studded his "cases." They were pleasant evenings; it was possible to forget for a time that Sandy deplored his reaction to the incident with the marauder, that Mama was referring to Will's homecoming with increasing frequency, and that there was a wall between Pa and him.

Meanwhile, Alison's game was having a twofold effect. It gave him a firmer grounding in legal skirmishing than any amount of reading could have done, and it gave him the pleasant companionship of a devoted and pretty friend. He could have spoken to no one else as he was able to do to Cousin Alison, he realized. He avoided disparately the over solicitous attention of Aunt Anne and the casual good humor of Sandy. Cousin Alison was his strongest link with the race of Adam.

Sam Dorfer was at loose ends, as well. Following the battle of Lovatt, he had tried to resuscitate the Lovatt company. As lieutenant, he was the ranking survivor. Without Tom's aid and encouragement, however, he could do nothing. It was doubtful that he could have accomplished anything even with Tom's help. The men of the company had taken orders from nineteen-year-old Will Kinyard because he had "been to the war." They were hardly inclined to take orders from a brace of six-teen-year-olds who had been nowhere.

"Anybody who wants can come down the mountain and take the town," Sam complained one morning near the end of Sandy's furlough.

Tom looked past the dried hollyhock stalks in the Dorfer's back yard at the mountain. The afternoon sun outlined trees at the crest; the eastern flank was already in deep and ominous shade. "Not very much we could do about it, even if the company started up," he temporized.

"I dunno," Sam replied. "You take it when the guer-rillas came, we held them off until the cavalry got here. If we hadn't put up some kind of fight, they'd have wrecked the place before the cavalry could get here."

"Whatever we did, we did as individuals, not as a com-pany."

Sam looked at him reproachfully. "Now, Tom; if it hadn't been for the company, Will Kinyard wouldn't have been up the steeple watching for them. And the rest of us wouldn't have had our weapons and been all together. You know that. That's why we need a company. And if Yankee spies come around, we could question them and examine their papers and things."

"And find everything in apple-pie order. They're pretty smart, you know."

"A person would think you didn't want the company to start up again, the way you talk."

"I don't," Tom snapped. "If everybody'd forget this foolishness, we'd all be a lot better off."

Sam grew pale with rage. "If you think the company was only foolishness, I reckon I don't want to hear any more."

"I mean the whole war. What right has anybody to decide who's going to die? Just because I'm stronger or pull a trigger faster, does that make me a better man than the one I kill? Maybe he's a better man than me."

Sam was surprised out of his wrath. "You've been thinking about all that? Why, Tom, that's plain crazy. That bushwhacker you shot, he would have killed your whole family."

"I know it, and I'm not sorry about what I did. But supposing he hadn't been what he was. Suppose he'd been like you and me?"

"I never thought about that," Sam admitted. "But if he was like us, he wouldn't be a bushwhacker or a Yankee, either one."

Sam's problems were easily settled. His only real problem was how to get his father to permit him to enlist in the army next year. Tom thought that that would be easy; no one could stand up to the steady friction of Sam's persistence for long.

Supper was a quiet affair that evening. Doctor Tanner was preoccupied with the need for obtaining quinine from somewhere. His Richmond supplier had been forced out of business by steadily rising costs which he had been unwilling or unable to pay. As a result, the doctor's own supplies had been cut off. If he was not willing to pay blockade prices, there were plenty of druggists who were.

It was a minor mishap in a time of great tragedies. The passing of one druggist was little noted; it would not be long remembered.

After supper, Doctor Tanner went to his office, presumably to take inventory of his supplies. In reality, he welcomed the opportunity to be alone. He was weary of Anne's unfinished sentences and depressed by Tom's moods. Heaven knew he had tried to understand the boy. But there was a point beyond which you could not go. How could you support the position that all killing was wrong, when you had another son who was developing into a fine soldier and a hero? He was sure that that was what was wrong with Tom.

Mary's conduct was disturbing, as well. She had taken to sewing for poor dead Will. He had discovered that quite by accident; one morning he had found an array of yellowed shirts and stockings in his drawer; upon questioning, Betsy divulged the secret.

"Miss Mary tell me her Will coming home one of these days, and she have to have new clothes ready for him."

"And since she had filled the other wardrobe, you had to make room by giving Will's things space in my drawers?"

Betsy nodded. "That's what I done."

"Lord, Betsy! You should have told me long ago."

"No, sir. You know he's gone, and I know he's gone. If she wants to think he's coming back, it's maybe because that's what she's got to have to live."

Thus Mary. The war was taking its toll of noncombatants as well. It was a little hard to remember that only two short years ago the Valley had been at peace and the war was something you read about in the newspaper. No, that was not quite right. Will had been dead two years.

Out in the night hoofbeats drummed along the Pike. Doctor Tanner turned down his lamp and went to the window. There were perhaps ten riders in all. The moonlight silvered their accouterments, made gray magic of their garb. Judging from the rough attempt to maintain a formation, they were not guerillas.

He dropped the curtain against the night. In the rear parlor there would be laughter and light and the sound of familiar voices. It would not always be so. A wise man would enjoy it while it was still present.

"I was just saying that we ought to get some fresh venison, now that Sandy is home," Mary smiled at him as he entered. "We have the services of two Nimrods, now."

"There's quite a shortage of percussion caps. I was unable to purchase any down at the store two months ago."

"I can help out," Sandy offered. "I did some unofficial requisitioning before I left. I can let you have about a hundred."

"What's unofficial requisitioning, Cousin Sandy?" Alison asked.

Sandy chuckled. "In better circles, one would call it borrowing. At a lower echelon, it's just plain stealing."

"I'm not sure I like that," Mary said firmly.

"It's not as bad as that, Mama. We capture stores and supplies from the Yankees and collect them for the army. Anyone who's short helps himself."

"In that case," the doctor said, "I think we might be able to risk a few rounds in the hope of getting a deer. How about it, boys?"

"Could you join us, Pa?" Sandy asked.

For a moment he let his mind soar off to the slopes of North Mountain. The golden sunshine fell dappled on the ground. A buck whisked through the brush, stopped. He raised his rifle; the front sight slipped into place . . . no. There was work to be done here. And it wasn't safe to leave the ladies alone.

"I'm sorry. I wish I could."

"You'll have Tom," Mary said. "It's a pity Will can't be with you, but Tom will show you how well he can shoot."

"Of course," Sandy said. He did not betray the fact that he had noticed the reference to Will.

"Tom needs the practice," Mary continued. "He'll be joining you next year."

"We'll see, Mary," the doctor said gently. "Tom's pretty young, still."

"Tom will do his duty," Mary said sharply. "I hope he kills a thousand of them."

Tom stood up. His face was pale, and his voice trembled. "I hope I never have to kill anyone or anything again!"

"Men are dying to keep you safe," Sandy said hotly.

"You'll do what you must do," Mary cut in. "If I were you, I'd be ashamed of what I had just said."

Tom half-bowed. "If you all will excuse me?" Without waiting for permission, he strode from the room. Alison slipped from her chair despite Anne's warning glance and followed him.

"Are you going to permit this?" Mary asked.

"It's a part of growing up, Mary. He's finding himself, and it's a painful procedure at best. We must be patient."

"My father had other concepts of what constitutes discipline."

"I'm sure of it, my dear. However, your father would be the last man in the world to criticize Tom for his views. Tom is merely exercising his rights as an individual. I disagree with him, but I will not suppress him."

"He needs a good talking to, Pa," Sandy said. "He'll get in trouble thinking that way."

"Angry words never changed ideas, Sandy. In time, he'll find his own answer. And in his own way."

Tom breathed deeply of the night air. It bore the faint perfume of faraway pines on North Mountain, the acrid odor of horse dung and dust. A party of horsemen had passed not too long ago. Nowadays the Pike seemed like a racetrack. Troops were forever moving down it in support of military operations in the northern part of the Valley, or else heading south for the railroad at Staunton, where they could be shuttled eastward to the Piedmont, or to the defenses of Richmond. During the nights, the Pike was claimed by all manner of men: bushwhackers who belonged to no side and preyed upon both, irregular cavalry or guerrillas, Federal patrols, and the hated Jessie Scouts: Federal troops in Confederate uniform.

Behind him the door opened. For a moment, a wedge of yellow lamplight fell across the darkness at his feet. Then the door closed and the brightness was succeeded by the silver haze of moonlight. "It's me, Tom," Alison said just behind him.

"I'm tired of pretending and hiding. It's time they knew."

Her hand rested lightly on his sleeve. "I understand."

"It's not something all cut and dried. Maybe I'll change my mind. But I have to think it out. It's not a thing you can jump into without thinking it out first."

"I was proud of you for standing up for what you believe in," she said. "Even if you don't believe in anything—or if you don't know what to do—it's better to say so and let them know."

Her skirt rustled, and the door opened briefly. It closed, then, and she was gone, and there was nothing but the silver-gray moonlight on the Pike and the eternal silence of the night.

CHAPTER 7

A Right Pretty Buck

TOM got up early the following morning. He had not slept well, and for the first time in weeks he had dreamed of the man he had killed. It was as though the knowledge of the disapproval of Sandy and of his parents had resurrected the incident, complete to the last detail.

It was still dark outside, and if he hurried he could probably get downstairs before the others were up. Last night, for the first time in his life, Mama hadn't said goodnight to him. All the rest of them probably felt the same way towards him. All of them except Alison, anyhow. The sooner he got away from the house, the better off he'd be. The better off they'd be, too.

Boots in hand, he crept down the stairs. Pa was snoring, and there was no sound from Will's room, now occupied by Sandy, since Aunt Anne and Cousin Alison had taken over Sandy's own room. So far, so good. Now if Betsy were up, everything would be perfect.

His luck held; Betsy was already busy with the fire in her stove. The light wood spat and snapped, and heat waves shimmered over the cooking surface.

"How come you're up so early?" Betsy asked.

"I'm going out in the woods today. Can you fix me something to take along?"

Betsy eyed him suspiciously. "You sure it don't have

78

nothing to do with what you told your ma last night? Miss Mary was right upset."

"I'm not running away from home, Betsy."

"That's good." She spread a clean napkin on the table and opened a cupboard. "All I got is corn pone."

"How about some of that mutton we had the other night?"

"Never you mind! There's just about enough for one more meal. You can make out on corn pone. You ain't starving."

"A lot you know," he teased. "I don't eat much at all. Just enough to keep body and soul together."

Betsy shaved a thin slice from the remnant of the leg of mutton and popped it inside a split pone. "Don't you tell on me. What you going to do out there?"

"Kind of walk around and get my bearings."

Betsy nodded. "You know what you want to do, only you don't know if it's right; is that it?"

"That's about the size of it. I want to get off where I can think things out. Or maybe not think at all."

Outside, the darkness was fading. In another half-hour, the sun would come up over the hills and it would be dawn. He stuffed the packet of food Betsy had given him into the pocket of his coat and took his bearings. The most remote place he could think of was Great North Mountain. That was a right smart piece for walking, as Will Kinyard would have said. For a moment Will's impassioned face swam before his eyes. Things had been easy for Will; he had gone to the war and been crippled, it was true, yet he had never deviated from his original purpose. To the day he died, he had been a fighter in a time when fighters were needed. Will had been the right man in the right place at the right time. He had never been obliged to buck other people's opinions; their opinions had always coincided with his.

Time was slipping past. Any moment now someone would awaken and discover that he was missing. Reluctantly he decided to take the bushwhacker's mare.

Brutus cocked a sleepy eye at him as he took down the saddle from the peg, and Sandy's big gray, Johnston, eyed him with open hostility. That horse was a killer, and no mistake! He led the mare into the yard, keeping to the grass so that the clash of her hooves would not awaken the family.

The sun rose abruptly when he was halfway to the foot of the mountain. Intervening trees hid the house and the village, and it was as if time had reversed itself and that once more there was nothing ahead of him but the almost unexplored wilderness of a hundred years ago. The land contributed to the illusion; it was uncleared, dotted with clumps of oak, with here and there a spreading stand of pine. The sun rose higher.

Now color came to the forms that the sun had burned from the mists and blackness of the night. All around him the summer smoldered, awaiting only the steady frosts of late September to fan it into flame. He paused on a gentle slope to look back. It was necessary to keep some sort of reference point in order to prevent being forever lost in time. The flights of mind are swift as lightning, and often more startling. He turned towards the mountain again, and all at once he saw beyond and over, into the valley beyond, and over the mountain beyond that. There was past and future, and they were together now, emphasized by the repetition of the seasons. He recalled Grandpa Hauser's favorite passage from Scripture: "While Earth remaineth, seedtime and harvest and cold and heat, and summer and winter, and day and night shall not cease." Thus it was and had been, and thus it would be. He soared into the void of eternity. . . .

A thin tendril of smoke rising from behind the trees north of Lovatt brought him back into the present.

80

Judging from the direction, it came from a cooking fire at McNair's or the Reverend Harmon's house. Somewhere behind him the world he had left was going about its business.

His gaze traveled southward; there was nothing to see but the endless succession of trees in the middle distance. He would have to climb still higher before he could hope to see the village.

Something moved across a clearing, far down the slope. He watched carefully. A rider on a gray horse. Sandy! For a moment he considered evading his pursuer; then he became conscious of the black trail the mare had left in the dew-drenched grass. Sandy was much too close, and the big gray gelding was more than a match for the mare. He dismounted and sat down to wait.

Sandy wore gray breeches and the soft, leather knee boots of the artillery, but his shirt was the old homespun he had always worn hunting, and he was bareheaded. Over his saddlebow gleamed the long barrel of Pa's rifle; the genuine Golcher that had been made in Pennsylvania before the War of the Revolution.

"See anything yet?" Sandy asked.

"Wasn't looking."

Sandy smiled disarmingly. "I owe you an apology for last night. I lost my temper."

"That's all right." He got to his feet. "Do you want to go further up?"

"Later, perhaps," Sandy said. He swung his right leg back over the saddle and dismounted with a fluid grace. No matter what he did, he did well, Tom thought with a trace of resentment.

"I saw tracks down at the edge of that far clearing," Sandy continued. "If we're lucky, we can get in a shot from here and save ourselves a climb."

The trees made a narrow alley that came to a point

some three hundred yards away. The end of the clearing was still in shadow, but it would not be that way for long. The sun was already nibbling at the shaded area. In another ten minutes it would strike the clearing directly and pinpoint whatever moved in it.

"Long shot, isn't it?"

"Not for the Golcher," Sandy replied. He measured powder from the horn and poured it down the barrel. With finical care, he seated the ball on a linen patch and drove it home with the ramrod. Pa had had the Golcher converted to percussion caps years ago, so there was no need to prime a pan.

"You'll be shooting into the sun."

Sandy grinned. "You're chock-full of objections this morning." He pointed to a small tree to one side of the horses. "In a minute or two, there'll be enough shade to keep the sun off the barrel. We can lie down on the slope there and shoot over that log."

The magic of the early morning was fading now. It had passed beyond the mountain, traveling ever westward. Soon this would be just another summer day.

"Where's your rifle?" Sandy asked.

"I didn't bring one."

Sandy's eyes flicked over him disdainfully. "It strikes me as a foolhardy thing to do. You, of all people, should know that the woods aren't safe for an unarmed man."

"I told you last night that I wasn't going to kill anything. Oh, I'll hunt, I suppose, if we really need meat. But I'm not going to kill anybody."

"What are you going to do when you go in the army?"

"I'm not going."

Sandy's face went white with rage. "I never thought I'd find out my brother was a coward."

"I reckon that's a matter of definition. If being scared is being a coward, then I'm a coward. But that's not the point. The point is that you can't solve anything by killing anyone."

"There are men who are dying in defense of your rights this very minute," Sandy rasped. "And you stand here quibbling about right and wrong."

"Look, Sandy; what good did it do anybody for our Will to be killed? Or my friend Will Kinyard? It didn't solve anything. But the men who killed our Will probably thought they were defending some right of their own. And the man who killed Will Kinyard probably figured he had to kill him to keep from being killed himself."

"Maybe they did. That still doesn't mean that they don't have a right to fight. You'll grant that a man has a right to defend himself?"

"I suppose so."

"Well, he has an obligation to defend his family and his country, the same way. The way to defend your family is to serve in the army. That ought to be plain enough."

It was simple, the way Sandy put it, but it wasn't the way things were. They were complicated, and they had all sorts of subordinate conditions. He tried another tack. "Suppose the war ended tomorrow, Sandy. What would you do? Would you go back to school and study to be a doctor?"

"What's that got to do with it?"

"Don't hedge. Just tell me."

"I don't know," Sandy said slowly. "I might just stay in the army. It suits me now."

"But if nobody's attacking you, you don't have to defend yourself. Isn't it true that after a while you get to like killing? You're a brave man, I know. You rescued one of your guns practically single-handed; we read about it in the papers. You lost half your men at Sharpsburg, but you kept all your guns in action. All right, you're a hero. But how many men had to die to make you one?"

Sandy laughed harshly. "You fool! Do you imagine that I sacrifice lives to build a reputation?"

"I never knew a man's mind to be changed any by calling him names. I'm no exception. I didn't say you had done any of this to build a reputation, mind you; I only said that you had gained by it."

But Sandy had only heard the first part. "You a man? You don't even have the guts to resent an insult."

"Just because you say something doesn't make it so."

Sandy's hand flicked out, cracked across his face. "What does it take to make you fight?"

And then he knew that nothing would satisfy Sandy, nothing would convince him, short of a fight. It was Sandy's only answer to what he conceived to be his problem. It was Sandy's answer to everything. Physical courage solved all problems in Sandy's world.

"You can whip me," he told Sandy. "But you won't change my mind."

"How can I whip you if you won't fight?" Sandy jeered.

His left fist caught Sandy on the shoulder and threw him off balance. Even so, Sandy stopped him short with a smashing blow in the ribs.

He had to stay cool. It helped to realize that he wasn't angry, but that Sandy was. Sandy rushed him, his hands searching for a body hold. No. Wrestling was not for him. Sandy was much too strong. He sidestepped and jabbed at Sandy's face.

"Hah," Sandy grunted, and then he struck hard, once in the chest, once along the side of the jaw.

Tom felt himself plunging towards the ground, and suddenly he crashed into it with bone-jarring force. It didn't hurt, though. It was dark and quiet.

"Well? Give up?"

He opened his eyes to the bright day. "No." Awkwardly he got to his feet, enjoyed with a queer detachment the look of bewilderment on Sandy's face. "Come on!"

Sandy bored in almost straight, weaving only slightly to avoid the fists that hammered almost automatically now, and then he struck hard to the chest, battering Tom backwards on his feet until he stumbled and fell into the merciful pit of darkness and quiet.

"Had enough?"

His head cleared. He got to his feet.

Sandy stood still and watched him. "All right, that's enough. Just say it. Say you're wrong."

A bruise on his right cheekbone stung as a drop of sweat rolled across it. He grinned at Sandy. "There's nothing wrong with me."

"I don't want to hit you again. Don't make me do it."

"Come on!"

Sandy shook his head, and then Tom lurched forward. He slashed awkwardly at Sandy's face with fists as swollen as pumpkins and just about as heavy, too. He felt them strike, but not hard, not clean, because he was too tired; and then his face exploded in a bright shower of pain.

"Are you whipped?" Sandy asked, and he was almost pleading. "Is that enough?"

"I'm still right." He breathed deeply, and his wits returned. "Don't you see that there are some things you can't change with fists or a gun?"

Sandy wiped his face. His nose was bleeding, and his mouth was cut and swollen. "You're no coward," he admitted. "But it's not my way of doing things."

"It's mine."

"I reckon nobody'll dispute the matter with you," Sandy smiled painfully. "You've got a right to your opinions."

"Do you admit you were wrong?" Tom asked suspiciously.

"This time I was wrong. But not about the big thing. When the time comes, you'll see it, too."

"About going in the army? I'm not going."

Sandy grinned. "Stubborn cuss, aren't you? I'm not going to argue the point, but I'm pretty sure that when the time comes, you'll do the right thing."

"Join the army?"

Sandy chuckled. "Why don't we cross that bridge when the time comes? Let's go find us a spring where we can wash."

He had been beaten, but he had won, too. Sandy had not been convinced, of course; but that wasn't the point. Sandy had been forced to admit that he had a right to his own opinion, and that he couldn't be beaten out of it.

"All right; let's go."

"Friends?" Sandy smiled.

He grinned through the pain of his bruises. "Sure," he said easily. "Disputatious at times—but friends."

A brown shadow moved in the clearing, and he touched Sandy's arm and pointed. Gradually he made out the shape of the buck; the head, the antlers, the absurdly slender legs beneath the massive barrel. "He's a beauty!"

"He's yours," Sandy offered. "You saw him first."

He hesitated for a moment. Last night he had said he would never kill anything again. This morning he had purposely come unarmed as an act of defiance. Had the gesture indicated conviction? Or mere sentiment?

"Hurry," Sandy muttered. "We'll never find another one this close to home. And we could use the meat."

That was the real answer. What difference did it make, after all? Whether you shot a deer for food or ate venison someone else had killed? Survival seemed to be inextricably tangled with killing. He reached for the rifle.

"You're on half cock," Sandy growled impatiently.

His thumb curled over the hammer and pulled it back with a sharp click. He nestled the stock against his cheek. The slender barrel of the Golcher slid naturally into

86

place, pointing down the long, dark alley of trees towards the golden clearing where the buck stood feeding on a low-hanging branch. The blackened front sight dropped smoothly into the notch of the rear sight.

The buck stopped feeding and turned his head. He stood motionless, listening, scenting the air. A head shot would be good, but difficult. Besides, at three hundred yards the Golcher might not drill cleanly through the bones of the skull. A chest shot it would be. He dropped the barrel the merest trifle and squeezed the trigger.

The rifle cracked sharply, and the butt jolted his shoulder. A wreath of dirty blue-gray smoke was caught and torn apart by the breeze. The buck was gone.

"Did you get him? I saw him jump."

"I don't know. I think so."

Sandy handed him the pouch and the powder horn. "Here. Reload, and we'll go after him."

His fingers seemed all thumbs as he measured the charge and rammed the ball home. Sandy was already untying his big gray by the time he reached the mare.

"Hurry up," Sandy yelled as he set his spurs to his horse. Tom followed, keeping well to the side of Sandy's track to avoid the little clots of turf the gelding's hooves flung in its wake.

The buck had not gone far. They followed the trail of blood a few lengths into the thicket, and then he appeared, still standing despite his wound, but with his head bowed, his antlers drooping almost to the dirt.

"Careful, Tom; he might have more fight in him."

"All right."

Sandy waited. He had unsheathed his pistol. "We can't hang around here all day," he muttered. "Half of creation heard that shot."

"Take the horses, then. I'll finish him."

For a brief moment surprise showed in Sandy's eyes. And then it was gone, replaced by a look of ungrudging admiration. "Take this, then," he said, holding out his pistol. "You might as well use my ammunition. I can always get more."

Tom moved closer to the buck. A wounded thing was suffering, dying. Men were also suffering and dying on a hundred bloody fields. The pistol kicked in his fist, and the buck's forelegs gave way. It was over.

"Good work," Sandy said. "That was a right pretty shot."

"Luck, I reckon. The sun got on the barrel so I couldn't see too well. I kind of guessed."

"Stuff and nonsense," Sandy said cheerfully. "It was a fine shot. Let's put him on the mare. We can ride Johnston double."

"Can we get him up?"

Sandy nodded. "He's kind of young. Don't run more than two hundred pounds. If you get the mare to kneel, we can heave him over the saddle."

"Why not butcher right here?"

Sandy grinned. "I aim to eat this meat myself—not furnish a meal to a bushwhacker."

Tom led up the mare, and with a little coaxing, he got her to kneel. She sniffed the air and shuddered.

"She ever carry game before?" Sandy asked.

"Only the man I shot."

Together, they heaved the buck across the saddle. Sandy loosened a picket rope from his saddle and secured the buck by tying his front feet to his rear feet and taking a hitch around the saddle horn. Like a great many things Sandy did, it was simple and effective

The mare staggered to her feet while Sandy steadied the carcass. "Meat for the table," he said. "Let's move."

Tom looked back up the alley of trees. He could just make out the fallen log behind which they had lain to shoot. The sun was high now, and the golden tone of the morning had faded beneath its intensity.

"Cousin Alison'll be mighty proud of you," Sandy said. "That's a right pretty buck."

"Why Cousin Alison?"

But Sandy didn't answer. He only grinned and clucked to his horse.

As Sandy had intimated, the venison was a welcome relief from the fibrous pork and beef supplied by John Dorfer. Not that it was Sam's father's fault, Tom reflected. The best of the hogs and cattle were going to Richmond, there to be distributed to the army, it was hoped.

"Say what you like," Pa said from the head of the table. "There's nothing quite so succulent as fresh venison. It's fortunate that you boys found deer so close to home."

"Tom gets the credit," Sandy smiled. "He spotted the buck first."

"Isn't it delicious?" Aunt Anne exclaimed. "Alison; do you remember . . . no, of course you don't. You were too young. You won't . . ." The sentence died in midair.

"I remember you telling me what a good hunter Papa was," Alison said tactfully.

It seemed to Tom as if Cousin Alison was always helping somebody out. Last night she had championed him, and yesterday she had helped Mama go over all the things she was planning to send poor Will with never a word of protest.

Mama cleared her throat, and he looked at her, knowing she wanted him to; knowing too that she would not be able to bring herself to say she was sorry she had not said goodnight to him, no matter how sorry she really was, but that this was her way of making amends.

"It was a fine shot, Tom," she said. A touch of her all-but-vanished humor lurked in her eyes, in the corners of her mouth. "I was beginning to think we might go hungry, the way the price of beef is going up."

"I reckon I could take to shooting cattle if there's more money in it, Mama," he grinned.

He looked past her at the shadows in the corner of the room. For a moment it had been the way it used to be. Somehow, he could have sworn that time had turned back for the breadth of a moment, turned back to that other time before the war. What had caused them to come together again?

Pa put down his knife and fork with a clatter. "It's been pleasant having you home, Sandy. We really feel like a family again." He glanced knowingly at the bruises on Sandy's face and on Tom's. "Even with the honorable scars of battle," he smiled.

CHAPTER 8

Tom Makes a Decision

IT HAD been a fine summer for growing things. The wheat was ready for cutting in the fields around Lovatt, and the backyard gardens in town brought forth the fruits of their owners' labor. Mr. Hauser's corn was already three feet high; his lettuce was doing nicely and would continue to do so, if the cutworms would only keep away. There would be regular mountains of potatoes, too, come fall.

Jeems McNair stepped across the road to inspect the results of good gardening. "You've done right well, Andrew. You'd make a good farmer."

"Wasted talent, hey?"

"I'd say so. I can send Horace over to give you a hand any time you want."

"No, thanks, Jeems; I don't eat much of this. I just like to grow it. Hoeing is good exercise."

McNair chuckled. "Fact is, it's the German in you. They get hold of a piece of land as big as a pillow slip, and they plant everything from squash to peach trees on it."

"Speaking of peaches, I'm going to have some jim-dandies this fall. I figure on making peach wine."

"Giving me some competition, hey? How's Doc?"

"Fine, fine."

"He hasn't been stopping by as often as he used to."

"It was a hard spring for Joe. A lot of hard work and no rest."

By tacit consent they avoided the real reason; Mary Tanner had not been herself. Although the prolonged visit of Anne and Alison had been a strain on her, their departure in mid-August had only served to increase her periods of erratic behavior. It seemed to Andrew Hauser that the presence of another woman in the house had served as a check upon her manner.

It was part and parcel of the war. Nothing occurred that was not somehow tainted by the ever-present threat of invasion, the steadily rising casualty lists, and the unseen enemies: hunger and fear and despair.

"Mary's going to pay Anne a visit one of these days," Andrew offered. "Sort of return the compliment. She's more lonesome than ever since Sandy went back to the army."

"That so? I hope for the sake of Joe's stomach, she doesn't stay as long as Mrs. West did."

"I think it's just for a day. Joe figures it'll do her good to see another woman."

Jeems smiled. "Hope you're right. I'd better get back. Old Horace might take it in his head to sample the stock."

Tom finished sluicing down the buggy wheels. It was a real marvel the way the gumbo stuck to the spokes. Of course the buggy got hard service, especially the way Pa used it in all weather and with little time to work on it, but that was one of the things about being a doctor, he supposed. You never quite had time enough for everything that wanted doing.

Today was an exception. Pa had consented to ride the mare on his rounds, so that Tom could drive Mama over to visit Aunt Anne in Scottsburg; as a result, there was time to wash the buggy and grease the wheels. Brutus was taking a lively interest in the proceedings. Earlier, when Pa had saddled the mare, he had pretended not to care, although he had been quite properly jealous. Now, however, it was plain to see that he had been reserved for a special occasion. It had done wonders for his self-esteem, Tom thought as he went out to the orchard to fetch the old horse. Brutus raised his head and stamped his feet, as if to prove that age had nothing to do with him.

Tom harnessed Brutus to the buggy and led him around to the front door. As he tied Brutus to the iron hitching post, Betsy came out on the front steps with a hamper, carefully covered with a clean white towel.

"You take good care of this, Mister Tom," she ordered. "Miss Mary, she packed it herself, special."

"What's in it, Betsy?"

"Miss Mary put in a ham and all kinds of good things to eat for poor Miss Anne."

"All right, Betsy; I'll take mighty good care of it."

"You take good care of your Mama, too. She been good to you all her days."

Mama came purposefully through the door, her reticule clutched firmly in her hand. "I'm ready," she announced. "Will you be all right by yourself, Betsy?"

"Yes, Miss Mary."

"If you're frightened, we can take you up to Mr. Hauser's."

"And let any old body come around our house? No, ma'am. My place is right here."

"All right. Keep the doors locked, and don't go far from the house. We'll be back before dark, I trust. Doctor will be home for dinner, of course."

As always, Betsy was happy now that she was left to her own devices for the rest of the day. Today was cleaning day, Thursday; there was plenty to do and no mistake, but it was a happy kind of work. You could always see

93

right where you were, how much you had done and how much you had left to do.

The upstairs was easy. There were only two beds to make, because nobody was using Mister Sandy's room or Mister Will's room. She dusted the mantels and the chests with the windows open to air out the rooms as she went. Finally, she swept the floors and the carpets with her broom, using a pail of damp sawdust to keep the dust down.

It took time, though; when she had swept down the front stairs and the back, it was pretty close to the time she had to stop and make dinner for the doctor. Betsy was inordinately proud of the fact that she had learned to tell time after a fashion. She knew her hours and her half hours, at least; that was a great deal better than that ignorant Horace over at Mr. McNair's who came around to pester her on Sundays. Not that there was anything wrong in passing the time of day with Horace or anybody else, for that matter; it was just that he always seemed to come around when there was work to be done and she had no time.

Just when she was ready to start fixing dinner, the doctor came into the kitchen and announced that he was in a hurry, and did she have something he could take along with him? Betsy obliged by putting a wedge of sausage between two slices of bread and pouring him a glass of buttermilk. "You can drink that here," she said. "The rest you can eat on the way."

"Thank you, Betsy. Did anyone call this morning?"

"No, sir. Ain't been nobody."

After the doctor had ridden off, it was quiet again. Betsy fixed herself a snack of corn pone, liberally drenched with molasses, and washed down with a glass of cold buttermilk. Miss Mary wouldn't be home for a long time, yet. She would have plenty of time to get finished with everything except maybe the kitchen. That could wait until tomorrow, anyhow. Tomorrow she had to get after that old cellar, too. There were cobwebs all over the place. Not that the doctor or Miss Mary went down there very often; but she surely didn't want them to find cobwebs and dust when they did.

It was right warm and pretty near as quiet as she had ever known it to be. She opened the windows in the front parlor, so that it could air out while she was dusting. For a moment she remained at the windows, watching the faraway pines on the flank of the mountain, listening for the familiar shuffle of feet and the clatter of hooves on the Pike. There was no trace of life at all—only the pine trees in the distance and the sun beating down, and everything a little blurred by the dust so that it didn't seem quite the same as it did ordinarily, but unreal, belonging somewhere else and in some other time.

A faint sound came from the south. Betsy listened carefully. One horse, walking. Maybe Miss Mary was coming home early. Betsy turned away from the window and began to rub at the rosewood piano. Even the big family Bible was dusty. Maybe winter mud was better than summer dust! Too bad Miss Mary had to come back so soon. It would have been right nice to look at the pictures in the big Bible. Her favorite was the one about the people escaping from Egypt, with the sea divided to let them cross in safety.

As she spread the damp sawdust on the floor, the hoof-beats drew nearer. She stole another glance out the window. It was not Miss Mary, after all. It was a soldier-man astride a dusty horse. His figure was gaunt and erect, as though he were holding himself in the saddle by sheer willpower. A dirty bandage was wound about his left arm, and his floppy hat was pulled down low over his eyes.

As she watched, the soldier dismounted and pulled a

95

short gray jacket from the blanket roll behind his saddle. Donning this with some difficulty, he moved forward and tied his horse to the ring in the hitching post. A moment later, he walked up the steps and began to knock on the door.

If he wants to, she thought with frightening logic, he can get in no matter what I do. He's got a gun and I ain't. Even if I did, I wouldn't know which end to use. She opened the door.

"I'm looking for the home of Doctor Joseph Tanner," the soldier-man said. His face was just like leather, brown and tough, and his eyes were old and tired.

"Doctor ain't home, sir. Won't be back until tonight."

"I'll wait."

"Yes, sir. You can take your horse back to the stable."

The man nodded and walked slowly down the steps. His boots dragged across the brick as though it was an effort for him to raise his feet.

"You want to wash yourself, Captain? I can get you some soap and hot water."

He paused a moment, as if to digest the meaning of what she had said. Then without turning, he nodded.

Tom had spent a delightful afternoon at Scottsburg. As always, it held a sleepy, remote sort of charm by the very fact that it was not closely linked to the world beyond its immediate hills. Cousin Alison had taken him to her favorite haunts: an open hillside above the town, knee-high in wild hay, a tree-sheltered corner behind the house that seemed to have been put there for the special purpose of reading and daydreaming.

"I dream too much," Cousin Alison said, as she spread her skirts and sat on a flat rock half-buried in the grass. Overhead, the trees gave a steady rustling accompaniment to their conversation.

"Sometimes dreams are the only things that seem real."

96

"I know. There's so little to hope for until the war is over." She checked herself with a laugh. "At first everyone used to say 'until we've won.' Remember?"

He nodded. "It seems a long time ago, now."

"What have you heard from Sandy?"

"Nothing to talk about. That he's well and was made temporary commander of his battalion. I reckon he hasn't had time to do any writing. Sally Lou Barnes hasn't heard, either."

"We heard that General Longstreet had been sent to the Carolinas."

"Yes. So far, no one seems to know if we're winning or losing, but if the army can spare Longstreet, I reckon we're ahead. I rode down to Staunton the day before yesterday to see if I could get some further news, but the telegraph wire had been cut."

Alison smiled at him. "I wish you had stopped to see us. It gets lonely here, sometimes."

"It wasn't because I didn't want to," he said. "Pa was concerned about Sandy, because he hadn't written, so I had to hurry home."

Alison rose. "We'd better get back. Mama will wonder what happened to us."

He put out his hands and took hers. "I wish we could visit more often."

As she nodded, her bright hair flashed in the sun.

Back at the house, Mama was gathering her things in preparation for departure. Aunt Anne was vaguely protesting that it was early, and that they could easily wait until dark, because there would be a full moon to drive by.

"No, thank you," Mama replied. "There are Yankee cutthroats all around us, these days, and Tom doesn't carry a gun. We'll travel by daylight."

"Alison—Aunt Mary's hamper? In the kitchen, I think."

"I'll get it, Aunt Anne."

As he made for the kitchen, Alison followed. "Do they still bother you about not going armed?" she asked.

"Some. Not a lot. I guess I bother myself about it more than they do. I've got the pistol I took from the bushwhacker. I keep it in the bottom of my chest. Sometimes I think it might be best if I just went ahead and joined up."

Alison shook her head emphatically. "Not without a reason."

"I reckon not. Pa says the same. You ought to have a pretty good reason for anything you do."

"I wish you were staying longer."

He nodded. "So do I. I can't tell you how much I miss our law game and all. I'm hoping I can ride over during the fall. Pa wants me close by, in case there's another raid."

Alison smiled as Mama called out. "Tom? We're waiting for that hamper!"

He reached for it at the same moment as Alison, and their hands touched. He turned his head to look at her, unwilling to release her hand, and suddenly he wanted very much to stay with her, to always be near her.

"Alison?"

She nodded and smiled. "I wondered when you'd find out."

He bent his face to hers and kissed her. It was an awkward, unsatisfactory sort of kiss, and yet it was the beginning of something that would never be unsatisfactory. He knew it as well as he knew his name.

"I never kissed anybody before," he said. "I always figured it ought to mean something when you did."

"So did I," she murmured. "Come on! We have to go!"

"What were you two up to?" Mama said as they waved goodbye from the buggy.

98

"Nothing, Mama. We were talking."

"Some folks have a lot to talk about."

"Yes, ma'am. That they do."

After the first ten minutes, the little hamlet was lost from view, swallowed by the exuberant greenery of the summer and the irregular hills. Mama fell into a doze, and he was able to permit himself the luxury of daydreaming. Only last month he had driven Alison and Aunt Anne along this road. Had he loved her then? Probably. How much time they had squandered!

Still it was right pleasant to think of all the time that lay ahead of them. All at once there were about a jillion things to say to her. He hadn't even said "I love you." For a second, panic mastered him; maybe she didn't even know it! No, that was silly. She knew it without his saying anything, just as he knew she loved him. It was something you didn't have to talk about, as long as you had it. And if you didn't have it, talking wouldn't do any good.

As the buggy turned into the Pike, Tom looked back over his shoulder at the gloomy side road over which they had just come. It was as if he had left one world for another.

They reached the Centre Creek bridge just as the sun dropped behind Great North Mountain. They'd make it back before black dark with no trouble at all.

"Where are we?" Mama asked as she came awake.

"Pretty near home, ma'am. You can see the house from here."

Sure enough, the pink walls glowed warmly with the last of the daylight. It gave you a funny twinge, he thought; here you were and there was the house, and in a couple of minutes you would be there. And yet it wasn't a thing that would last. It was part of growing up, he guessed, realizing that nothing lasted forever.

"There's a strange horse out in back," Mama said.

Sure enough, a bay mare was tethered to one of the

trees in the orchard. Even at a distance it was easy to see that the mare had been ridden hard. She looked dejected, and the dried sweat was gray on her flanks.

"Why didn't he rub her down? It's a poor horseman who can't take care of his mount. You take good care of Brutus; hear?"

"Yes, ma'am. You'd better wait for me, Mama. No telling who that might be in there."

Quickly he unhitched Brutus and led him into his stall. He poured a measure of oats, and while Brutus ate, he rubbed him down and covered him with a blanket.

"Someone ought to take care of that mare," he said.

"Later, Tom. Let's see who owns her, first."

They came through the back door for convenience's sake. Betsy was kneading bread dough, clapping it against the floury table top.

"Evening, Miss Mary. There's a soldier-man inside to see the doctor. He looks like maybe he's sick. His arm's hurt."

"Thank you, Betsy," Mama said. "I'll go see what he wants."

He followed Mama through the shadows of the dining room into the hall. She went directly to the door of Pa's office and opened it. "There's no one here," she said with surprise.

Tom opened the opposite door, which led into the front parlor. Enough light still came through the west window to reveal the soldier, who was fast asleep in his chair. Despite his somewhat battered appearance and his obvious exhaustion, the man looked formidable. There was about him the indefinable, yet indelible mark of the man of action. It showed in the set of his jaw, the scar over his forehead, the scratched leather of his boots and the well-worn pistol holster at his belt.

Tom cleared his throat, and the man came awake all

at once, the way a cat does. It was as if he had not been sleeping at all, but merely waiting for the right moment to stand up and assert himself.

"I beg your pardon. I must have dozed. I was waiting for Doctor Tanner. Captain Jonathan Marle, at your service."

"I am Mrs. Tanner. This is my son, Thomas."

"I regret exceedingly . . ." Captain Marle hesitated as if he wished someone would help him with a word. No one did. "On the occasion of the third of September," he said formally, "your son Ambrose was mortally wounded."

Sandy. Dead. In a flash Tom remembered Sandy: solemn, as on the morning they had stalked the deer; riding hell-for-leather with a grin of sheer deviltry on his face; smiling at a pretty girl at a party. But always alive. No one had ever been so alive! The hot tears welled into his eyes.

"Thank you for telling us, Captain. Where is my son?"

Tom looked at her in amazement. She was holding herself as proud and steady as if nothing at all had happened.

"Under a guard of honor, ma'am. I was unable to get transportation from Gordonsville. I thought that I might find a wagon hereabouts."

"It will be attended to. Has Betsy seen to your wants?"

Captain Marle stared at her. "I'm all right, Mrs. Tanner. Are you sure you wouldn't like to sit down for a while?" He coughed tactfully. "I realize what a shock this has been."

Mama shook her head ever so slightly. "My three sons expect us all to be courageous."

CHAPTER 9

The End of Valor

CAPTAIN MARLE'S wound had been dressed by Doctor Tanner, and the captain and Tom had gone to Gordonsville for the body. It had been embalmed, the captain explained with a show of pride, the expense being borne by the officers and men of Sandy's old battery, now Marle's own. Marle's wound had made it possible for him to be detailed to escort the body home.

Aunt Anne and Alison had arrived to help with the funeral arrangements, and a continuous flow of visitors now surged through the parlor, where the coffin lay on two trestles, banked with flowers.

Mary Tanner was alone. The doctor was in his office, to which he had retreated to vent his grief in a way he would not have permitted himself before others, and she had come upstairs to be by herself.

There were certain things she had to do, things which could not be done by anyone else. Sandy's sword and pistol were still in her bedroom, where she had put them after Captain Marle had given them to her. Now she took them to Sandy's room. For the time being, they could stay on the mantel; later, she would hang them on the wall. Beside them she placed the ambrotype Sandy had had made shortly after his promotion to captain.

They had told her William was dead, but the coffin

102

had been sealed so that you could not know with certainty whose body lay within. She was still positive that they had been mistaken, that Will was a prisoner of those terrible people who had set fire to the barn. Almost positive. For now they said that Sandy was dead; the son she had most loved and cherished. She had never really believed it possible that Sandy might die; there had always been an aura of immortality about him that was only now being refuted. If Sandy were dead, then perhaps Will was dead, too, and all the food and clothing she had parceled and given to Betsy to give to the Yankees in the woods to take to him had never reached him at all.

No. That was what Papa and Joseph wanted her to think. She knew very well that they thought her entrapped by a delusion. It might well be that Sandy wasn't dead, either. Perhaps they had found some dead boy who looked like him and rushed to the conclusion that it was Sandy. In all honesty, the boy in the coffin did look somewhat like Sandy. But there were differences. Sandy's face was not so pinched and drawn. Sandy's hair was a luxuriant, glossy black; it wasn't dry and brittle. And Sandy was always smiling.

But if this was not Sandy, why hadn't Sandy returned to his unit? Her imagination encompassed wounds, capture, a dazed condition that would keep him from remembering who he was or where he belonged. Any of these were possible, of course. Her glance fell upon the weapons on the mantel. The saber he had carried in battle and on his furlough last month. The pistol with his initials cut into the butt. These were his, had been used by him; if they were here, then he must be here. And if he were here, then he must be dead.

She began to weep in the frightened way a child weeps when it has discovered that infallibility is not an attribute of humans, and that somewhere all things have an ending.

Tom shared his room with Captain Marle, who slept in the bed while Tom occupied a pallet in the corner. Sandy's room was unoccupied, of course, and Aunt Anne and Cousin Alison were now in the room that had been William's. Mama had voiced no objections; it was as if she had belatedly realized that her actions must conform to the expectations of others.

Marle's saddle bags were in the corner. They had some of the attributes of their owner, Tom decided: a tough surface, impervious to minor outside influences, and a decidedly practical aspect. Marle was different from Sandy, in that Sandy had almost invariably found humor in the routine of life. Marle, on the other hand, was grim, almost puritanical. He had been here two days now, waiting for the funeral and giving his wound a chance to heal. Meanwhile, his possessions gave tangible evidence of his tenancy, even when he was absent.

Across the hall in Sandy's room, he heard Mama moving about. She was taking it well, not panicking or fainting. She didn't even cry; her grief had turned inward. But grief there was. It took on the form of hating anyone who had no active part in the war. Yesterday she had refused to speak to the eldest Dorfer boy, and towards Jeems McNair she had only a frigid bow that partook more deeply of insult than of courtesy.

As for himself, Tom was left with no one who understood him, except for Alison. And there were some things you couldn't explain, even to Alison, the way you could to Sandy. There would be no one to go hunting with, to sit cross-legged before a fire roasting chestnuts and swapping droll stories.

Following a discreet tap on the door, Captain Marle

104

entered. "I wanted to clean up some before the funeral," he said easily. "I hope I won't disturb you."

"No, sir. You go right ahead."

"They're fixing to start directly." Marle got a rag out of one of his saddlebags and rubbed his boots. It didn't help much. Even Betsy had been unable to apply a lasting polish to them.

"How was Sandy killed?" Tom asked abruptly.

Marle glanced at him. "In a little action that didn't even get in the papers. He was going to fetch a gun that we left behind," he continued patiently. "A Parrott shell struck his horse and exploded."

"Was it something he had to do?"

"Being what he was, yes. He was the bravest man I ever knew. He never counted odds. He just jumped right in and did what had to be done." Marle tucked his boot rag back in the pouch. "They'll be looking a long time to find a man who can take his place."

There it was again. No one could help but love Sandy; now that he was gone, he would be missed in some way by even the most casual of acquaintances. Tom turned away from Marle to hide the tears that burned his eyelids.

"Reckon you'll be joining up soon," Marle said.

He turned on his heel, glad to take refuge in anger. "Hasn't there been enough waste of life already?"

Marle stared at him for a long moment. "That's not the point," he said finally. "But I reckon you're entitled to your own opinions. I'll see you downstairs."

There was no hearse with gleaming jet-lacquered panels and tossing sable plumes. Dave Dorfer had gone off to Staunton to see to it, but for some unaccountable reason he had not returned. Doctor Tanner decided not to wait; they had not had a hearse for Will, either. The coffin was placed in the wagon in which Tom and Captain Marle had conveyed it from Gordonsville, and covered with fresh flowers. The hot sun drew forth the perfume of the roses and the acrid tang of road dust and the sweaty clothing of the people waiting to follow the wagon through the town to the burying ground on the hill behind the church.

A new grave, dug that morning by Horace, gaped at the edge of the wood. Beside it, the slab that marked William Tanner's resting-place was already somewhat weathered. It had been over two years since Will's death.

The sun beat down warmly as Mr. Harmon began the service. The men stood, hat in hand, while a faint breeze from the eastward slope of the mountain bore the redolence of pine and of cool places.

"I am the Resurrection and the Life," Reverend Harmon began.

The Dorfers stood together; young John was away at the army, of course, and Dave had not yet returned from Staunton. Sam looked at Tom, nodded, and looked quickly away.

Sally Lou Barnes stood beside her father. Her face might have been cut from stone, so rigidly did she maintain her expression. As Tom watched, she looked at him, flicked him with her glance, and looked away once more.

Some grieved, as did Pa, their hearts melted with sorrow. Some grieved as did Captain Marle; a friend was gone, a valued officer who would be hard to replace. And some grieved with bitterness and resentment, as Mama did, and Sally Lou.

"A paladin has fallen," Mr. Harmon said.

A paladin has fallen, Sally Lou's glance seemed to say, and you who are inferior to him in every way are still alive. He squirmed uncomfortably. The contrast between himself and Sandy was great. And he owed a debt to

Sandy that he had never owed to Will: a debt for lessons learned by observation. Sandy had taught him by his very example to lose graciously, to accept with fortitude whatever might befall him, to look with humor on the otherwise embarrassing incidents that happened to everyone.

Sandy was gone. Who would replace him?

Pa and Grandpa Hauser stepped forward with shovels. The first clods thumped hollowly on the lid of the coffin, and somewhere a girl sobbed. Pa's face was swollen from suppressed tears. He looked ill.

Captain Marle touched Tom on the arm. "I suggest we take the ladies home."

Tom looked at his mother. She was holding a handkerchief to her mouth, and her jaws were tightly clenched to prevent any sound from escaping.

"Mama?"

She nodded, and he led her towards the buggy.

As they passed McNair's tavern, Captain Marle edged his mare closer to the buggy. "What's the next town up the Pike from here?" he wanted to know.

"Staunton, sir."

"You reckon that's where the smoke's coming from?"

Away to the south a column of black smoke spiraled threadlike into the sky. He squinted to see it better. If it were as distant as Staunton, it would hardly be so clear.

"No, sir. It looks like they've got a fire somewhere between here and Staunton. Maybe five or six miles off."

"I can guess what kind," Marle muttered savagely. He edged his horse away again, as if to concentrate more thoroughly on the smoke. Maybe that was part of being a soldier, Tom thought. Maybe Sandy would have done the same thing, had he seen the smoke at Marle's funeral.

He quelled an insane desire to chuckle. How could there be laughter with Sandy dead?

To the left of the Pike a faint dust cloud betrayed the hurried passage of a horseman. Tom watched, vaguely curious as to why anyone in his right mind would elect to cut across broken country and ford Centre Creek to boot, instead of riding on the Pike and crossing by the bridge. Marle slapped a rein end across his mare's neck and shot forward.

"Where is he going?" Mama asked.

"I don't know, ma'am. I reckon he wants to see who's coming through the fields, there."

Mama leaned forward. "He's headed right for our house!"

Marle veered off the Pike to intercept the stranger, and a moment later the other horseman broke out of the trees.

Mama clutched his arm. "Is it Will?" she demanded. "Tell me, is it Will?"

"Mama, Will's dead," he said gently.

"Yes," she murmured without conviction. "That's right. Will's dead, and Sandy's dead, too."

As they drew nearer to the rider, Tom recognized Dave Dorfer. Captain Marle was questioning him; questions to which Dave's answers were apparently of the yes or no variety. His horse was twitching with exhaustion. Another five miles at that pace would have killed it.

Marle turned to them as the buggy came level. "He says there's maybe a squadron of Yankee cavalry on the Pike near Staunton."

"They're burning a house," Dave gasped.

Marle swore. "Get your horse on home, boy, and take care of it."

As Dave led his foundered horse towards the back of the house, Grandpa Hauser's rig pulled up with Pa, Aunt Anne, and Alison.

"What's happened?" Pa asked. "Why didn't Dave bring back the hearse?"

"Yankee raid, sir," Marle replied. "He rode right into it. They started chasing him, and he only just got away."

Pa shook his head, and the merciless sun showed the gray creeping into his fair hair. "When will it end?" he asked of no one in particular.

"They'll be collecting troops at Gordonsville," Captain Marle was saying reflectively as Tom walked towards the stairs. "We can't let a whole squadron of them sit here; they'd cut our railroad communications with the West. I'm going to ride down to Gordonsville and see if I can be of any use."

"Betsy will give you some supper," Mama said, and then Tom climbed away from the voices to the upper hall.

A pale ghost that was Alison stood there waiting for him. "Oh, Tom," she murmured. "I just can't believe it."

He nodded. "It seems like there's no one to replace him."

"I never could talk to him, though. Not like I talk to you, I mean," she said with swift loyalty. "Remember two days ago? I felt I never knew anyone so well as I know you."

"I love you, Alison," he said quietly.

"Oh, Tom! Are you sure? We're awfully young!"

"I'm sure." He put his arms around her and drew her to him gently. She came willingly, eagerly, and she put up her face to his.

He remembered the first kiss, only two days ago. An eternity had passed since then. Sandy was gone, and there was no one to whom to look for guidance, the way a boy had to look to someone to learn what was right to do and what was not. Now he would make his own decisions, do his own thinking. The long wait in limbo was over; he was a man, and he had a man's part to play. He knew now who must take Sandy's place.

Aunt Anne called from the foot of the stairs. "Alison?"

"I have to go, my love," she whispered.

He watched her walk down the stairs, and then he went into his room. Marle's saddlebags lay as they had before; they were strapped and ready for instant departure. There would be no excess baggage to delay the captain's leaving.

Carefully, he folded the black broadcloth suit of Will's that he had worn to the funeral and pulled on the old gray trousers that had once belonged to Sandy, and his boots. An old flannel hunting shirt all but completed his attire.

Only one more item remained. The pistol that had belonged to the bushwhacker. He went to his chest to get it.

Jonathan Marle wiped his mouth and got up. The fixings were first-rate here, and no mistake! It was too bad he couldn't spend another night. When a man passed thirty, he appreciated good cooking and a soft bed. But he might be of some use over to Gordonsville. If not, it was plainly his duty to get back to the battery as soon as possible. Sergeant Harrison was capable, but he lacked imagination.

Out in the front parlor, the Tanners were still sitting with Mrs. West and her daughter. Nobody was saying anything. That was the trouble with good manners; folks had to sit around and be courteous, when what they really wanted was to go off by themselves and bawl until they got it out of their systems. The boy was still upstairs. He probably had a lot more sense than the rest of them, even if he was against the war. He wasn't a coward,

110

either. You could smell cowardice a mile away. Marle knew.

Marle cleared his throat self-consciously as he walked into the parlor, and Sandy's father looked up. "May I assist you with your luggage, sir?" he asked.

He tensed himself to keep from chuckling at the compliment that had been paid his antiquated saddle bags. "No, thank you, sir. I reckon I can manage them just dandy."

"Perhaps Thomas . . ." The doctor stopped, and Marle followed his gaze. The boy stood in the doorway, a pair of shabby gray pants stuffed into high boots, obviously in an effort to achieve the effect of a uniform. A new black holster and belt were buckled around his waist. The U.S. on the belt catch was quite prominent.

"Captain Marle, I have the honor to offer my services to your battery," the boy said quietly.

"Tom!" the doctor cried out.

Mrs. Tanner stood up. For a moment it was as if Sandy was standing there, the light of battle in his eyes. "I knew you wouldn't fail me, boy," she said clearly. "Will and Sandy expect us all to be brave."

Marle looked around the room. Whatever the boy did was going to be all right with Miss Alison. You could see it in her face. Even the doctor was coming around. Poor devil; he was the only one of them who knew without being told what the boy was letting himself in for. Mrs. Tanner was looking for vengeance. That was plain to see.

And what about the boy? He had made his play; was it just that? A bid for attention?

"I'm going upstairs to get my saddlebags," Marle said abruptly. "And then I'm leaving. Will you be ready?"

The boy nodded. "I'm waiting for you, sir," he said pointedly.

111

CHAPTER 10

The Schooling of a Gunner

OCTOBER came in with a succession of rainy days that laid the dust and turned the roads into bottomless quagmires, impassable for wagons and guns alike.

"The war's over for another year," Corporal Walker announced with an air of wisdom born of almost three years of continuous service.

Tom huddled beneath the square of oilcloth he had gained by swapping his Barlow knife and nodded. It was difficult to believe that anyone would want to fight a war in this kind of weather. It was too wet to do much of anything except shiver and wish he were somewhere warm and—above all—dry.

"Do we just live out like this, Ben?"

"Shucks, no!" Corporal Walker said spiritedly. "Another month or so, we'll start building huts, and then it'll be fine. You wait and see!"

"Don't the Yankees ever move in winter?"

"The first winter they didn't. Last year they tried it at Fredericksburg, but that didn't work out so well." Walker grinned. "In fact, they got whipped to a frazzle."

"Well, any time they start building huts, let me know."

The rain and the mud were a far cry from the day he had ridden to Gordonsville with Marle. Just by closing his eyes, he could bring back the freshness of the air, the grass waving in the fields alongside the road, the warm afternoon sun beating down upon their shoulders, and the fine white dust rising beneath their horses' hooves like smoke.

He no longer had the bushwhacker's mare. He had offered her to Captain Marle, who had suggested that he sell her to Colonel Hulme, who was always on the lookout for a good bit of horseflesh. The mare was one of the last links between Private Tanner and the boy who had shot a man in his own kitchen. He was as glad to see her go as he was to receive the hundred and fifty dollars in Confederate notes from the colonel.

Day ran into day, sliding past with a devastating sameness, with only an occasional highlight to set any one apart from the rest. The first day had been important: he would never forget accompanying Marle through the street of Gordonsville in search of someone with authority to organize a pursuit column to advance on Staunton and drive the raiders or destroy them.

They had been too late; Marle, belatedly remembering his responsibility to the battery, had led the way out of town, pointing out the sights as he went.

"See that platform by the railroad tracks? That's where General Jackson stood a year ago last spring, when he took his corps down to Richmond." Or, "There's where the ladies had a whole barrel of lemonade set out for us in sixty-one."

Just out of Gordonsville, Marle drew rein. Instinctively, Tom turned his head and looked west. Somewhere out there lay Lovatt and Scottsburg, sleepy in the twilight. Alison was there, perhaps thinking of him even now. Pa, Mama, Grandpa, Sam—the faces flickered in his mind in stylized poses, like a collection of ambrotypes.

"The army is northeast of here," Marle was saying. "We're still holding a line along the Rappahannock

River. I figure on sleeping out as soon as we find a good camping place, and then we can push on tomorrow."

He nodded, only half understanding Marle.

"The thing is," Marle said, toying with the ends of his reins, "you're kind of young to go into this. If you wanted to change your mind during the night, I wouldn't hold it against you."

"I'm going on eighteen, and I don't figure on changing my mind, Captain. I'll be here in the morning."

Marle grinned his relief. "Shucks, boy; no offense meant. I only didn't want to take you if you had cold feet."

He forced himself to smile, and the ambrotypes in his mind shattered into kaleidoscopic fragments, and then there was only the dust and the easy, familiar odor of warm horseflesh and the unfamiliar tug of the black holster riding on his right hip.

"My feet are just fine, sir."

"Well, what're we waiting for?" Marle asked. "Let's get moving!" The pale bandage on his arm led the way, for all the world like a white banner furled on its staff.

He and Marle had joined the battery somewhere west of Fredericksburg, on the banks of the Rapidan. Colonel Hulme had bought the mare, and from then on Tom walked with the other gunners, trying to learn as he went, trying to persuade himself that he could some day become the sort of officer that Sandy had been, and knowing in his heart that he could not. It was a matter of inspiration: you had it or you didn't. He didn't.

Sergeant Harrison had drilled him in the groundwork of artillery handling, giving him an unusual amount of attention, and Ben Walker had continued where Harrison left off.

He could perform almost any duty on the piece: packing ammunition in the chest with tow between the

114

rounds, passing rounds and cutting fuses, laying the piece, and even substituting for Walker in firing the piece. The mysteries of pricking the woolen cartridges through the vent, thumbing the vent to prevent hot air from prematurely igniting the cartridge, preparing the tube with a primer, were mysteries no longer. Never again would he mistake cannister for shell. He knew, in the best of all possible ways, the way the right arm of Number One ached after ramming ten consecutive rounds in half as many minutes. He adjusted the piece for lateral deflection with the trail spike until his back creaked with the strain.

But it was no good; he did not progress beyond the mechanics of firing. He could not, as Walker or Harrison could, direct fire with one eye and search for new targets with the other.

In truth, there had been but little opportunity to attempt to see things through any eyes but those of an ammunition passer. They had only fought one battle, an ineffectual action at Rappahannock Station. There was a background of heat and dust and smoke against which his gun moved into firing position and added its own small clamor to the general din. The powder sacks were passed in the same way they had been passed at any one of a hundred practice drills. And if you blanked your mind to the peculiar howl overhead and the white puffs of smoke on a hillside a mile away, it was possible to ignore the fact that you were shooting at actual men, and that they were shooting back at you.

"That's because we had no casualties," Ben Walker warned. "You wait until a charge of grape comes through a gun position, and then you'll know there's a war going on."

He thought of telling Walker that violent death was not a new experience to him, either. All he had to do was to remember how he had obtained the pistol belted around his waist, and he knew all he wanted to know about killing a man. But to tell Walker would be in the nature of bragging, he decided, and since it was an act he wouldn't particularly care to brag about, he kept silent.

Meanwhile, it was autumn, and they were back on the south bank of the Rapidan, and the rain made little clots of water on the greasy brass tube of Number Two gun.

"She's an old soldier," Walker said affectionately.

"Have you always been on this gun?"

"That's right. She was one of the two original pieces. I was Number One at first, and then the gunner took sick and died, so I got to be gunner." Walker grinned. It was the grin of a small boy who has suddenly come across the cookie jar with no one near to restrain him. "The major—your brother—he got the Parrott when they reorganized the first time, back in the spring of sixty-two. Everybody wanted to go work on the Parrott, because she was new and big and could shoot further. But I stuck to old Number Two."

"Why?"

"Well, which is easier to clean: a rifle or a musket?"

"I reckon a musket. It doesn't have rifling."

Ben nodded happily. "Just the way I had it figured. As far as accuracy, the Parrotts are better at long range because they're rifled. But at short range, the old Napoleon has one edge: if you're using solid shot, the Napoleon won't sink her rounds in the dirt like a rifled piece. She'll send them skittering along the ground like a bowling ball. If you miss your first target, maybe you'll get another. With the Parrott, if you miss, that's the end of it."

"It sounds good."

Ben coughed and pulled his waterproof tighter. "You know, you could be an officer if you worked at it. Shoot, Tom, you're a right smart fellow."

"Not smart enough to figure out how to stay dry."

"That don't take brains. All that takes is a big enough piece of oilcloth."

"Which I don't have."

"Me, neither," Ben said. "We all figured you was coming in to be an officer."

"I reckon I never really wanted to be an officer, Ben. I never even wanted to be a soldier after—well, not for a long time." He rubbed his hands together to drive out the chill. "When I came with the captain, I wanted to take Sandy's place. If that meant being an officer, I was willing to be one. But that's not much of a reason."

"Not to be a good officer, no," Ben agreed. "There's all kinds. Take Harrison, now; he wants to get himself a commission just because he never had one in the old army. Marle wanted to fight, and he figured that being an officer was the best way to do it."

"What about Sandy?"

Ben wiped the rain from his face. "I reckon your brother was one of the best officers I ever knew. Shucks, Tom, he *was* the best. But why he was, I don't know. Harrison is good as a sergeant because he loves his guns. It don't matter whose guns they really are. He could have been happy in anybody's army, just so long as they gave him a battery to keep him happy. He could have stayed in his own army, except he saw a chance to get further with ours. But the major? I don't rightly know."

He nodded. Maybe Ben was right. Maybe all the fine talk about patriotism and individual rights didn't make a good fighter. It only made a person vulnerable to emotion, to sentimentality.

"But you take Marle," Ben continued. "Now he's a man who believes in the cause right down the line. Maybe I don't figure slavery is right. Maybe you don't figure we should have seceded. But Marle? He's death on anybody who don't think just the way he does. He even hates some Confederates he figures ain't as red-hot as they

117

ought to be." Ben lowered his voice. "You watch that man, Tom. He acts like he's a real good fellow, but there ain't nothing inside him but a hard core of hate."

"Sandy wasn't at all like that. I don't think he ever hated anybody."

"No," Ben agreed. "The major was one of the finest men I ever knew. I know one thing about him, though. He liked being an officer. He liked to run things and people. He'd get in a spot, and then he'd figure out some way to get out of it. It was kind of like a man running up the side of a mountain to see can he do it."

Autumn deepened to the tunking of axes as the army prepared for winter. While the leaves turned rusty along the Rapidan, the gunners dug emplacements for the pieces so that they commanded the nearby fords and their approaches. Although the main body of the Federals could be expected to stay in similar encampments north of the river, there was always the possibility of a cavalry raid for sheer nuisance value. The days when the Federal cavalry closed up shop for the winter were over, the veterans agreed. Always well armed, the Unionists took better care of their mounts now, and increased self-confidence was followed by ambitious plans and daring execution.

"It's not the way it used to be," Sergeant Harrison said with terse accuracy. "They've learned as much as we have, and they've got better horses."

Horses were becoming a problem to the artillery, as well as to the cavalry. Overworked during the summer campaign, they now faced winter with the prospects of too little forage. An epidemic of hoof disease late in October took a heavy toll. Some of the survivors were herded south in droves for rest and forage in areas not yet stripped by the army.

Meanwhile there were details for "browse"—the tender

118

bud ends of branches which would keep a horse alive, if not in good condition—and for wood to shore up the gun emplacements, for building huts, and for firewood.

Tom enjoyed the firewood detail. If the work was hard, it at least kept you warm. Besides, there was always a fire kept burning to warm your hands, and that made it possible to rest more comfortably than in the damp, cold huts they had built of sticks and mud. Last, but perhaps most important, it was possible to augment the cornmeal ration for the day with a squirrel or rabbit by combining wood chopping with hunting. The officers were inclined to overlook the expenditure of government ammunition for hunting, assuming that ammunition by itself would be of little use unless there were reasonably healthy men available to use it.

It was almost like being on a large-scale hunting party; the men worked cheerfully, aware that the benefits of their labors were to be enjoyed by themselves, and re- lieved that the enemy would not have to be faced for another three months, if they were fortunate. They were a friendly lot, the men of the battery, now that they knew that Tom was not an army politician. If Sergeant Harrison was dissatisfied with his progress as a teacher of the fine art of artillery, he was also mollified by the fact that Tom had not attempted to advance himself by the use of his brother's name. Ben Walker had become al- most as good a friend as Sam Dorfer had been, back in Lovatt.

And there were others; Hodges, a lean, undersized mountaineer, semi-illiterate, who had enlisted Tom's aid in writing a letter home, and who thereafter allowed his gratitude to outweigh his natural suspicion of strangers. There was Hunter, the conscript from Richmond, a boy of nineteen who had wanted to study for the ministry, but who was caught up by the long arm of Winder's provost guard and packed off to the thinning ranks of the army. And there was Marston, a languid aristocrat from the Tidewater, who read from a battered copy of Plato, and who had little knowledge of—and less interest in—the working of the gun to which he had belonged for two years.

These were his friends; to them he spoke as he could not have spoken to anyone save Alison. He depended upon them for entertainment, for sociality, and for the necessities of life that the army was unable to provide.

First snow fell like a thick powder, with a thin, keening wind to drive it. Out on the picket lines, the smudges of surreptitious fires outlined the positions as clearly as a map would have done. Tom squatted in the corner of the hut he shared with Ben Walker and hammered at the stiff clay of their chimney with a stick. Somehow the fires never drew the way they should. They had a tendency to become smoky and peter out, usually at the coldest part of the morning. Ben had said there wasn't much that could be done, but he was at least going to have a try.

A lump of clay broke off and fell to the hearth. Good. That ought to widen the chimney a little. Now if he could only find a barrel to set on top of the chimney and give it a good draft, he'd really have something. But that was like looking for hard cash in a private's pockets, as Ben said. All the barrels that had not been appropriated as chimneys had long since gone up those same chimneys in smoke. Maybe a few sticks plastered to the top with clay would help.

The light from the doorway disappeared as Hodges crawled in. "Sure glad it ain't raining," Hodges grinned. "What you doing now, Tom?"

"Fixing the chimney, I hope."

"Cain't fix a clay chimney once she's up. You got to build her right the first time around."

120

"That's what Walker said."

Hodges nodded, obviously pleased to find authority on his side. "Walker says he's taking out to get some wood. You want to come?"

"Who's going?"

"Me and you and him. And Marston and Hunter, if he can find them."

Tom considered. The chimney probably couldn't be made better. He might even knock a hole in it or tumble it down, and then where would they be? "Fine. Wait until I get my warmer on."

His warmer was a piece of tarpaulin salvaged from the wreck of a tent; he had stitched it into a crude cape that fell to his knees. Wooden buttons, whittled with the Barlow knife of happy memory and now the possession of Hodges, made it possible to close it at the front as far as his waist. It was not particularly stylish, but it was reasonably effective in keeping off the wind. As long as his boots held out, he was in good shape, he thought wryly. A good deal better off than those whose shoes hadn't lasted, at any rate.

Ben Walker was waiting for them just beyond the battery position. "Hunter'll be along with the axe directly. Marston couldn't be found." He scanned them with a professional eye for detail. "Got your pistol, Tom?"

"Under my warmer," Tom smiled.

"Old Tom, he totes his tent along with him," Hodges chuckled. "All he's got to do is cut hisself a pole and stick it down his back, and he's in bivouac."

"Handy, ain't it?" Tom jibed, refusing to snap at the bait.

Hunter came running up. "Sergeant Harrison says don't lose the axe or . . ."

". . . he'll make us wish we'd never been born," Ben finished "I've heard that one before."

"Where are we headed, Ben?" Tom asked.

121

Walker looked around. The guns stood muffled in the snow. To their front, a picket trudged along his post, his rifle slung muzzle down. "We're going over towards the river," he said with an air of conspiracy. "Some of the boys on picket yesterday said they swapped with the Yankees."

"Probably got cheated," Hodges grumbled.

"Shucks, no. They got hard-bread and bacon."

"What did they give for it?" Hunter asked suspiciously.

"Tobacco and a C.S.A. belt buckle."

Hodges stamped his feet in the snow. "Are we going to talk or trade horses? Let's get going!"

The picket waved a limp hand at them as they passed. A short distance from the guns, the ground fell away sharply towards the river. The trees had already been cut here, both as a source of wood and to provide open fire lanes for the guns. Down in the bottom lands where there was danger of rifle fire from the Union pickets, the trees still grew thickly.

"We ought to strike our advance line pretty soon," Ben Walker muttered.

Footprints in the snow showed where someone had recently passed. "He went in the bushes and the hogs ate him up," Hodges snickered.

Walker smiled. "Maybe he went over to the Yankees."

"Doggone it, Walker, you ain't got no call to talk that way about a man you don't know."

"Simmer down, Hodges. I didn't mean for you to take it seriously."

Abruptly, the trees fell away, and they were at the river's edge. A gray sheet of water; wide, but still reminiscent of Centre Creek. Was there ice on the creek now? And beyond the creek lay the road like a tunnel through the trees, the road that led to Scottsburg. Was Alison in the front parlor with its booklined shelves, perhaps this moment thinking of him? Alison . . .

"Well, who wants first turn?" Walker asked.

Hodges rested his rifle against a tree and rubbed his horny paws together. "Give me that doggone axe. I'll show you how to make chips fly."

"The rest of us'll keep a lookout for Yankees," Walker agreed.

Hodges selected a small scrub oak and swung his axe in a flashing arc. The wood was green, of course, but the dead wood had long since been hauled away and burned. Besides, oak made a good hot fire, once you got it going.

Tom unfastened the flap of his holster as a concession to Walker's warning and thrust his hands beneath his arm pits to get them warm. It was always a little surprising to him to see Hodges bring down a tree. Undersized and apparently as lank as a lock of his tow-colored hair, Hodges looked as though he could just about lift an axe and no more. Yet he was far and away the most accomplished woodsman in the battery.

Something sparkled in the thicket across the river, and Tom moved to the shelter of a tree. "Something moved over there, Ben. What do you want us to do?"

"Hodges!" Walker called sharply. "I think we've got some company. Hold it up a minute until we find out for sure."

Hodges rested his axe on the ground and peered across the river. "He's got hisself behind a tree over there. You must've seen his bayonet shine." He grinned happily. "The tree's too small for him. His tail is sticking out. You want, I can shoot him for you."

"Shucks, no! We want to trade."

"Hey, Yank!" Hodges called. "We-uns are going to let you off today. You can come out from behind that old bee gum."

"We won't shoot if you don't!" Walker added.

A face peered around the tree. Apparently satisfied, the Federal stepped out into the open, holding his rifle

123

at the ready. He was an older man, dark-complected and bony.

Hodges poked Hunter in the ribs. "Doggone, boy! Look at them britches! I should have shot me that Yank anyways. It's downright sinful to wear good clothes like them there."

"What's going on, Johnny?" the Federal called.

"Nothing much. We're cutting firewood," Walker explained. "You can go back to sleep."

"You're making too much racket!"

"I'll keep a-cutting," Hodges said to Walker. "It don't pay to act eager-like when you want to trade."

Tom chuckled to himself. When it came to trading, Hodges was probably a match for the best peddler the Yankees could muster. His innocent expression masked an innate shrewdness that was coupled with the acquisitive desires of a pack rat.

The Federal picket stamped his feet and grounded his rifle. "Awful cold, ain't it, Johnny?"

"Sure glad it ain't raining!" Hodges called.

"You fellows got any tobacco?"

"Reckon we can spare some," Walker said, relieved at having the Federal initiate the bargaining. "What can you offer?"

"I got some hardtack."

Walker considered. "How about bacon?"

"Ain't got none. I can get ration beef, though."

"How much tobacco've we got?" Walker inquired of the others.

The tally amounted to two plugs and a pigtail, with Hunter offering to donate a leather notebook in lieu of tobacco, which he did not use. "It doesn't seem like much to offer," he remarked. "Not for beef, anyway."

"It all goes according to how much he wants to smoke," Hodges said knowingly. "Besides, you ain't seen the beef."

124

"Two plugs and a pigtail," Walker sang out.

The Federal thought it over. "It ain't much, Johnny. What else you got?"

"How much beef did you say?" Hodges bawled.

"Shoulder joint. I can throw in some beans, too."

"We got a genuine leather notebook with paper."

The Federal shook his head sadly. "I can't write so good, Johnny."

"Doggone stupid Yankee," Hodges growled, quite forgetting that he himself was all but illiterate. "Hey, Yank —good beans?"

"Yesiree, Johnny!"

"How about some of that hard-bread?" Tom called. "I can throw in a C.S.A. belt buckle."

The enemy surrendered. His friend had access to a boat, he said, and would complete the exchange. Hodges returned to his chopping, happy in the knowledge that he had made a good dicker.

A short time later, a flat-bottomed skiff pulled away from the northern shore. Tom took off his hat and put his spare belt buckle inside. "Deacon's taking the collection, gentlemen," he said. The plugs, the pigtail, and the notebook followed.

"You do the swapping, Tom," Ben said. "We'll cover you."

The boat glided close to shore and stopped perhaps twenty feet out. "Let's see what you got, Johnny," the red-faced oarsman said cheerfully.

He held the hat so that the Federal could see the contents. "Let's see the meat."

"It's in a sack."

"Come on in, then. We won't hurt you."

The Unionist looked troubled. "I ain't supposed to."

"You're not supposed to be where you are right now, if it comes to that. Come on, if you want to swap."

The beef looked tough and fibrous, and the beans had a greenish tinge to them, but the hard-bread was fine. On the whole, it was a good swap. The red-faced man examined the belt buckle. He was apparently satisfied. "Had me one of these and lost it," he explained. "You fellows got more stuff to swap, we're here pretty near every day."

"You're not going any place?" Tom smiled.

"Not for a while, Johnny," the Yankee grinned. "Not for a while."

That night, they huddled together in the tiny hut. The beef and beans bubbled merrily in a tin kettle Hodges had managed to pilfer. Hunter had donated a packet of salt, precious beyond telling now. Ben stirred at the soup with a peeled twig, while Tom fed the fire with small chunks of wood. It might take all night, but they were going to have one good meal.

"Hungry?" Ben smiled.

"You bet I am."

Hodges' head lolled back. He snored gently.

"How much work does it take to be a lawyer, Tom?"

"Generally you read with a regular lawyer for three years, and then you go before a judge and let him examine you. I don't reckon it has to be three years either. You could do it in less time."

Ben nodded. "I was thinking maybe I'd like to be a lawyer when the war is over. I always had a natural bent for it."

"Maybe I could help."

"Say, now! That would surely be fine!"

The fire washed a knot with flame. It popped loudly in the silence. "Funny thing; when I was talking to that Yankee in the boat, I never thought once about Sandy. It was just as if there wasn't a war."

126

Ben smiled. "While you two were palavering, I was busy keeping Hodges from shooting him. Hodges thinks Yankees ain't quite human. No matter what you do, he thinks it's all right if you do it to a Yankee."

"One of them killed Sandy. Another one killed my brother Will. But I didn't feel like killing either of the Yankees we saw today."

"How many of them do you reckon you've killed, serving the gun?"

"It seems different, somehow."

"It ain't, though," Ben said. "The major was killed by a shell that was aimed by one man, loaded by another, and fused by a third. A fourth man pointed the gun and pulled the lanyard. It gets to be a kind of general thing after a while, Tom. You can swap and talk one day and shoot to kill the next. It was different in the beginning, though. I hated their guts. I reckon most of us did."

"What changed things?"

Ben rubbed the spiky black beard on his jawbone and stared into the fire. "Well," he said finally. "The ones who really hated most volunteered first. There ain't many of them left now, because they were shot at over a longer period of time, and the law of averages caught up with them. The new men coming in don't feel that way because they would have volunteered if they had. Those of the old-timers who are left have got it figured out that hate kills the man who hates. It burns him up inside. You can kill a man who'll kill you if you don't get him first. But you don't have to hate him. Shucks, Tom; win, lose, or draw, we're going to live in the same world with them after the war. Are we going to go on hating them the rest of our lives?"

"I agree, Ben. I don't think Sandy hated them, either."

"No. The major was a different breed of cat. He had an ideal to fight for. But there are almighty few ideals

127

left; it's a different war, now. We've got one hater left, though—Marle. He's a dangerous man, Tom. Watch out for him."

"He said he wanted me to try for a commission."

"You aim to?"

"I don't know. I reckon I owe it to Sandy."

Ben leaned forward and gave the soup a stir. "That don't sound like an awful good reason to me," he said quietly. "Back in sixty-one it might have been. But it's a different war now. An officer has to be good enough to take care of his men. If he isn't, he's got no business being an officer."

Hodges blinked his eyes and eyed the kettle. "Ain't that about ready, Walker?"

"Pretty near."

"You all like a drink?"

"Of what?" Ben asked suspiciously. "Snow water?"

"Whiskey. Good whiskey. Leastwise, it come outen Marle's saddlebag; it ought to be good."

Tom held the bottle gingerly. He had never had anything stronger than wine, yet to refuse to drink would be unmannerly.

"Here's to your lawyering," he said to Ben. "The best of trading, Hodges." The raw liquor burned its way down, all but strangling him, but he forced himself to hold back the choking coughs that threatened to erupt.

"You done good for a church going man," Hodges chuckled. "Help yourself, Ben."

Ben stared into the amber depths as if he could read the future therein. "I hope we're never any worse off than we are tonight," he said quietly. Then his eyes danced in the firelight as he looked at Tom.

"Here's to your soldiering, boy," he said.

128

CHAPTER 11

The Sounds of Spring

WARM winds came up from the south, and the dogwood flowers in the thickets were like pale ghosts of the winter's snow. For some weeks there had been no trading at all with the Yankees across the river. The pickets on both sides had been increased, and their officers encouraged the exchange of shots with their opposite numbers. The men themselves were willing. Winter, the common enemy, had gone; the time of peace was at an end, and the machine of war began to move once more.

Rumors that the Federals had got themselves another new general were succeeded by the grim fact that the enemy had taken the initiative and was crossing the river in force. As the advance developed, small groups on each side broke off from their parent bodies in vain efforts to turn the enemy's flank. Over roads that bore the name by courtesy, through the tangle of scrub and underbrush that was rightly called "the Wilderness," the armies moved; clashing at unexpected points due to the blindness entailed by the nature of the terrain, they often failed to locate enemy positions in an attack for the same reason.

The iron-shod wheels of the Number Two gun bounced over exposed roots or churned through last year's leaves as its starving, bone-rack horses tugged it along in an effort to keep abreast of the invaders. Once they forged ahead

129

and dug positions on the south bank of a small river; the enemy failed to walk into the trap, electing to sidestep and advance by another route, and so the chase began again while the weather grew warmer and the casualty lists grew longer.

It was a different sort of war, Ben Walker had said last winter. Tom could believe it. All the principles of artillery fire that Marle and Harrison had tried to teach him were violated daily. The artillery was seldom in position in time to support an infantry attack; often, the guns had to receive a counterthrust by the enemy without any aid from the infantry. It was as if the army had lost its coordination, had been thrown off balance by its adversary, and no longer was capable of rendering unified, powerful blows.

They rested in a grove of trees near a nameless road. Behind them rifle fire sputtered in the wood. No matter how often Marle referred to their movements as "flanking" or "tactical maneuvering," the men of Number Two knew better. They had cut their teeth on Harrison's drill, and they had followed Sandy Tanner down the long road from First Manassas. They were retreating, and that was all there was to it.

Marston lay on his belly, his head pillowed on his arms. He was not sleeping, Tom knew; he was just "conserving his energy," as he would say if Harrison asked him.

"I wish we had some infantry up here," Ben grumbled. "I feel about as naked as a jaybird."

"The rest of the battery is supposed to join us, isn't it?" Tom asked.

"Some time. All Marle told me was to take Number Two and hold the road until he came. He said there was going to be infantry to support us, but I'm switched if I can see any."

Hodges peered over the tube of the gun. "There's Yankees coming, Walker."

130

"So's your Aunt Hattie."

"Boom!" Hodges yelled. "I got me about a jillion of them."

"Will someone silence that larrikin?" Marston drawled.

"Boys, listen to him!" Hodges chortled. "Old Marston is the best educated man in the whole doggone battery. He can call you more names without backtracking than the Yanks have sutlers."

Hunter smiled at Tom. There was a long-standing, albeit good-natured feud between Hodges and Marston. Despite the raillery, however, Hodges respected Marston's ability to remain aloof where work and promotion were concerned as much as Marston secretly admired Hodges' self-reliance and independence.

Hodges turned back to the piece, pretending to sight it on the angle where the road turned out of the wood. "Hey, Walker!" he called after a moment. "There really is something out there."

"All right," Ben called. "Take your positions, boys. Load! Cannister!"

"Reckon they've seen us, Ben?" Tom asked.

Walker nodded briefly. "They know we're here, all right. They don't know what support we've got, though. That's what they've been waiting to find out."

Now they could hear the crackle of breaking twigs as the skirmishers of the Federal advance fanned out under cover of the woods. Ben Walker motioned the crew to the prolonge ropes. "Pull her downhill a way, like we were fixing to pull out."

Encouraged by this apparent sign of retreat, the Federals set up a chorus of catcalls: "Where's Jeff Davis? Even my grandma don't run out on a fight! Where's your mama, Rebel?"

Hodges dropped his end of the rope and ran back to the crest of the hill. "Go back to your mama, you blue bellies!"

"Hey, Rebel! Pat your feet if you can't talk!"

"I don't talk through my doggone nose like you all!" Hodges yelled. Quietly he spoke to Walker. "There's a slew of them going to rush us from the road, Ben. They're waiting for the gun to get harnessed."

"Let's oblige," Ben grinned. He gave the appropriate orders, while the men on the ropes and the trail rested. One man jangled the securing chain and banged the coupling pin against a tire. It sounded very realistic.

"What're you all waiting for?" Hodges yelled. "We got the whole army back here."

The answer was an impromptu volley by half a dozen of the skirmishers. The balls droned overhead, and Hodges dived over the crest to safety. "They're a-coming," he gasped.

As the snout of Number Two cleared the crest of the hill for the second time, Ben sighted over the hausse and depressed the muzzle. The blue cloud of skirmishers had already come within two hundred yards of the position, yelling a chorus of hurrahs. "Stand clear!" Ben yelled. "Fire!"

Hunter, the Number Four man, pulled the lanyard. Dust and the smoke of the muzzle blast obscured the scene for a moment. Tom fumbled with a fresh cartridge while the rammer swabbed the tube to extinguish any embers of burning cloth that might have remained in the bore. The survivors of the attack pushed ahead, leaving half a dozen fallen on the ground behind them. For a moment Tom remembered the bushwhacker falling towards him, the smoke from the derringer eddying in the room, and he paused.

"Double cannister!" Ben yelled. "Come on! Load that charge!"

The moment passed, and he shoved the charge in the muzzle to be rammed, his eye on the Number Three man now, to make certain that the vent was stopped to prevent

132

a premature discharge. If you didn't kill them, they would kill you. It was as simple as that.

The second round was decisive. The smoke hung over the dead and wounded like a gray pall. Nothing moved in the clear area between Number Two and the wood. He pushed the third charge in the muzzle, preparatory to ramming, and stepped back. Someone in the field below was calling for Papa. It was the voice of a young boy, perhaps his own age.

And then something went "spat" just behind him, and Hodges yelled, "Who's hit?"

Ben Walker put his hand on the left wheel of the gun and gripped it until the sweat stood out on his face like water. Tom looked down at the rapidly spreading stain on Ben's right knee. So it had happened. The law of averages, as Ben would have said, had caught up with him.

He took Ben in his arms and laid him down beside the gun. "We'll fix it, Ben," he said. "Give me your knife, Hodges."

Carefully he cut away the trouser leg. The knee cap was shattered; you didn't have to be a surgeon to see that. There was a lot of blood, too. That called for a tourniquet. He worked the severed trouser leg around the lower part of Ben's thigh, knotted it, and twisted it tight with a stick.

"What's going on out there?" he asked sharply of the faces crowded around. "The Yankees could walk right over us."

Hodges turned to look. "There's more of them piling up in the road around the bend. I can see them between the trees."

He stood up, knowing what he had to do at last, and accepting it, because there was nothing else to do.

"Marston? Take one of the new men and make a stretcher for Ben. Then carry him back the way we came

133

until you find him a doctor. And then get back here as fast as you can."

Ben opened his eyes for a moment. "I reckon I'll have time for lawyering now," he murmured.

Tom bent over and wiped Ben's face with the tail of his shirt. "It'll be all right, Ben."

"God willing," Ben whispered. "Maybe we'll be partners, Tom. I'd like that."

"Them Yanks in the woods are bunching," Hodges said.

Ben looked at Tom. "Take care of the boys," he said, and then he fainted.

Tom straightened and walked over to Ben's old position, to the left of the breech. "Load with solid shot; the charge is in."

The others looked at him in surprise, and then they obeyed. The loaders passed the ball from the caisson up to the muzzle of the piece. The rammer slammed it home and stood back. Number Three uncovered the vent, and Number Four—the gunner—pricked the charge and inserted the primer tube.

Over the coarse sights of the hause, the trees at the bend in the road were plainly visible. Here and there a patch of blue cloth showed as the new attack wave was formed. The gunner raised his hands, and the men stepped back. The gunner looked at Tom.

His hand chopped down in the familiar signal. "Fire!"

Number Four's arm swept backwards, pulling the lanyard.

Now it was June already, and there had been no letter from Tom since May, when he had written briefly to say that he was well, that his boots were still whole, and that it seemed likely that the army would be moving again. Mary Tanner smiled pleasantly at the pale young man who sat on the edge of the veranda; it would have been nice if

134

he had brought some sort of message from Sandy, as well; but then, he had obviously been under a great strain.

"They had to amputate above the knee?" Joseph was asking the young man. "Was there no other way?"

"No, sir. It was a minny ball; they expand when they hit something. And this one hit my knee right square."

"The surgeon did a wonderful job," Joseph said kindly. He had examined the wound earlier in his office. "Very neat indeed, the way he stitched the flap across the stump. Does it still pain you, Mr. Walker?"

"Some—not a lot, sir. Not like when they first took it off."

Mary cleared her throat, and at once the conversation stopped. "How is Tom progressing, Mr. Walker?"

"Well, ma'am, he took over the gun when I left and one boy who come out right after me said he made corporal. I reckon he can handle the job."

"What does he do, exactly?" Joseph asked.

Mr. Walker smiled. "Well, sir, by rights a sergeant is the gun chief, but we haven't been getting promotions. Tom is gun chief—that was my old job. He decides where the gun ought to go into action, what kind of ammunition should be used, and then he goes ahead and sights the gun and gives the crew whatever orders he has to, to get the piece loaded and fired."

"I had hoped he would be an officer by this time," Mary said. "Have you seen my son Ambrose recently?"

Joseph gave a start, and Mr. Walker hesitated briefly before replying. "Last time I really saw the major, ma'am, he and I were going back from furlough. My pa—he's a conductor on the Virginia Central railroad—he fixed the major up with a whole car to himself. Him and that big gray horse of his."

"You knew Sandy from the beginning, didn't you?" Joseph said quietly.

135

"Yes, sir. We came a long, hard way together."

"What will you do now?"

"Well, sir, Tom and I got to talking last winter about law. I figured I'd start reading law. You don't need to have two legs for that."

A rig pulled off the Pike and headed towards the house. "Reckon this here's my ride," Mr. Walker said. He slid from the veranda and hitched his crutches under his armpits with unexpected dexterity. "Ma'am. Sir. It's been a great pleasure meeting Tom's folks."

"God keep you," Joseph said quietly. "Come back when you can. My father-in-law is a lawyer; perhaps he can give you some advice."

As Mary Tanner watched the boy make his way out to the ramshackle buggy, she remembered the first year of the war, the way the boys had looked in their gray, cadet cloth uniforms. It had been a comic opera sort of thing, where no one got captured or lost or—or killed. Of course that hadn't happened to her boys. But it did happen.

On the brighter side, perhaps Thomas would show them all in the long run, even though he had been so reluctant at first. A corporal wasn't much, but it was a start. And it was a duty to rise as high as one could. Tom owed it to them, no less than to his country.

"Tom will be an officer, too," she said firmly.

Joseph nodded absently, almost as if he had not heard her. "He'll be a fine lawyer," he said.

Sometimes Joseph was so exasperating. He just didn't seem to be able to concentrate on the practical things in life.

Betsy sat down at the kitchen table with her Bible. Since Miss Mary had begun to teach her how to read words, she had taken a good deal of pleasure in trying to find words that she knew. The first part she knew anyhow. In the beginning was the Word, and the Word was God. It was easy

136

to figure out the words in that piece. "God" always had a great big front part, important-like, the way God ought to be. "In" and "the" she knew. She could walk up to either one of them on a dark night and know what it was right off.

It was kind of like the part about casting your bread upon the waters, the way Miss Mary had picked up since she had started the reading sessions. Miss Mary had finally gone and broken that old law about not teaching colored folks to read, and it seemed to take her out of her own troubles. She still made up packages for poor Mister Will, and she wrote to poor Mister Sandy the same like she wrote to Mister Tom, but she didn't go to brooding on them the way she used to. She couldn't write so many letters now, anyway, because they were pretty near out of paper. The doctor was using an old roll of wallpaper and leaving a little room between the lines so Mister Tom could answer in that space. What the doctor would do when he ran out of wallpaper, she didn't know. Maybe start peeling it off the walls.

A shadow flickered across the doorway, and she looked up to see Horace's grinning face. "What you doing here, this time of day?" she demanded.

"Come to see you," Horace replied pleasantly. His eyes darted here and there, inspecting the room, finding it wanting. "Ain't you cooking?"

"Is that what you come here for? You act like nobody never feeds you over to McNair's."

"I eat good," Horace said. "Only it's my cooking. It ain't never so good as somebody else's."

"You better get used to it. There ain't nothing for you around here."

Horace shrugged his shoulders and looked at the Bible. "Who you trying to fool, woman? You cain't read that book."

Miss Mary had cautioned her not to tell anybody about

137

the reading lessons. Doctor Tanner knew about them, of course, but he was the only one. While she struggled between her desire to tell Horace and set him back a place or two and her duty to remain silent, he assumed the offensive.

"I been hearing things, Betsy. The Yankee soldiers are coming."

"Who says?"

"Folks come by. One man, he tell how they give every black man a new suit of clothes and a mule for riding. And we are all going to be free, we don't work or nothing. This here's the Year of Jubilo. Lord Jesus, he come back to set us black folks on the Glory Road."

"Who's going to feed you?"

"White folks. The Yankee soldiers make 'em."

Work was nothing to run away from. If you wanted to eat, you had to work, and that was right and proper. But new clothes! Ah, she hadn't had any material to make a new dress since the beginning of the war. Still and all, nobody gave nobody nothing without getting something in return for it. And white folks stuck to white folks, North or South. Anybody wanted to be friends with a black man, let the black man watch out!

"It sounds like somebody's been funning you, Horace. Them Yankee soldiers don't care about you and me. They got to fight the war, the same like our boys."

Horace shook his head. "Father Abraham, he's coming. And when he comes, we're going to be free."

"I'm free right now," Betsy said. "I know you ain't. If you want to run away North, that's your business. Maybe I don't blame you for wanting it, but don't count on nobody giving you nothing. Whatever you get, you're going to work hard for."

When Horace had gone, she pondered over the things he had told her. Everybody knew that the Yankee folks had

138

recently started to make big promises. She had overheard the doctor repeating some of them to Miss Mary. The new clothes and the mule weren't the half of it. They were going to turn the white folks out of their houses and share out all the Confederate gold. It all sounded like a great big bunch of lies, when you heard it, but there was the possibility that a little bit of it might be true.

Nobody knew exactly where the rumors started. Maybe some of them started as wishful thinking in Horace's head. It was mighty hard to tell just what was true and what was not. There was one thing, though. She didn't want anything that wasn't hers. She had her own money that the doctor put away for her. When the war was over, there'd be a new dress and new shoes, just like before all this foolishness had started.

What it all came down to was the Yankees were going to give away what wasn't theirs. It was a good thing to set all the black folks free; nobody ought to have to stay where he didn't want to. But to take other folks' property, that was a horse of a different color.

An aura of decay had settled over Scottsburg, Alison decided. She had noticed it even last fall, when she and her mother had returned from Lovatt, following Sandy's funeral. It was apparent in the odors of damp rot from the houses that had been abandoned last year and during the winter. It was audible in the sound of a loose shutter banging in the wind this gusty spring, in the echo of voices that once had come from the children next door, and which were now heard only with the ear of memory and wishful thinking. But above all, it was a feeling, a sense of being alone, with no one to turn to in time of need.

Not that there was a particular sense of want. Even in the dead of winter Mr. Hauser and Doctor Tanner had kept them well supplied with meat, and now that the corn was ripening, they would be well prepared for the summer. It was to be hoped that the yams and squash would do as well, although the corn was more important. In the autumn, there would be white potatoes, also.

But the feeling remained, no matter how hard she worked, no matter how often Mama dredged up stories from the past to entertain her. It was not that things were difficult now; it was that something was about to happen. Time had been arrested; soon it would begin to move again. Perhaps this feeling meant the end of the war; they heard no news save that which Mr. Hauser might bring. It could very well be that the embattled armies had made a peace, Mama suggested when she mentioned the feeling of presentiment to her.

"No, it's not that," Alison replied, as the gunfire drummed in the Wilderness, a hundred miles away. "It's a restless, disturbed spring."

"We must accept what God sends us," Mama said gently.

"I know, Mama. It's just that it's been so long now. It's June already."

"And you want Tom to come back," Mama smiled.

In truth, she didn't know what she was hoping for. Probably only that the war would end and that she and Tom could begin their life together. In this year of 1864, very few Confederates envisioned a victorious conclusion to the war. Both sides might stop fighting, but that was all.

Out in the bright morning, she took down her hoe and searched on the shelf near the barn door for the file. The corn was doing beautifully, but the weeds had to be kept down. The "wheet, wheet" of the file on the blade of the hoe sounded abnormally loud to her in the still morning air. It was as if there were no other persons in the world, save her and Mama.

No. There was another sound. Horses headed from the west. A steady, rhythmic beating against the earth. It must

140

be a team of four, at least; maybe more. The sound swelled and she put down her hoe and walked toward the house. The time of waiting was almost over. Something was about to happen.

She and Mama stood in the front parlor and peered from behind the faded drapes as the riders trotted up the street, their dark uniforms appearing black in the sunlight, their accouterments gleaming as though burnished. Yankees. The enemy from the North, just as the Bible stated.

There was a strange inevitability about them, as though they had somehow been destined to come, if not now, then in another morning, riding into the sun on their sleek, well-cared-for-mounts, with their handsome sturdy uniforms and their well polished boots. She contrasted them with the worn tunic of Jonathan Marle, the pale starveling ghost that had been Sandy, and she felt a new kind of resentment. Granted their opinions might differ from hers: but what right had they to be well fed and well clothed when her Tom was not?

She went quietly upstairs and checked the priming of the pistol she had found in the attic last winter. It was not the easiest thing in the world to conceal beneath her apron, but she owed it to Tom to resist the enemy as valiantly as she could.

But no one tried to enter. Six riders led by a sergeant with bright yellow chevrons cantered back up the road and turned off at the vacant house next door to theirs. They dismounted, and the sergeant hammered the door open with the butt of his carbine. Two of the troopers led the horses behind the house, presumably to graze, while three of them sauntered off into the trees beside the road. It was all done in an assured emotionless manner that defied criticism. Even the act of breaking into the house was not vindictive. There was a house which could offer shade

141

from the sun and concealment from a possible enemy. That was all there was to it.

Despite the heat, Mama closed the windows and bolted the doors. "I'll feel safer," she said to Alison. "But I wish you'd put away that silly pistol, dear. It might go off."

She nodded absently and put the weapon on the parlor table. It would be convenient, if needed. There was nothing to do but wait. She crossed to the rosewood piano and picked at the yellowing keys. The piano had a decided twang; a tendency to give a plaintive, minor-key sound to whatever melody was played upon it. It had last been tuned by a roving journeyman in the summer of fifty-nine. She seated herself and placed her hands upon the cool ivory. Softly, she played the first few bars of "The Bonnie Blue Flag." They had a long-ago, faraway sound, as though they belonged to someone else and in some other time.

"Alison!"

She crossed to the window beside Mama and peered through a chink in the blind. Two troopers were walking across the side lawn towards the back yard.

"Let's go upstairs," Mama urged. "Perhaps they won't know anyone is here."

A sudden inspiration came to her, and she raced to the kitchen door. Sure enough, the great lumps were breaking off half-ripe ears of corn and trampling the potato plants in the bargain. Without further thought, she flung open the door and stepped out on the porch.

"Will you have the goodness to leave our garden alone?"

The shorter of the two turned around and she could see the flash of yellow on his sleeve. He touched the brim of his forage cap with the tip of his index finger. "Do you live here, Miss?" he asked stupidly.

"I wouldn't be standing here if I didn't."

The sergeant considered the logic of her remark. "I guess you wouldn't at that. We're just taking some corn."

142

"I am well aware of that," Alison said sharply. "It happens to be the only thing we'll have to eat this summer, thanks to you all."

"Well," the sergeant said. "We were told to go forage."

He wasn't much older than Tom, she decided. It was only the short and carefully tended beard along his jawline that made him look as old as he did. She considered a new approach. "I don't think your mama would approve of your stealing from poor people."

The sergeant blushed. "We're not stealing. We're foraging from enemy territory," he said angrily.

"If you think you're justified, why are you getting mad?"

He began to laugh, then. "Pa always said no man could ever win an argument with a woman." He turned to the other trooper. "Leave it, Joe. I know when I'm licked."

"You mean it?" Joe asked.

"I mean it." He turned back to Alison. "We aren't all monsters, you know."

"Thank you for sparing us," she replied, still rankling from the injustice of being obliged to a stranger for her own corn.

"I'll see to it none of my men take any," the sergeant promised.

She nodded, unable to humble herself a second time, and then she turned away. For all the sergeant's good nature, she could not forget that some day he might meet Tom in battle. It was a sobering thought, and it served as a reminder of the inner war that must linger, long after the guns were stilled and the banners furled.

Later the sergeant and his men rode back towards town.

She watched them from an upstairs window, safely concealed behind the drapery. As the sergeant rode abreast of the house, he turned in the saddle and half-raised his hand in greeting. She moved swiftly back into the room, amused, yet angered at the presumptuousness of the man. If it had only been Tom riding by!

During the night the patrol moved out towards the Pike. She could hear the thud of hooves cutting across the deserted yard next door, the drumming as they struck the harder surface of the road. Although no orders were given, she could hear the jingle of saddle rings and the clink of steel upon steel as a carelessly grasped carbine touched a saber scabbard.

When she went outside next morning, she discovered that most of the corn had been trampled underfoot by the riders who had sought a short cut to the main road.

CHAPTER 12

Village in the Moonlight

As HODGES said, it looked as if the Yankees had worn themselves out chasing the army. They had fought their way from the Rappahannock down to the outskirts of Richmond without once being able to pierce the thin line of defenses that blocked their approach to the capital at every step. Once the Federals blundered badly: they sent wave after wave of infantry in an attack which was under artillery fire from three sides. It lasted for perhaps half an hour, and as long as he lived Tom would remember the screams of the wounded lying in the blazing sun for two days without water because the Federals refused to accept a truce.

"It's their own men!" he said in disbelief.

"Remember that, boy!" Marle grated, his eyes glittering. "Yankees have plenty of men to throw away. They don't care how many they lose."

Even Marston was shocked out of his usual lethargy. "It's sheer butchery. I was glad to see it end."

"I wasn't," Marle said briefly. "The more of them we kill, the better I like it."

There was a new edge to Marle's bitterness these days. Tom thought it stemmed from the recent invasion of his home state of Mississippi by the Federals. Whatever its cause, Marle had become a man obsessed with killing. He was no longer fighting to bring the war to a successful conclusion; he was fighting to kill as many men as possible. There was a difference.

In truth the war had changed, as Walker had said during the winter. The days when gray-coated cavaliers rode gaily into battle to the blare of a brass band were over. That there had been casualties in that halcyon time, none but the most simple-minded veterans would refuse to admit. But now there was a bitterness which ripened in proportion to the crops and homesteads which were destroyed by the invaders. Ideals had been obscured by hatred and revenge.

To Jonathan Marle, the time between the first action of the year in the thickets along the Rapidan and the final attack at Cold Harbor was the longest he had ever known. In the days before the war, five years had slipped past with less to recommend them. Yet this newer period had been of short duration: from the beginning of May to the middle of June, roughly speaking.

Now they were only marking time here in the emplacements near Cold Harbor, too weak to attack the Yankees, waiting for the enemy to make the first move. They weren't real emplacements, either. Field fortifications was a better name for them. Earth scooped out and thrown up as a parapet, with a few logs tossed on for good measure. He looked down the line at the Number Two gun.

Sturdy pieces, Napoleons. This one had been in service right from the beginning. The tires had been renewed two or three times and the wheels had been replaced once, but she was still the same old piece for all of that. Tanner kept her looking well, too; it was just too bad he didn't have some of Sandy's genius. He would probably never get any higher than corporal. Well, Marle had done all he could; his conscience needn't twinge on that account.

"Yankees steal one on you, Jonathan?"

He turned to find Colonel Hulme behind him, a sheaf of papers in his big fist. "Just checking, sir," he grinned.

"You looked mighty possessive. I'd hate to try to walk off with one of your pieces."

"I'd hate to see what Harrison would do. He'd take the guns to bed with him, if he could."

Hulme nodded. "He's a good noncom. Best sergeant in the battalion." He cleared his throat. "I want you to keep this to yourself, Captain," he said formally. "Only the battery commanders will be given this information. It must go no further."

"I understand."

"We're moving out."

"It figured," Marle said. "The Yankees ain't fired more than five rounds all day. They're going to flank us, and we have to move to block them."

Hulme grinned. "Not this time, Jonathan. Some of the army is going to sidestep and keep in front of them, but we're headed west. To the Valley." His voice was charged with emotion as he spoke the last words. It was as if he had said "we're going home."

To the Valley! The scene of the first victories. The stage where the immortal Jackson had first appeared. Despite himself, Marle felt a thickness in his throat. Maybe this would mean an end to the bad luck that had dogged the army since Gettysburg!

"Maybe this is it, Colonel."

"A lot of us hope so, Jonathan," Hulme replied.

They moved out of the lines on June 13, 1864. They were Early's Corps, now, the old Second Corps of Dick Ewell, conceived at Chancellorsville in the long-remembered spring of sixty-three, born in that same hot June, and baptized in blood on the slopes of Culp's Hill. They were as was their general: tough, hard-bitten, lean, pro-

147

fane, tobacco-chewing veterans who had marched the long, hard road from Manassas under Jackson and D. H. Hill before they had become a corps with a separate entity and a new dignity to maintain.

"I'm Jubal Early's soldier, and Dixie is my home," they sang as they marched, and "A hundred months have passed, Lorena." They chanted "Praise God from whom all blessings flow," and without a pause for the sake of propriety swung into "The Georgia militia, eating goober peas."

They were "Lee's Miserables." They were the ragged, barefoot boys and old men who were fighting, not for some abstract ideal, nor for a slave empire, nor for the pale, cold president of the Confederacy; but for their homes and for their liberty. They were a corps pretending to be an army. They were the embodiment of the American legend of the victorious underdog.

They were magnificent.

In the beginning, the battery went afoot, since the Federal cavalry was out on a raid and no man knew how long the Virginia Central might be expected to operate west of Beaver Dam. On the second day of the march, June 14, trains came downtrack and began to shuttle the infantry forward. Hampton's cavalry had beaten Sheridan soundly, the trainmen reported, and the track was safe for the time being. Eventually, someone remembered the artillery, which was popularly believed to ride and which never did, owing to the weakened state of the horses.

"You all don't know where we're going," Hodges crowed.

"I suppose you do," Marston yawned from his perch atop the gun trail.

Two of the four guns of the battery and their limbers and crews had been hustled onto flatcars under dire threat of being left behind. They had been waiting two hours, now, until the horses could be cajoled into boxcars with special slings to support them.

"We're going up the track and shoot Yankees," Hodges announced with an air of triumph. "Boom!"

"From this flatcar, Hodges?" Tom queried.

"Doggone well right."

"How're you going to shoot from a moving train?" Sergeant Harrison chuckled.

"Double cannister!"

"End of gun. Fall out, gun crew," Tom smiled.

Up ahead the engine gave off an exploratory cloud of steam and jerked the slack out of the couplings. The train began to roll off the siding on to the main line.

"Whooee!" Hodges yelled. "We ain't got horses, but we're sure a-going."

"The horses are up ahead," Marston said solemnly. "The engine can't pull this big train all by itself. It only makes a noise to keep the horses pulling."

Hodges cast a suspicious eye at him. "You funning me?"

"Of course not. See for yourself."

Hodges scrambled under the trail and peered over the side of the car. "I cain't see no horses. Doggone you, Marston!"

"There aren't really any horses," Hunter explained. "Come on over, and I'll show you how an engine works."

Of them all, Hunter showed the most patience in his dealings with the other crew members and with his superiors. The Richmond conscript was a little like Will, Tom thought. He was generous to a fault, sharing whatever he had with the others, writing letters for the illiterate men and furnishing the precious paper as well. The main difference between him and Will was his sunny disposition. Religion had been a duty to Will; it was a joy to Hunter.

149

Marle strode across the splintery flooring. "Beats walking, don't it?" he grinned.

"Yes, sir," Tom agreed. "It does that."

"I reckon you got an idea where we're headed?"

Tom chuckled. "Well, Captain, it looks like maybe we're going to hit Gordonsville. That's mighty close to home for me."

"Staunton's closer," Marle said smoothly. "You ought to be seeing your folks pretty soon now."

And Alison! When Marle had passed to the next car, he closed his eyes, and the road to Scottsburg came clear in his mind as it had so often in the past year; the overhanging branches freighted with leaves, the turns and twists to avoid rocky outcroppings, and finally the village itself, with its strange air of being in a time all its own, with no past and no future, but only a "now" that was magically separate and distinct from all other "nows."

On the sixteenth they reached Charlottesville and left the train. The news was bad; Hunter's cavalry had raided up Valley as far as Lynchburg. They had occupied Staunton and Lexington; now they threatened Lynchburg.

The Second Corps pushed on, and by evening they were occupying the trenches that the citizens of Lynchburg had dug to protect their town.

On the following day, Federals appeared in some force and began to lob shells at the town. The long-range pieces engaged the enemy successfully, and after a short time the duel ended in favor of the Second Corps. By the eighteenth, the Federals were in full retreat, and the Second Corps were snapping at their heels.

They were in Staunton on the twenty-sixth.

The town had turned out in force to greet them. Small boys huzzahed and yelled as the scarlet battle flags borne by the color guards flamed through the narrow streets. The bands, with understandable optimism, struck up "Maryland, My Maryland." It seemed possible now that they would not only drive Hunter from the Valley, but reach Maryland as well. The warm sun was kind to bare feet and rags; it draped the worn-out harness and the battered limbers in a golden aura.

Alongside a building someone yelled "Tanner!" and Tom looked over his shoulder to see Ben Walker leaning on a set of rude crutches, grinning happily.

"It's Ben!" he called, and they turned to call greetings to the man who had commanded Number Two almost from the start of the war.

Home! I'm coming home! he cried silently, even as he waved to Ben. He couldn't trust himself to speak.

The bivouac that night was a peaceful one. The cavalry had been able to push the hostile forces ahead of them with little or no opposition, according to a courier who had ridden through camp on his way to report. Curiously enough, the Federals had elected to flee over the mountains to the west. The Valley was thus free to the Second Corps.

"Thinking about home?" Hunter asked gently as he ladled out the mush for their supper.

"Not at the moment. I was thinking about how long it would take the Yankees to get to wherever they're going."

"You live north of here, don't you?"

Tom nodded. It was a fortunate chance indeed that had sent the enemy off to the west. Supposing they had stopped to fight at Scottsburg? Or Lovatt?

"Have you thought about going home?"

"You mean now? Tonight?"

Hunter grinned. "Harrison heard from a friend of his

that we're going to have a general inspection tomorrow."

"What a time for an inspection!"

"It's not as crazy as it sounds, Tom. They want to see which batteries aren't going to be able to keep up. The best batteries will probably get the best horses from the others. I think some of the worst outfits will be sent back."

That made sense. Apparently General Early intended to do some hard, fast marching.

"Reckon I'll go nose around and see what I can find out," Tom said as he finished the last of his mush.

Sergeant Harrison was eating a similar dish in the company of Captain Marle when Tom located the sergeant. The two men were seated companionably atop the limber of Number One, holding their tin plates in their laps. Marle's chief virtue, Tom decided, was his ability to overlook rank and still maintain his authority.

"Climb up, Corporal," Marle ordered. "I was just thinking about you."

"Sir?"

"I just learned from Colonel Hulme that no leaves are to be granted for any reason whatsoever. I had thought that you might be able to spend a day at home."

He tried to conceal his disappointment. "Thank you for trying, sir."

Harrison grinned. "Never say die, Corporal. The army never lets a good gunner down."

Marle nodded. "We're having an inspection of men and equipment tomorrow afternoon. You'll stand it with the rest of the battery. But this evening and tomorrow morning I want you and one of your men to patrol in the direction of Lovatt, speak with the inhabitants, and learn what you can of the enemy activity in that area."

"Yes, sir!"

"Colonel Hulme had a fine mare he bought from somebody a while back. He's donating her for the patrol. My

152

horse is available for the man you choose to accompany you."

Tom showed the pass Colonel Hulme had given him to the outpost guard, who nodded sleepily and waved him on. Hodges nudged him and grinned happily. "Heyo, Tom; this is something, ain't it!"

"I agree."

He had decided to take Hodges in preference to Hunter or Marston on the strength of Hodges' aptitude for fighting. Hodges could be depended upon to keep up, no matter what the cost; he could also be relied on to stay awake, to shoot straight, and to have no mistimed twinges of conscience before he did so. If he left something to be desired as a conversationalist, his other attributes and his good nature more than compensated for that flaw.

"I saw Sal and Sal saw me, up in the crotch of a sour-apple tree," Hodges bawled lustily.

"Hold it, boy," Tom cautioned, trying to keep the laughter out of his voice. "There could be Yankee stragglers around."

"That's right, ain't it? I got a good present for them, if they want it. Buck and ball."

Hodges was armed with one of the old .69 caliber muskets which normally was loaded with one ball and three buckshot. Up to a hundred yards, it was effective, although not nearly as accurate as the rifles.

"How far we going, Tom?"

"Ten miles. To Lovatt, if we can. Only first I want to stop somewhere else."

Hodges nodded wisely. "I can watch out for her folks for you."

"Not necessary," Tom chuckled. "This is the girl I'm going to marry."

"Oh." Hodges considered the statement at length. "That's a serious business, marrying."

"It sure is."

"I reckon a man has to be pretty sure in his own mind he's picked the right girl before he goes to tying himself down," Hodges hinted.

Tom laughed. "Don't worry about it, boy. I'm sure."

They rode on in silence as the dusk gathered at the foot of North Mountain. He wondered if the mare remembered the road to Scottsburg. It had been better than a year since he had ridden there, and the last time had been with Mama in the carriage. How long would it be until the next time? The years crept slowly by, indeed!

As soon as they entered Scottsburg he could sense the change. The moonlight accented the black and empty windows, and the odor of damp and decay was heavy. They left the road and passed through a deserted back yard. The sharp odor of horse dung came to his nostrils. Not too fresh, he decided. Maybe a week ago a large number of horses had been here.

"Yankees?" Hodges asked.

"I don't think so. But they've been here." He flapped the reins, and the mare walked across the remainder of the open space into the shadow of Aunt Anne's barn. Hodges slid from the saddle and turned into the door's black void, quickly and silently. Even in the unfamiliar interior he made no sound. A moment later he appeared.

"Nobody here," he said. "You want me to take the horses in the shed?"

"Good idea. I won't be too long."

A candle was burning in the window of one of the upstairs rooms, but there was no other sign of life. He stood before the back door waiting, listening. "Alison?" he called gently.

The door opened abruptly, and she came out of the darkness into the moonlight. For a moment she stopped,

154

as if she were unable to believe that it was him, and then she came into his arms, suddenly and easily, and put her face to his.

"Alison?" Aunt Anne called. "What are you doing down there?"

"Cousin Tom's here, Mama!"

"Good evening, Aunt Anne."

For a moment there was silence, and then Aunt Anne said, "Lord have mercy! I'll be down directly, children; come in out of the night air."

They clasped each other tightly, urgently, as if that could somehow void the long time that had passed and the time that must pass before they could meet again.

All too soon light appeared in the kitchen. "Come in!" Aunt Anne ordered. "Come in and let's have a look at you!"

They sat around the kitchen table where a home made tallow candle guttered in a pewter holder.

"Your grandfather says your folks are fine, Tom. There was a battle up near Lovatt, but nobody you know was hurt."

He wrenched his mind from Alison with an effort. "Have you seen Mama?"

Aunt Anne shook her head. "Not for quite a while, Tom. Not since you went away. But your grandfather rides over here once a week or so, and he tells us all the news."

"He brings us meat," Alison added. "We have a garden, so we're quite well off."

"Do you still have Sara?"

Alison shook her head. "She ran off when the Yankees came. I take care of the garden myself."

"That must be mighty hard work."

"I couldn't blame Sara for wanting to be free. I wouldn't like it if I had to stay where I had to ask someone's leave to do the least little thing. And as far as the work is concerned, I didn't want to have to ask for help."

He nodded his understanding. It wasn't just blind, stubborn pride with her. It was the desire to show his parents that she could stand on her own feet and not be a burden.

"Are you going to see your folks, Tom?" Aunt Anne asked.

"Yes, ma'am. If I get time. I have to be back in Staunton tomorrow noon."

Disappointment clouded Alison's face. "You haven't much time, if you want to see Uncle Joe and Aunt Mary. It'll take you a good hour or more to get there."

"I'll have time. Before I go, though—Aunt Anne, I'd like your permission to ask Alison to be my wife. I know it's right sudden, but it seems like there isn't so much time any more." It was a blunt way of putting it, he thought. But was there any other way, given this time and this place? He looked at Alison, who smiled happily at him.

"Well," Aunt Anne began, "I have no objections, Tom, so long as you don't rush into things."

"I feel, ma'am, that we should wait until the war is over." He looked at Alison, and she nodded her agreement.

Aunt Anne did a surprising thing. She bent over and kissed him on the forehead. "If you're going to do any courting and see your folks and get back to your army, you'd best get started." She stood up and turned to the door. "Goodbye, Tom; and God bless you." And then she was gone.

They took the candle to the front parlor. It was just as he remembered it, he thought. An easy, comfortable room where two people who loved each other could talk or be silent with no sense of strain or urgency.

"I've imagined you here so often," Alison murmured.

"I reckon I've imagined myself here just as often," he smiled. "I don't know where we'll live, but I hope there'll be a room like this."

156

"We'll see to it, dear."

"I haven't had a chance to study law, but I don't think I'll have too much to catch up with. Not with Grandpa helping."

"He's a wonderful man, Tom. One of the finest men I know."

He took her in his arms, and they were together while time was still and past and future merged.

Out in the shed, the mare snorted. Hodges would be getting restless, he thought.

"What time is it?" Alison asked drowsily.

He fished for his watch. "Just past midnight."

"Oh! I'm selfish keeping you here!"

He kissed her gently, and the candle flame flickered. Time had begun to move again.

"Tom, darling—you have to go."

Blindly, he nodded and released her.

"Goodby, my own. Come back to me!" She was gone.

After a moment he stumbled across the room to the door. On the table, the candle smoked and guttered in the draft. He went back, stooped over, and blew it out.

Hodges tugged on the reins, and the moonlight skittered crazily on the barrel of his musket. "This here your place?"

Tom nodded as he watched a ghostly Sandy and Will alighting from a phantom buggy.

"Doggone," Hodges said. "This here is one jilly of a house."

The ghostly image vanished, and then there was only the moonlight in the empty yard, over which brooded the dark and vacant windows. Tom leaned forward, passed his right leg over the saddle horn, and stepped to earth.

"Let's tie up in back, Hodges. It's safer there."

The rear door was bolted, as he had expected. He flipped a pebble at the window of his parents' room. Perhaps Pa would awaken and come down. He waited while Hodges tied the horses.

A second pebble pinked against the window, and then a pale blur showed for a moment. The sash went up abruptly, and Pa leaned out. "Who is it?" he asked testily. "What's the trouble?"

"Pa, it's me; Tom."

For a moment Pa stood frozen as if he couldn't believe it. "Thank God," he said at last. "I'll be right down."

Hodges ate steadily and methodically at the kitchen table; he ate the bread and yellow cheese and pickles as if he hadn't eaten in a year. Even Tom found it difficult to keep up with him, although for the time being his own manners had been overruled by hunger. Mama apparently didn't fancy Hodges' manners any, Tom thought with an inward chuckle. Maybe she didn't think too much of his own.

The war had accomplished one thing at least, he reflected; it had brought together individuals from every station and cultural background. For better or for worse: it could make for a logical extension of Mr. Jefferson's democracy, but it could also lead to a breakdown of the barrier which had kept the ruling classes firmly in the saddle, with a tight rein on the accumulated hatred of Hodges' class.

"You're looking well," Mama said. "Sandy should be home soon. And Will. I hope they're half so fit."

"Yes, ma'am." He shot a glance at Hodges, but Hodges had apparently not noticed her remark.

"Have you seen much fighting?" Pa asked Hodges.

"Yes sir," Hodges mumbled through his bread and cheese. "A right smart. Old Tom here, he pretty near got made lieutenant. And they come close to making me a sergeant," he added with becoming modesty.

"How have things gone here in Lovatt?" Tom asked.

158

An expression of bewilderment passed over Pa's face. "Until just recently, pretty well. The bushwhackers were active this winter, but there was no trouble close by. Your grandpa and McNair and I got a band of irregulars started to protect the town, and we all had plenty to eat. That's one thing; the Yankees haven't burned us out here in the upper Valley. Except for Lexington, that is."

"Lexington?"

Pa nodded soberly. "It was their General Hunter. He's kin to the Virginia Hunters, you know. Well, he burned the Institute because it had furnished officers for the army, and because the cadets went out and whipped Sigel back in May. He burned Governor Letcher's house and some others. Why, some of his officers went in one house, ate dinner, and then set fire to the place. It's beyond understanding how he could condone such a thing, let alone order it."

For a moment Marle's face came before Tom, the savage eyes giving animation to the strong, stubborn lines. "The more of them we kill, the better I like it," Marle had said. What would Marle do in enemy territory, given any sort of leeway for individual action?

"It's a funny sort of war, Pa. We fight the enemy and they fight us, and the civilians get trampled in between."

"This was no accident," Pa said sharply. "It couldn't have happened if our cavalry hadn't run off."

"You look like this was all news to you, Tom," Mama said. "Don't you hear anything about what's going on?"

"Not an awful lot, Mama," he smiled. "We've been kind of busy ourselves."

"It started with that Breckenridge," she said. "I never trusted that man. Too handsome for his own good."

The picture came clear. Sigel's Union forces had come up the Valley in spring. Breckenridge's Confederates, with the aid of the cadets at the Institute had beaten him. Then

159

Sigel had been replaced by Hunter, who had wiped out the Confederate cavalry only two miles from Lovatt and swept south into Staunton and Lexington, where he had stayed until Early's Second Corps, of which Marle's battery was a part, had chased him off.

"I packed some things in the buggy and went out to offer my services," Pa said quietly. "Several of our surgeons had been captured, and they were working along with the Yankee surgeons. I had a hard time getting through; so many of our men were coming up the Pike trying to get away from the Yankees. But I finally made it. Your grandpa took Brutus for me, and I went the rest of the way on foot. It was horrible."

"Were you in the battle, Pa?"

"No, I missed that part of it, thank God. But the men! They were ragged and filthy. And the wounds were of every description. I performed four amputations, prevented one of our butchers from performing as many more unnecessary ones, and treated perhaps twenty-five stomach, chest, and head wounds. There were men who had been shot through the body with a rifle, men who had been wounded by a stray bit of shell or shrapnel, men who had been brained with rifle butts."

Hodges stared across the table at Pa. "I reckon you ain't never seen nothing like that, Doc?"

"I have not!"

"It goes on all the time," Hodges said easily. "After a while you kind of get used to it. Tom, here, he can tell you. But you're right about one thing. Some of them sawbones are a caution. They'd saw off a man's head, if there wasn't somebody around to stop them."

"Sam Dorfer and Todd Harper were riding with Jones," Pa said, hoping to change the subject. "They only just managed to get away."

"How is Sam?"

160

"Fine. Just fine," Mama said, quickly disposing of Sam. "Is he still in town?"

"He's off with the irregulars," Pa said. "We recruited the survivors from Jones's outfit and some of the lightly wounded. Sally Lou Barnes stopped by the other day. She asked after you."

"That's nice," Tom replied, stifling a yawn. "And Grandpa?"

"He's about as frisky as he ever was," Pa smiled. "He worked with the irregulars for a while doing scout duty, but now Sally Lou scouts the north end of town for us. She's a girl with real spirit."

"I'd like to get over to see Grandpa."

"At three o'clock in the morning? Somehow, I don't think he'd relish company at that hour. When must you leave?"

"We have to be back in Staunton by tomorrow noon."

"You had better get some rest," Mama said. "You will use Will's room, and your companion may sleep in your own."

Hodges smiled amiably. "I don't aim to be no trouble. I can sleep in the barn, far's that goes. It don't make me no never mind."

"No such thing," Pa said heartily. "Tom can show you to your room. And if you boys want a good wash, the tubs are still in the washroom."

Later, Tom lay between the clean sheets on Will's bed and watched the stars burning icily in the pale sky visible through the window. Mama had put him in Will's room because she couldn't bear a stranger being there. But even he would never be allowed to stay in Sandy's room. That was a fact; you knew it without being told, just as you knew that there would be no answer forthcoming should you question the motive behind the fact.

161

It was a part of Mama, just like hating the Yankees. Except for Captain Marle, he had never known anyone else who could hate strangers with such intensity. He couldn't. They had burned buildings and on occasion killed prisoners, and once they had left their own wounded to die of thirst in the hot sun. But we might have done the same things, given the same opportunity, he thought. Not kill prisoners, of course. That could never happen. Or were the rumors of life in the prison camps a true reflection of what went on? Well, the Yankees had prisons, too, and they were probably just as bad.

One thing was certain: the Yankees had to be driven from the Valley. Even Scottsburg was no longer safe. They had to be driven back to where they belonged before he would feel right in his mind about Alison, before he could resume his law studies, before they could get married.

Another thought came to him. Why hadn't he told Pa about Alison? Something had stopped him each time he wanted to tell. He didn't think that Pa would disapprove; Pa had always liked Alison. And then it came to him; he hadn't wanted Mama to know. Somehow she would find a way to make it all seem like a childish game; she would compare him and Alison with Sandy and Sally Lou. It was bad enough to play second fiddle to Sandy's ghost. He couldn't help that. But he wasn't going to let Alison play second fiddle to anybody on earth! He'd tell Pa in the morning, if he could get him alone.

He closed his eyes and tried to compose himself for sleep by thinking about the new gray jacket with brass buttons Mama had been saving for him. It was a good jacket, short, as was the new style, due to the exorbitant cost of material caused by the blockade.

Drat the Yankees!

CHAPTER 13

Thrust and Counterthrust

THE wheels of Number Two gun rumbled down the Valley Pike, past Lovatt, through Winchester. They splashed through the Potomac and they made ruts in a meadow outside Washington City when the battery went into firing position to shell one of the forts. The crew could see the unfinished dome of the capitol on the horizon, and they knew somehow that they were unique, the only Confederate Corps ever to reach the Federal capital. They also knew that it would never happen again. It had to happen now, the capture of the Yankee stronghold, or it would never happen at all. It didn't happen.

The wheels broke free of the ruts and retraced their tracks, while July came to an end, and the Yankees followed warily. The pursuit turned into a game of Dodgem, with each side seeking to give battle under the most favorable conditions, and neither side finding the conditions favorable enough.

On the twenty-ninth, Confederate cavalry under General Early's orders burned Chambersburg, Pennsylvania, when that town refused to pay a ransom of one hundred thousand dollars in gold. On the seventh of August, they were surprised and badly beaten at Moorefield, Virginia. The fact that they had been surprised was a sad commentary on the lack of discipline that was becoming prevalent in all branches of the service.

163

Jonathan Marle took a gloomy view of the situation. In his opinion there was nothing wrong in burning a town. That was no more than repaying the blue bellies for the burning they had done in Lexington and a few other places as well. He didn't have to think very hard to remember the shambles the Yankees had made of Fredericksburg. No; a few towns like Chambersburg might teach the Yankees to be more careful with other people's property.

The thing that irked him most was the apparent unwillingness of the high command to come to grips with the enemy. The Federals were mighty strong—they outnumbered the corps by about two to one. But still there ought to be some way of driving them into a position where their numbers need not be the decisive factor. Some day, one of the Federal generals was bound to slip up, perhaps fail to maintain contact with the rest of the army. Then! Destroy him!

"There's not much we can do about it, Jonathan," Colonel Hulme said with a trace of bitterness. "We can't go tell the general that his cavalry is all but useless because they're more interested in looting than in fighting. And we can't tell him that he's going to get whipped good and proper if he insists on fighting his corps one division at a time."

"It wouldn't take much right now to make me apply for transfer," Marle said grimly. "The only thing is, the cavalry's gone to pot since Stuart was killed."

"Wade Hampton's pretty fair, they say."

"He ain't Stuart." Marle creased his gloves in vexation. "I tell you what, though: no matter what Early does with the rest of the corps, this is one battery that's going to have discipline. No Yankee is going to catch us napping!"

In the warm September weather the battery drilled under the joint supervision of First Sergeant Harrison and

164

Captain Marle. Every man was given an opportunity to learn afresh every other man's job, right up to laying and firing the piece. Crews were switched to give the crews of the two Napoleons a chance to learn the operation of the Parrott, and its new running mate, a Brooke rifle.

The Brooke was a lovely piece, as Marston said when he first saw it. Designed and manufactured in Richmond at the Tredegar works by the ordinance officer whose name it bore, it had a slender tube, reinforced by a breech band. Similar to the now famous Parrott, it was safer and supposedly more accurate. Its graceful look belied its deadly calling.

"How'd you like to swap?" Hodges asked the gunner of the Brooke.

"For that peashooter of yours? Ho!"

"It ain't no peashooter! If you wasn't a natural-born floppy-eared jackass, you'd know a good gun when you saw one."

The gunner stepped forward swinging, and it was only with difficulty that a fight was averted. It was a sign of the temper of the army, Tom decided. Everyone was feeling the strain of inaction. It was nerve-racking, knowing that the Union forces were only waiting for the right moment to step in and smash the Second Corps. Any action would have been better than the period of enforced inactivity.

Dimly he remembered having felt this way once before. When? And then he remembered that, too. It had been early in spring, and the idleness of the winter had eroded tempers, while in the background lurked the shadow of death.

The next day they had gone into the wilderness.

Doctor Tanner put down his cup. Parched-wheat coffee wasn't bad drinking, but it couldn't begin to compare with the real thing for breakfast on a chilly morning. And the

165

mornings were getting chilly with a vengeance, now that it was September already.

"Are you going through town, Joseph?" Mary asked.

"Yes, my dear. I want to stop in and see your father to learn if he's had any word from Tom."

Mary smiled. "You're a good father, always so concerned. Papa was that way, too."

"Perhaps you'd like to come along for the ride? I think old Brutus should be able to manage."

"No, thank you. I was there only yesterday, and Papa's housekeeping leaves a great deal to be desired. If only my poor mother had lived to look after him. He needs someone."

In that respect, Mary hadn't changed a bit, Doctor Tanner reflected as he entered Lovatt. She was always "taking care" of someone or other. Of all the candidates she might have picked, though, Andrew Hauser was the least in need of special attention. He was about as self-sufficient as a man could be.

A rider trotted up the Pike past the church. Sally Lou Barnes. Doctor Tanner raised his hat, and she turned toward him. What a change the war had made in her! She was like everyone else these days, living from now to five minutes from now, because that was all the future anyone could count on.

Sally Lou's complexion was unfashionably brown. It was no wonder, the doctor thought; she rode in all kinds of weather.

"No one north of here," she said briefly. "I went down Pike a mile or two to make sure."

"That's fine." He still found it somewhat embarrassing to carry on a conversation with Sally Lou; he was forever attempting to reconcile the lovely, high-spirited girl who had been Sandy's betrothed with the hard-eyed rider who wore a navy Colt buckled around her slender waist and concealed by her pelisse.

166

"I wonder if it's quite prudent to carry a pistol," he suggested. "The Yankees might construe that as a sign of hostility."

"And hang me?" she smiled.

"They're capable of it."

"I'll take my chances. Life is much less complicated this way. I don't have to worry about making anybody a good wife or being a perfect lady, or anything like that. All I have to do is watch out for Union soldiers and use this if they get too close." She touched the butt of the pistol.

This was what it came to in the end, he thought wearily. Will dead and Sandy dead and Tom Heaven-knows-where. Mary's mental condition rapidly deteriorating and Sally Lou fighting a bitter, personal battle, neither asking nor giving quarter. This was the end of all the proud dreams of independence, of the new empire which was eventually to embrace Mexico. Mexico, indeed! They'd all be lucky to get out of this without being hanged.

When the doctor left Sally Lou and rode on to Mc-Nair's, he found Andrew Hauser in the taproom, talking with Jeems.

"Come in, Joe," Andrew said testily. "Come in and hear the news."

"I met Sally Lou Barnes outside. There's no one on the Pike north of here."

Jeems raised a quizzical eyebrow. "There will be," he said briefly. "Early's been whipped up near Winchester."

Fear froze him. What of Tom? "Where'd you hear that, Jeems? Maybe it's just a rumor."

"No chance," Andrew Hauser put in. "A rider came down from Harrisonburg early this morning. He said he was sent by White's irregulars to warn us. The Valley's wide open to the Yankees."

Jeems nodded. "It's true enough, Joe. That new Yankee general Sheridan caught Early just north of Winchester yesterday and rolled him up. Early pulled out and was supposed to make a stand south of Winchester. But he must have lost a lot of men. The man I spoke to said he didn't think Early could hold with what he had left."

The end of all proud dreams. "What can we do, then?"

"Get set to help any survivors who come our way," Andrew Hauser said. "Help them reorganize so that they can fight as irregulars. And be prepared to offer our services to the army, if it can use them."

By that afternoon the survivors of the battery had completed their emplacements and had leisure to inspect the other arrangements which had been made to contain the enemy. A line had been drawn from Great North Mountain on the west to Fisher's Hill on the east. Just in front of the battery's positions, the remnants of a company of Alabama infantry had scooped out shallow rifle pits under the direction of their black-bearded sergeant. A tall, yellow-haired man who said his name was Judd Davison had come to Tom to "borrow the loan of a spade."

It might have been a pleasant enough afternoon, but the Federals appeared in their front on the opposite side of a shallow creek that paralleled the line and attempted to force a crossing. The infantry climbed out of their holes and ran forward whooping and yelling. The Federals went back to their own side, and then some of their supporting Parrott guns drove the Alabamians back to their rifle pits. By the time that was over, no one was in the mood for visiting. It was getting cold, too; the sun had gone behind the mountain, and a breeze that hinted of the coming of November murmured over the field.

Tom realized that they had been lucky to get away with the gun and the limber. Some of the gunners in the battery next to them at Winchester had cut the horses loose and fled, leaving their guns to the enemy. But three men were missing from the crew of Number Two. He was left with Hodges, Marston, Hunter, and a replacement named Watson. These were barely enough to serve the piece, providing the action was not too sustained or too intense. He could double as gunner, laying the piece as well as sighting it, and observing the effect of his fire. Watson would have to tie the horses behind the position and serve in Number Five position, bearing the ammunition from the limber. That would leave Marston as Number Two, loading and checking on Watson's fuse cutting. Hodges would ram the charges, and Hunter would prepare the primers and fire the piece.

In any case, it wouldn't matter very much; there wasn't that much ammunition left. Ten rounds of cannister. Five round shot. No shell. That had been expended yesterday at Winchester or lost with the reserve ammunition in the caisson.

"It's getting cold," Hodges grumbled. "I'm sure glad it ain't raining, though."

"What did you expect?" Marston retorted. "Summer in September?"

"I didn't figure on freezing until November. Reckon them blue coats are going to fight us tomorrow, Tom?"

"They probably will. They'd be fools if they didn't."

"I don't see how we'll stop them," Hunter said quietly. He had been pessimistic ever since they had heard about the Chambersburg raid. It wasn't right to burn the town, he had said; they would have to pay for it in one way or another.

If Hunter was in the minority as regarded his dislike of the burning of Chambersburg, it was by no means a small minority. His logic was faulty, though, Tom thought sardonically; if the burning of a town meant losing a war, the Federals would have lost a long time ago.

"We'll whip them easy," Hodges flared up. "What're you talking about?"

"They've been gaining ever since July, Hodges," Marston said wearily. "Ever since we failed to take Washington. The only surprising thing about yesterday was that it didn't happen sooner."

As the sun went behind the mountain, rifle fire broke out on the west end of the line. They could even see the tiny jets of flame lick out at the darkness. There wasn't enough firing to be particularly concerned about, Tom decided; an attack would be preceded by shelling from the batteries across the creek. It was probably a Yankee trick to keep everybody jumpy. They had tried that before.

Captain Marle came up and stood beside Number Two. "I think it's just a little noisemaking party to scare us," he said finally. "But keep your eyes open. They might try to cross the creek in the dark."

As Marle walked away, a heavy drumming came from the Federal positions, accompanied by a momentary glow far behind the trees. A moment later, the first shells began to fall among the rifle pits in front of the gun emplacements.

"Doggone," Hodges muttered in the lull that followed. "They're shooting straight even in the dark."

A wild burst of yelling towards the west announced a successful attack on that part of the line.

The shells began to fall again. In the brief flashes of the bursts they could see the Alabamians coming towards them, falling back in good order. They walked past the gun, and then they were swallowed by the gloom.

Marle reappeared. "We cain't fire a target if we cain't see it," he said reassuringly. "We're dug in good, so we'll just sit this one out. If you see anything move ahead of you, though, fire on it. I'll be at Number Four."

For a time the shells burst harmlessly in the zone formerly occupied by the infantry, and then the position next to theirs on the west erupted into a small-scale battle in which rifle fire predominated. As though on signal, the Federal artillery ceased fire.

170

A gray-clad figure burst out of the gloom from the west. "They're rolled up the line!" he screamed, and then he was gone.

"Swing the gun left!" Tom yelled.

With some difficulty they levered the Napoleon up the slope and brought it to bear on the ground to their left. "Double cannister!" he ordered.

Somewhere behind them Sergeant Harrison's voice rose above the crackle of small-arms fire. "Hold to the guns, men! Fight your pieces!"

There undoubtedly were Federals in the next position, fighting hand-to-hand with the gunners. There were Confederates there, as well. He hesitated while Hunter waited, lanyard in hand. If I don't fire, he thought, we'll be overrun. And then a figure with a forage cap appeared before the gun. A Yankee! The time for thinking was past.

"Fire!" he bawled, and the gun leaped back in recoil.

A shell whistled overhead and flame erupted in the gloom behind him. Hunter hammered on his shoulder to attract his attention. Hunter was yelling, but he couldn't hear what he was saying, so he turned around to look. An ammunition caisson or limber had been hit and the rounds in it had exploded.

"Marston was helping Watson," Hunter shrieked. "They're gone! That was our limber!"

It was something that happened to other guns and other crews, but it couldn't happen to you. Only now it had and there were just the three of them, him and Hunter and Hodges, and all the Yankees in creation would be on top of them directly.

"That was the last round," Hodges yelled. "The rest were in the limber."

"Spike her with the priming wire, Hunter," Tom ordered. "Let's get out of here."

Hunter jammed the wire in the vent. Suddenly he fell forward across the hot breech. Hodges helped Tom pull

171

Hunter away, but already they could smell the singed cloth of Hunter's jacket. Hodges bent over Hunter for a moment. "He's dead, Tom," he said. "Let's go."

The burning fragments of the shattered limber cast a lurid glow that made them prime targets. It also disclosed one of the battery horses straining at his picket rope. The other three were gone, apparently well on their way to safety. Hodges cut the picket rope with his knife as rifle balls whizzed overhead or ricocheted off the tube of the abandoned gun. "Get up," Hodges said. "I'll hold him."

A grimy ghost on a sorrel gelding came towards them. "Tanner? What happened?"

"The limber blew up with Marston and Watson. We've got no more ammunition, so I spiked the gun."

Captain Marle nodded. "Let's travel. They'll have their cavalry out directly. Harrison's dead, and Number Three blew up with its crew."

Something rapped Tom sharply on the left forearm. It felt like bumping into a table in a dark room, but when he tried to move the limb, the pain was almost more than he could bear.

"Anybody hit?" Marle asked suspiciously. Suddenly Tom knew that whatever plan Marle had in mind had no room in it for a wounded man. If Marle suspected that he had been hit, Marle would ride off with Hodges and leave him behind.

"I'm all right, sir," he said. "Come on up, Hodges."

They trotted off into the illusory safety of the dark.

The wound bled somewhat at first; he could feel the drops trickling down his fingers, but it didn't seem like anything to worry about. He hooked his left index finger through the top button hole of his coat. In that way, the arm would be in roughly the same position as if it had been in a sling. After a whole the bleeding stopped, and

172

the arm grew numb. He dozed for a while, awakening just in time to prevent his mount from bumping Marle's.

"Must be around ten or eleven o'clock," Marle said conversationally. The noise of firing was still audible behind them, but it was faint and spasmodic, now. In the gloom, Tom could make out other riders near them, moving in no particular formation. They had not been alone in running.

"We'll dismount and rest the horses," Marle said. "Then we can keep on until morning."

"What happens then, Captain?" Hodges asked.

"God knows. If we find the rest of them, we'll reform and fight as infantry. It looks to me like we got whipped good. If One and Four crews got away, we'll still have a battery, but I doubt if they did. One was west of you fellows, and Four only had three horses left. If they didn't make it and if we can't find anybody else, we'll take to the hills. I always had a hankering to be a horse soldier."

Hodges had already dismounted. Tom slipped his right leg over the broad back of the draft horse. As he slid down, he struck his wounded arm. The pain was worse than any he had ever known. For a moment he hovered on the edge of unconsciousness, and then he drew breath sharply and the night became clear around him again, the breathing of the horses, the sound of hooves and voices on the road beside them.

"What's the matter?" Marle snapped.

"I've been hit."

"When?"

"Back at the gun, I reckon. It didn't feel like anything then. I figured it was a spent ball."

Marle fumbled in his saddlebag for a moment. A match sputtered, and flame lanced from a candle stub in a small tin lantern. "Hold this," Marle ordered Hodges. He slit Tom's left sleeve.

"Busted," Marle said tersely. "I can tie it up, but that's about all. You'll have to see a doctor."

"Here's a piece of wood," Hodges offered. "I can hold it while you do the tying, Captain."

"All right." Marle tore a strip of cloth from the tail of Tom's shirt and began to bind the arm. "It's better if you keep talking; you won't feel it so much that way. Got any preference in doctors?"

Nausea washed over him. "No—yes, I do. My Pa."

"Doggone, boy! He's fifty miles from here."

"Ohhh!"

"Easy does it," Marle said. "I'm pretty near done." He divided the strip at the end and secured it with a knot.

Off in the darkness someone bawled, "Blow out that light! You want to bring the Yankees down on us?"

"Blowing out a candle ain't going to stop them," Hodges muttered. "You all right, Tom?"

He nodded. Now the delicious numbness was coming back where Marle had bound the bandage.

The captain pulled a flask from his coat pocket. "Have some of this."

He sputtered as the liquor burned its way down, but he felt better almost immediately. He was warmer, and he could feel his strength returning. "Thank you, sir. I feel fine."

Marle chuckled. "I can see that."

"How about Pa?"

"If you want to try, I won't stop you. But you better see a doctor before you get there. That arm's in bad shape." Marle turned to Hodges. "You go with him; hear?"

"Why, sure, Captain."

"When you get him there, report to the first unit you see until we reorganize and you can rejoin the battery. If there's a battery to rejoin," he added bitterly.

"How about you, sir?" Tom asked.

174

"I'll leave you. I want to look for the colonel when it gets light to see what I can do. If I can't find him, I'll collect some of these stragglers and form my own army." He mounted and waved to them. "Good luck. Rejoin as soon as you can." And then he was gone.

They traveled another ten miles before dawn; Tom rode while Hodges trudged along leading the broken-down draft horse. From time to time they stopped while Hodges rested and passed the flask, which Marle had donated to the expedition. At first light, Hodges led the horse into the shelter of a small wood near the road. "We'll rest up here for a while," he said laconically. "Until we figure which way the wind blows."

During the morning, the refuse of the Second Corps streamed past. No guns. Small groups of cavalry, huddled together for company. Individual riders who shunned all companionship. Once, an officer madly spurred on a group of riders, berating them for cowardice. Although the tableau took place a good two hundred yards from the thicket, Tom could hear the words floating up as though from another world. At first the riders paid no heed; but then, almost as an afterthought, one man drew a pistol and shot the officer from his saddle. No one seemed to notice the incident. Except for the dead man in the road, everything was as it had been before.

Tom unsheathed his own pistol and laid it on his lap for company. If he had been forced to shoot to save his life, he didn't think he could have. The moving panorama flickered and jumped before his eyes like something in a dream in which he had no part.

Hodges awoke about noon and took the watch, while Tom lay back and tried to sleep. But sleep would not come. There was only a blank oblivion disturbed from time to time by Hodges bending over to see how he was.

Fever, Hodges said once. I'll be switched if I know what'll be when the liquor's gone, he said another time. And then the blackness washed mercifully over him.

They left the wood at dusk. There were fewer stragglers now, Hodges said, and that was a bad sign. No guns had come down the road, and so there was nothing to keep the Yankees back.

He nodded obediently without knowing what he was agreeing to. Moments later it came to him that Hodges had told him to shoot anybody who tried to take the horse. If he could. He probably couldn't even hold the pistol now, let alone cock and fire it.

They came to a town and he saw McNair's tavern clear as anything, but Hodges wouldn't stop. "This ain't it, Tom," Hodges said and kept on walking. Night fell, and then there was a ghost of a town with all the shutters fastened and not the faintest light to brighten the dark night of defeat. He slumped forward on the neck of the horse, and then the other darkness came on.

He had to get to Pa to get his arm fixed, because it had looked bad when Marle dressed it. There were little white chips sticking out of the crust that had dried, and even though Marle hadn't said anything, he knew that they were splinters of bone. An army doctor would just get out his bone saw, and that would be the end of his arm; he had seen what happened to wounded men in innumerable field hospitals from the Rapidan to Winchester. But Pa could do anything, even with a messed-up arm like this one.

That was why he had to get home to Pa. He just had to!

CHAPTER 14

The Coming of Winter

THERE was a faint light pressing against his eyelids now. He was drowsy, and they were gummed together, and he didn't really want to open them. There was a monotonous clicking sound from somewhere; it was regularly spaced, like a clock.

Abruptly he came awake and opened his eyes. Across the room a familiar clock with gilded leaves rationed out minutes. He was at Grandpa Hauser's, and for some reason they had laid him on the old table at which he used to do his Latin translations. He tried to sit up, but there was no strength in him to do more than turn his head.

Pa's hand rested for a moment on his forehead. Big, strong and capable, there was no mistaking it.

"Pa?" he murmured. "Is it all right, Pa?"

"It's all right, Tom," Pa said gently. "It won't hurt you any more."

"Where's Hodges? He brought me here. He's my friend."

"He's a fine boy," Pa said. "He left to join up with the army. They've been coming through here for more than a day now." Pa shook his head sadly. "What will happen to us, I don't know."

"It's not the end of the world, Joe," Grandpa said from the doorway. "We got whipped, but we'll come back. Tom, you tell your father that no good Rebel ever accepts a temporary setback as a final defeat."

He managed to smile. "It's mighty good to be here, sir."

"I don't see how you ever made it," Grandpa continued. "That boy said you came all the way from Strasburg."

"The whiskey helped." His eyes burned with the unfamiliar light. "Can I sit up?"

Pa glanced quickly at Grandpa, and then he turned back. "It's all right," he said. "I'll help you, son."

"I can do it now." He braced himself with his hands, but suddenly there was a sharp pain above his left elbow, above where the wound had been, and there was no feeling at all below that point. He looked at Pa and saw the compassion written on his face, and then he knew what had happened, even before he looked down and saw the bandages where his left arm had been.

"There was no other way, Tom," Pa said. "It was gangrenous. If I hadn't amputated, you would have died. I used chloroform so it wouldn't hurt."

He closed his eyes, and immediately he could see the bone saw in Pa's operating case, shining and sharptoothed. Perhaps it was the very same one that Sandy had used the day he cut the checkers out of the willow twig. "It's all right, Pa," he said gently. "I know you did what you had to do."

"Your friend left you something," Grandpa said. He opened his eyes again and turned his head. Grandpa was holding the Barlow knife he had given Hodges a year ago in trade for a square of oilcloth.

"How can I use a knife with only one arm?"

Grandpa smiled. "Your friend had faith in you, boy. He said you'd figure out a way if anybody could. That was quite a compliment."

He was able to sit up for an hour that evening. Someone had bathed and shaved him, he noticed. He was wearing someone else's clothing, too.

"The clothes were my contribution," Grandpa said. "Your Pa washed you before he operated. He said a few

178

minutes wouldn't matter, and that you might as well be clean and comfortable when you woke up."

"How's Alison?"

"She's just fine."

"Can I see Mama?"

Grandpa sat down heavily. "I don't think it would be advisable, Tom. Your mother has not been herself, and your Pa felt it best that you remain here. You see, the war has sort of stopped for her. She's back in 1862 and we're winning—or at any rate, we're not losing—and Sandy's going to be home directly when that colonel of his gives him a furlough. If she saw you, there's no telling what the shock might do."

He nodded wearily. There were so many things you couldn't understand, and yet you had to live with them.

"As a matter of fact," Grandpa continued, "I felt it desirable to keep your presence here a secret for other reasons. Unfortunately, you can't trust everyone the way you used to."

"Surely we don't have spies in Lovatt?"

"You remember the Trojan horse, I see. Nothing so dramatic, I fear. It's just that people get tired and hungry, and the first thing you know somebody passes a bit of gossip in the wrong place in exchange for a pound of sugar or coffee, and there you are. We have Union guerrillas over the mountain, now, and they're always on the alert for information."

Something more than a battle had been lost that day at Winchester, Tom realized. The old army of the Valley was gone, and with it had disappeared the faith and trust of the Valley people. What would take their place?

"What do you figure on doing when you recover, Tom?"

"Go back to the Petersburg lines, if they'll take me. Or fight as a guerrilla." With the army gone, someone had to defend the Valley.

An older, drier Jeems McNair crossed the road that

179

night to pay his respects. "We're proud of you, Tom," he said. He carefully avoided looking at the bandaged stump.

"Have you a company in Lovatt?" Tom asked in an effort to recall the days of the militia company.

Jeems shook his head. "Your Pa and the Barnes girl keep watch as best they can. Andrew and I keep our rifles loaded. That's about all we can do."

"How about the Dorfer boys?"

"They're away with the army now. Sam, he joined up with Gilmor's partisans, and Dave was in the Laurel brigade, the last we heard." Jeems shook his head. "It ain't the way it used to be."

"No question about that," Grandpa agreed.

Jeems cleared his throat apologetically. "If you're not too tired, Tom, maybe you could tell us what we're up against. What was the Yankee strength up there at Strasburg?"

"I heard they had two army corps. I know they've got a whale of a lot of cavalry in support. Some of their prisoners told us that."

"How much would you say?"

"Maybe the equivalent of four brigades, not counting whatever irregulars they had out against us before the battle."

Someone tapped at the door, and the two older men exchanged furtive glances. "Trouble," Jeems said, as Grandpa went to open the door. "There's always trouble nowadays."

"Who's out there, Jeems?" he asked suddenly.

"Now how would I know that, Tom?"

He smiled. "I'm thinking there's very little that goes on around Lovatt that you and Grandpa don't know. Like the way you asked me about the Yankee cavalry. What could Lovatt do about it, if the Yankees sent a brigade up

180

this way? There's not even a militia company here, you said."

"You exaggerate my importance, Tom," Jeems said pleasantly.

"Maybe. The way I see it, I'm not going to be much of an artilleryman any more. No good for infantry, either. That leaves irregulars. Only I might have trouble finding a company to join."

Jeems grinned. "When you're ready, we'll find the right company for you to join."

Grandpa appeared in the doorway. The sense of anxiety Tom had seen earlier had gone; he seemed positively exuberant.

"Good news, sir?"

"It's an ill wind that blows no good. Jeems, that was Barnes. He says Todd Harper rode in with a report that the Federal guerrillas brushed with Gilmor's men this afternoon. They're headed this way. Gilmor is taking up the chase, and we've got to hold the Yankees until they get here."

Jeems nodded happily. "A nice fat bait in the trap and then—click!" His face stiffened. "We've got to get Tom out of here, Andrew. They'd shoot him before they'd take him prisoner."

"How do we get him out? He can't ride."

"Joe can take him, then. I'll send Horace down there with a note. Horace can use Joe's horse and buggy."

It was all adding up, Tom decided. Grandpa and Pa and Jeems McNair were all part of an impromptu intelligence service that furnished information to Confederate guerrilla forces in the upper Valley. Perhaps they even helped to organize some of the companies, as well.

"When I'm ready to rejoin, who do I see?" he asked.

Grandpa smiled. "You just get better, boy. When you're ready, somebody'll probably drop around to tell you where

181

to go. I wouldn't be a bit surprised if that was what happened."

"I wouldn't be surprised if you were the somebody who dropped around, sir."

"We old fellows do what we can, Tom," Grandpa said modestly. "But we don't talk about it, especially to a wounded boy who might be captured and tortured before we could get him to safety."

He nodded. There was only one question in his mind. "Where am I going?"

Grandpa chuckled. "To Scottsburg, boy. It's the best place I know for a wounded hero."

There were different ways of being awkward. One was when you got out of bed in the morning and found that you were lighter on one side than you were on the other. You invariably staggered somewhat until the lost sense of balance was restored. Another was getting dressed. You had to lean against the wall to hold your trousers up until you could button them. You had to toss your shirt and catch it with your head or else crumple it until you could grasp the neck and the bottom hem at the same time. But the worst way of all was to see other people, to be courteous in the face of their courtesy, pity, or indifference. Invariably he said the wrong things and made the wrong responses.

If he had been alone with Alison, he wouldn't have worried. She had put him at ease immediately, neither making light of his misfortune in an effort to cheer him up, nor withholding the consideration that he needed.

"They only stare because it's unusual," she said one day in mid-November. They were walking through the village on what Aunt Anne was pleased to call "Tom's airing."

"It makes me feel like some kind of a freak." He kicked angrily at a clod. "Have you thought about what it'll be like being married to a cripple?"

182

"I'm not marrying a cripple. I'm marrying Tom," Alison said quietly.

He ducked his head in confusion. "I'm sorry, Alison. I reckon I was taking it out on you."

"Yes, you were! You were feeling sorry for yourself, and there's no reason to do so."

"I can think of a few."

"Well, I can't! Suppose you were a woodsman or a carpenter and you needed two hands to earn a living. Then I'd pity you. But you don't need two hands to be a lawyer, my dear. You have a fine mind, and you're going to be a great lawyer. I just know it!"

"I haven't made a lot of myself in the army. I didn't even get to be an officer."

"Are you comparing yourself with Sandy again? I won't have it. When the war is over, nobody'll remember whether you were an officer or not. The thing that counts is what you make of yourself then. Besides, your brother was nowhere near the man you are, even if you did lose an arm!"

Already, the leaves had fallen from some of the trees. It wouldn't be long until winter came. Perhaps the Yankees would let up then. But after winter came spring, and another new campaign was sure to follow.

"Would you care to go back?" he asked.

She nodded. "I've had about all the fresh air I can stand for one day."

"I'll have to chop some wood when we get back." He had taught himself to use an axe after a fashion, shortening his grip on the haft and taking short strokes.

"It's a strange thing, the way you grow up," Alison said abruptly. "Sometimes I wake up and I have to consciously remember I'm eighteen. I feel about a dozen years older."

"Just think of the experience we're getting, though," Tom quipped. "By the time we're thirty, we'll probably be smarter than Grandpa."

183

She laughed delightedly. "That's the first time you've made a joke since you've been back."

"I haven't been a very cheerful companion," he said penitently.

"Under the circumstances, I'd say you've been very cheerful . . . Tom?"

"Yes, dear."

"Wouldn't it be lovely if you didn't have to go back? If we could get married right away?"

He nodded. "It would be lovely, indeed. But I'd only be a drain on you until I can earn a living for us. It's not going to be the easiest thing in the world."

"As I said," she replied, "you don't need two hands to be a lawyer. You could study here, just as well as at Lovatt."

"Even so, I feel I ought to get back. It's not even that in a way I owe it to Sandy. It's that everybody who can has to fight now, since the army has been lost."

"You'll do what you have to do, I know." She smiled ruefully. "Sometime I wish you weren't so conscientious, my love. But I wouldn't want to change you if I could. You know that, don't you?"

"I would," he grinned. "I mean change me. I bet I'm an awful person to live with. Ornery and moody and selfish."

"Sometimes," Alison replied seriously. "But you keep working at it. You always try to do the right thing, and that makes it all right."

He had made some progress, he reflected as he set out in search of a deadfall to drag back to the yard for cutting. His use of the axe during the last month had strengthened his good arm, and he was even able to use the stump of his left arm in a limited fashion, gripping items between it and his body, pushing away an unwanted object, and the

184

like. It was a painful business at best, but the pain was lessening as the lacerated tissues slowly healed.

Pa had been to see him almost every day, and Grandpa Hauser rode by at least twice a week. Grandpa had made him a pad to wear on the end of the stump, according to Pa's directions. Now he didn't jump out of his skin every time he bumped into something.

He had even learned to load his pistol. It was a slow procedure, but at least he could do it if he had to. That was the important thing, although it didn't seem as if he would have to use it, since the Second Corps, which had reformed after the disaster at Fisher's Hill, had been all but annihilated at Cedar Creek. At first they had beaten the Yankees, but then some of the men had stopped to forage in the abandoned Federal camps, and the enemy had taken advantage of that pause to regroup and counter-attack. Now the Second Corps had ceased to exist except in the rolls of memory. One of these days he'd have to get down to Staunton, though. There had to be something he could do.

He spied a fallen pine some distance away. It hadn't been down long, not long enough to rot, anyhow. He could cut off a fair-sized limb and drag it back to the house for further chopping. How much could he drag with one arm? A limb eight inches across and maybe six feet in length. That was about his limit. He began to hack away at a branch.

"How about giving me a try at that?"

He turned to see Hodges standing just behind him, a big grin on his face.

"Where in the world did you come from?"

Hodges took the axe and pumped his good arm enthusiastically. "If you ain't a sight for sore eyes! I asked for you up at the house, and they told me I'd find you out back."

The axe flashed expertly in Hodges' capable hands. "McNair passed the word you was pretty near fit, so Marle sent me on down to get you," he said between strokes.

"Captain Marle?"

"I run into him up at Cedar Creek. We kind of stuck together and a bunch of other fellows joined us, so now we got a company. Old Walker, he's got a peg on that stump of his, and he's riding with us." Hodges sunk the axe in the severed branch. "You tote my carbine, and I'll fetch this."

The carbine was a new model Sharps, shiny and well oiled. "Got it off'n a blue belly didn't have no more need of it," Hodges explained laconically.

"What's been going on?"

"The devil's loose," Hodges said tersely. "Them Yankees have orders to burn all the barns and crops in the Valley. It's like a big cinder up around New Market. There's nobody left to stop them, either; only us and a couple of other companies like us. You feel like you could sit a horse?"

He nodded. "I can do what I have to do."

"If you ain't ready yet," Hodges said smoothly, "I could tell Marle you need more time."

"I'm ready. When do we start?"

"Directly. We got to be on Massanutten before dawn."

"I'll tell them inside."

Alison was stirring a bowl of batter for johnny-cake when he entered the kitchen.

"I have to go back," he told her shortly. There was no other way of putting it.

She nodded. "I mended your jacket. I was planning to surprise you, but you'll be needing it now."

"I reckon so."

She opened a cupboard and brought it forth, neatly

186

folded. She had washed the jacket and pressed it into shape. Even the buttons—rescued from Sandy's oldest uniform coat—had been burnished until they shone, and the rents had been so carefully mended that they hardly showed. The left sleeve was stitched up at the elbow, and the superfluous material had been cut away. "I used it for patching," Alison said.

"It's a beautiful job, my dear."

She looked at him steadily. "Will it ever be this way again, Tom?"

She didn't have to put it into words. The feeling of security that they had had in being together was tacitly understood. No explanation was necessary.

"We have to keep hoping that it will."

They held each other tightly until the sound of the axe stopped and Hodges clumped up the back steps. "Time to go, Tom!" he called.

"God keep you, my darling," Alison whispered.

CHAPTER 15

Marle's Army

MARLE'S company of ten riders was a cross section representative of any army. There were idealists, such as Walker, who had joined after the Cedar Creek disaster, and Marle himself; rejoined stragglers who felt that they should fight even though they had long since abandoned hope of winning; and out-and-out opportunists who saw only an opportunity for plunder. The latter differed not at all from the bands of bushwhackers who had preyed on lonely villages in the early part of the war, except that they limited their choice of victims to those who remained loyal to the Union. Theoretically at least, the Confederate guerrillas operated only at the expense of Federal troops or avowed civilian Unionists.

The day following Tom's arrival, the company rested. "We can't work in daylight," Ben Walker explained. "They'd gobble us up for an appetizer and then look for the main dinner. We have to strike at night, raid their camps, hit stragglers. And we have to get you a horse."

A pall of smoke hovered over the lower Valley, where the burning had begun. Clearly visible from Massanutten, it was like nothing Tom had ever seen. The very immensity of the deed was in itself horrible. An area of about two hundred square miles was being systematically put to the torch. It made the burning of isolated homes in the early days of the war seem of no consequence by comparison.

Worst of all was the indisputable fact that the Federal armies were making war on a helpless civilian population. The Valley had supplied the armies of the Confederacy with food for almost four years of war; the Federals were making sure that this would never again be possible. If a few thousand civilians starved as a result, it was regrettable but necessary. Tom thought of the scanty supply of corn in the pantry at Scottsburg, and he shivered.

Marle's ten rode out at dusk with sleet falling gently out of the gloom as if to mitigate the harsh glow of the fires that dotted the night. Mounted behind Hodges, Tom clung to his belt as they passed down the mountain on a meandering trail and made for the nearest fire.

"If there ain't too many down there, we'll take 'em," Hodges said. "Then we can get you a horse."

As they came near the fire, Marle circled the yard cautiously, although the farm seemed unoccupied. A shed was burning brightly, despite the sleet; and as they watched, the roof tumbled in with an accompanying shower of sparks. Marle dismounted and walked across to the house. While he knocked on the door, some of the men moved closer to the burning shed to warm themselves.

Ben Walker edged his mount close to Hodges'. "How are you making out, counselor?" he asked Tom.

"Fine. If Hodges can put up with me."

"Why, sure. Only we better get down before this Yankee crowbait gets too tired." Hodges stared at the house. "Looks like old Marle went inside."

A moment later the captain reappeared, holding a lighted lantern. "Leave two men to hold the horses," he ordered. "The rest of you come in here."

The place was a shambles. Not content with burning

189

the shed, the raiders had ransacked the house in search
of loot. Furniture had been overturned and smashed, and
clothing was strewn over the floor. Hodges shook his head.
"Yankees? Or bushwhackers?" he asked.

"What difference does that make?" Marle snapped.
"They're all the same to me. Come in here."

They followed him through the splintered remains of a
door into a second, smaller room. Marle swung the lamp
high, and in a far corner a girl raised her hand to shield
her eyes from the glare. She was slumped against the wall,
half-lying, half-sitting. An ugly bruise marked her temple.

"No; please, no," she murmured in a monotone.

"If anybody here forgets this," Marle said evenly, "I'll
shoot him the same way I intend to shoot the scum who
did this."

There was nothing to be done for the girl, Tom knew.
There was no time to put out the fires and bind the
wounds and hide the grain from the invaders. There was
only time to kill and to run so that they could kill again.

An hour later they found a Federal trooper leaving a
haystack he had fired. He was only a boy, perhaps seventeen or eighteen, and he said he had been separated from
his command.

"There's your horse, Tanner," Marle said. "Take his
pistol, too. You could use another one."

Tom slid down from his perch behind Hodges and went
up behind the trooper. He pulled the boy's pistol free of
the holster and thrust it into his belt. Then he ordered
the boy to remove the belt and hand it to him.

"I never did nothing," the boy kept saying. "Them was
our orders, to burn the haystacks."

Marle nodded in a friendly manner. "We don't shoot
soldiers we take prisoner. Only murderers and thieves."

Tom mounted the trooper's horse and pocketed the
boy's cap box and cartridge pouch. They could be fastened

190

to his belt later. He looked around the circle of riders, at their taut faces glowing in the light of the burning stack, and suddenly he knew that the boy was dead already.

"Turn out your pockets, Yank," Marle ordered.

"There ain't nothing there." He looked from one to another in the forlorn hope that someone would speak and save him. "You can't shoot me! I'm a prisoner!"

"Turn out your pockets."

With trembling fingers, the boy obeyed. A small brooch fell to the ground; the chain of a locket winked in the light. "This here was my mother's."

The girl in the house could have been Alison. The brooch could have been Mama's. Rage mastered Tom, a cold and emotionless rage that suddenly made him stronger than any of them. "Hand me that locket," he ordered.

By the light of the fire he examined the bauble, made out the inscription on the back. "What was your mother's name, Yank?"

The boy turned towards him, his eyes wide with terror. "It was just laying there on the table, Johnny!"

He dropped the locket to the ground and twisted the reins around his wrist. Then he pulled the boy's pistol from his belt. He looked past the trooper to Marle, who was watching him. Marle nodded, and suddenly the boy plunged towards him, racing for the protection of the darkness beyond.

Tom turned his horse and leveled the barrel of the pistol at the running figure. For a moment he wavered.

It could have been Alison.

The heavy Colt jerked in his hand.

No one who rode in the Valley of Virginia in the winter of 1864–1865 ever forgot it. The snow lay deep in the upper Valley, hampering the movements of friend and foe alike.

191

It covered the charred beams and scorched foundations of barns and granaries and houses with merciful grace; but it also made movement impossible without leaving telltale tracks, and the barren trees offered little concealment. The horses were fed browse because there was no grain, and the men ate what they could hunt or beg from the starving citizenry. Stewed horsemeat was an esteemed delicacy that helped to lessen the tragedy of another man being dismounted by reason of the starvation of his horse.

What had begun as an attempt to stop the Federals in their policy of looting and burning now became a grim battle for survival. The primary purpose of raiding a Federal outpost was no longer to punish the enemy: it was to obtain fresh horses and food, weapons and ammunition, stout boots and warm blue overcoats. Occasionally, the food stores captured on a raid were shared with a needy family; more often there was not enough to go around, and the defenders of the Valley turned to its starving inhabitants for grain, buried before the Federals had been able to burn it. Aid was given, in most cases willingly. After a time, however, the irregulars became almost as unpopular as the Yankees.

"What difference does it make who takes my corn?" one aggrieved farmer complained. "Whether it's Yanks or Rebs, I still get the short end of the stick."

"We won't burn your barn," Marle said hotly. "That's the difference."

"Mighty big difference, seeing as how there ain't nothing left in it now anyways."

Once Tom had imagined war to be a matter of bugles, colorful uniforms, and fluttering pennons. He had seen the last of battle flags and guidons, he thought grimly. The company carried no standard, and only Marle wore a saber. Ragged jackets dyed butternut brown topped Yankee blue trousers, and more often than not a Federal overcoat covered the heterogeneous attire. Gallantry and pageantry had died somewhere in the headlong flight from Cedar Creek, and the Second Corps had died with it, leaving a group of loosely connected bands of irregulars to prey upon the invaders as best they could.

Now that formal military discipline had all but broken down, they were closer to each other, he thought. The first line of "The Bonnie Blue Flag" that ran "We are a band of brothers and native to the soil" had a fresh and valid meaning as the irregulars fought their last grim battle on the soil of their beloved Valley.

Heavy snow in December marked the end of fighting for a time. Movement was very nearly impossible, and they settled down in an abandoned hut on Massanutten, leaving the area only twice during the month to strike a Federal outpost on Great North Mountain. The first raid had been highly successful; they hit a six man outpost and managed to overwhelm the six without arousing the nearby camp. The extra horses were taken as spares, and Walker found two whole boxes of hardtack and a side of ration beef in the guard tent.

On the second raid they rode into an ambush. They netted no profit; on the contrary, four men were missing when they reached the rendezvous point, and Hodges' mount had a bullet wound in the shoulder.

Two nights later, the two guards Marle had detailed to watch the approaches to the camp rode off on Marle's and Walker's horses, the pick of the lot. Now there were only four of them; Marle, Hodges, Walker, and himself. It didn't seem to bother Marle beyond the momentary irritation of losing a good mount and a good saddle. He was too busy planning for the future.

"Once the weather gets warm," he was fond of saying, "we'll pick up another ten or fifteen men. Then we can raid up North."

"How far north we going, Captain?" Hodges asked artlessly. "Maryland?"

If Marle realized that he was being teased, he showed no sign. He even had an alternate plan; they would ride south in the hopes of joining the main forces of the army, which reputedly were south of Richmond, near Petersburg. But that was a last resort, he insisted. Come spring, Early would be back from his winter quarters near Staunton to gather up the men like themselves who had elected to remain in the theater of action. Then they would sweep the Valley clean!

In March, Sam Dorfer and Todd Harper, Mr. Barnes's hired man, joined the band. They brought two other cavalrymen with them. The four had been forwarded by Doctor Tanner, Jeems McNair, and Andrew Hauser. Early's decimated force had been wiped out near Waynesboro, far to the south, they reported.

"The Yanks are crawling over the Valley like fleas on a dog," Todd Harper said gloomily.

It was good to see Sam again. For a while it was almost as if time had turned back and they had re-entered that glorious state of irresponsibility that is boyhood. They reminisced happily for the first day or two, and then the novelty wore off.

"Let's face it, Tom; we ain't getting younger."

"If they had told me when I was eighteen that I'd be older than Pa by the time I was twenty, I'd have said they were liars," Tom grinned.

"Shucks, I was born old," Hodges chimed in.

"We're none of us going to get much older, if we don't get out of here pretty soon," Walker prophesied. "My horse can eat grass, but I can't."

The horses were in fairly good shape now. Rest and the young grass had worked wonders, and when the cavalrymen produced currycombs and groomed them to a reasonable facsimile of inspection standards, the company looked a little less like brigands, a little more like soldiers.

194

The episode of the wounded man occurred in early March. It was typical of the contradictory nature of events in that mad spring when even Nature seemed to have become intoxicated by the fatigue of what historians later would call "four years of arduous war."

Marle's band had been on a night raid, and towards morning they had run full tilt into a Federal picket near the Harrisonburg Pike. In the exchange of shots, each side had scattered, and when Tom regained familiar ground he discovered that he was alone. It was a wet morning, as almost all mornings were wet that spring; soon it would be light, the sun (if there were a sun) shafting through the gray tendrils of mist. He was near the flank of the mountain, and with luck he would be able to reach its shelter before dawn. It would take luck, though; already the sky was distinct from the blackness of the trees.

Perhaps the Yankee had become confused and lost his way in the same skirmish; one minute there was no sign of another human being, and in the next the boy and his horse loomed out of the mist. Tom crammed the reins in his mouth and drew his pistol and fired.

The Federal's mount screamed with fright and reared. Its rider slid lifelessly from the saddle and fell heavily to earth. Tom turned his own mount to interpose it between him and the fallen man and dismounted.

The Yankee was young, perhaps eighteen or so. His uniform, however, was hardly better than Tom's own which indicated that he had served at least through the winter, when even the Federals had been unable to supply their forces in the Valley properly. The slug had struck him on the right upper arm, ricochetted off the bone, and gone along his chest before it emerged.

Lucky Yank, Tom thought. Lucky to be alive. But perhaps he was not too lucky after all. The arm might well be broken; if it were, Tom was aware of the possible consequences. The loss of the arm might seem like a minor point to a man with two arms, but Tom knew better. He stood over the boy, hesitating. Clearly this was one Yankee who would do no more fighting for a long time to come, if ever. It was not necessary to linger over him; he could simply take away his pistol and ride off. If the boy were found by his friends, he would live. If he were not found at all, or found by someone like Marle, he would die. Marle was the last man in the world to bother with the formality of taking prisoners, especially wounded ones. Marle would have shot the man five minutes ago and been halfway up the mountain by now.

The wounded man opened his eyes. His mouth rounded silently in terror as he saw the drooping pistol barrel aimed at his head.

Tom decided. "Pull your gun with your left hand, and pitch it down near me. Slow!"

The pistol thudded wetly on the turf. It would be a simple matter to pick it up and ride off, but the result would be the same as if he were to put a slug through the boy's head.

"If you kill me, Johnny, it ain't going to make no difference to this war, one way or another."

The mist at the crest of the mountain was bright; in five minutes it would be light enough for anyone to see him. He remembered the bullet that had struck his arm the night of the rout at Fisher's Hill and shivered. Scared? All right, he *was* scared! Suppose the Yankee talked? Told his friends which way the one-armed Rebel had ridden?

"Please, Johnny!"

It would make no difference to the outcome of the war. But it would make a big difference to him. It would make an even greater difference to the boy on the ground, pleading for the life God gave him. And as for the pos-

196

sibility of the man talking, you couldn't go on living without ever trusting anybody.

"You'll die if I leave you, Yank."

"Maybe not. Maybe they'll find me. I've got a chance."

He slid the pistol back in its holster. "I'll help you," he said quietly. "Can you sit up?"

The slug had apparently failed to penetrate the chest, although the boy was bleeding copiously. Tom wadded the unfamiliar yellow scarf against the chest wound. "Button your jacket over that. Can you move your arm?"

The boy nodded. "Some. It hurts when I do."

"All right, then. Hold your left hand right above it and press down hard!"

The flow of blood ebbed to a trickle. Just below them the outline of a muddy road emerged from the mist; fresh wagon tracks indicated that the road received a fair amount of traffic. The boy followed his gaze. Then Tom turned and looked at him.

"Know where you are?"

"Yes, sir. I think so."

"I'm not an officer . . . can you get down to the road by yourself?"

"I think so. Yes."

He nodded, satisfied. "Get on down there, then, and find yourself a place to sit down and wait. Something's bound to come along. If you're on the road, they'll see you and stop." He thought quickly. "Don't walk any further than the road, hear? If that pad slips, or if you let go of that arm, you could bleed to death."

The boy wagged his head. " 'Thank you' ain't enough, but it's all I can say, Johnny."

"That's all right." He touched his empty sleeve. "I know what it is, Yank."

He was sure that no one had seen him, even though it was bright dawn before he reached the illusory shelter of the trees. Even so, it was risky traveling during daylight hours with strong concentrations of Federal cavalry available to trail stragglers back to their rendezvous.

"You're the last man in," Marle said peevishly when he rode into the clearing. "What kept you?"

"I got confused in the dark and went off too far west."

Todd Harper slouched over. "You get hit?"

"No."

"How come there's blood on your coat, then?"

Marle's eyes narrowed. "Where've you been?"

He swung down from the saddle. If Marle was crazy enough to shoot him, he wanted to be on the ground. "As I said, I went off to the west, thinking I was going south. Then a Yank rode in front of me, and I shot him."

"How'd your coat get bloodied up? How much did you take off him?" Todd inquired.

"His scarf," Tom replied. "I bandaged him with it."

"You did what?" Marle yelled.

"I put a bandage on his chest where I shot him."

"What!" Marle bellowed. "You let one of them . . ."

"The man surrendered, Captain," he said flatly. "I respect the rights of prisoners."

"I reckon we all do," Ben Walker said just behind him. "The captain just didn't understand how it was. Ain't that right, Captain Marle?"

"It makes a difference," Marle said reluctantly. "But how can you be sure you weren't followed?"

"The man was bleeding like a stuck pig," he said briefly. "His horse had run off, and he could just about stand. If you'll excuse me, I must see to my horse."

Little mention was made of the incident after that. Ben approved of his action, as did Hodges. "You couldn't leave the poor jackass die," Hodges reasoned. "You had to shoot him or help him, one or the other." Todd Harper, how-

198

ever, made no bones about what he would have done in a similar situation: "The more of them there are, the less I like it," he said.

Marle said nothing at all, but he didn't have to. It was plain enough to everyone how Marle felt about Yankees. The fact that they might be prisoners would make no difference to Jonathan Marle.

Was this what happened in war, Tom wondered. Did normally decent men become transformed into killers who respected no law? He took a long, hard look at Marle's company, and he saw that the distinction between some of the men and the bushwhackers was a slight one, indeed.

In late March Marle rode off on a solitary scout and returned with exciting information. A battalion of enemy cavalry was stationed up near New Market. They had outposts, of course, and one of them was on the flank of Massanutten.

"It's like falling off a log," he crowed. "They've got a squad on duty, and they're watching the mountain. Now we can get between them and their main camp. They won't be expecting us from that direction."

"What good is it going to do, sir?" Sam Dorfer wanted to know. "Wouldn't we be of more use heading south to join up with the army?"

"Why, sure," Marle said easily. "But we might as well go back with a full belly and plenty of cartridges."

The conversation was effectively ended.

"I don't think he wants to go back," Sam said when Marle had fallen asleep.

Walker motioned towards the door and picked up his cane. Sam and Tom followed him out into the wet spring morning. "I'll tell you how it is with the captain," he offered. "He's got a chance to do what he wants when he wants to do it, for the first time in his life. Whether he knows it or not, he's going to hang onto it."

199

"What about the rest of us?" Sam demanded.

"I don't know about you all, but I'll stay with him. I've soldiered with Marle pretty near back to the beginning. He joined us after Second Manassas, so it's been ever since then. I reckon I'm used to him."

Maybe that was it, Tom thought. He, too, was used to Marle; attracted to him despite his cruelty because he had been Sandy's friend; bound to him by all the memories that still kept Sandy's face before him when he closed his eyes at night.

"What about it, Tom?" Sam asked. "I'll go along with you."

"I'm used to him, too. I'll stick."

CHAPTER 16

Marle Makes a Move

THEY followed Marle along the ridgeline as closely as they dared. It was dark, not black dark, but pretty nearly so. At Marle's order, they all wore scraps of white cloth on their right arms as a means of identification. Marle led because he knew the way, and Todd Harper brought up the rear because he was stronger than the others and could be depended upon to assist Tom or Ben in the event they were unhorsed. Tom thought he might be able to mount without assistance, even if his horse became excited, but Walker would be another matter. A peg leg wasn't a foot, no matter which way you looked at it.

"Hey, Tom!" Walker called softly. "How about a three-legged race?"

He chuckled to himself. It was typical of Ben to joke at a time like this. And a good thing, too; it relieved the tension.

"You reckon between the two of you, you could make a whole man?" Hodges jeered.

Marle swung his horse abruptly and Hodges pulled up. "Shut up," Marle rasped. "We're pretty near there."

Now they moved downhill, headed for the Valley floor. Once or twice Marle stopped to check his position, and then they moved off into the gloom. Lights appeared like golden pinpricks in the night. They were a long way off, and they looked lonesome, all by themselves in the wall of darkness.

"That's the town," Marle murmured, half to himself. He turned to the others. "They'll have a fire going. You all stay behind me and let me do the talking. When they challenge, I'll answer. We'll try to do this without shooting, but if you cain't help it, remember that there's a whole regiment just outside the town, and don't sit around and wait for them. Run for your lives."

They moved slowly forward along a well defined trail until the gleam of the fire showed clearly through the intervening bushes. Someone gave three short whistles, and Marle stopped. He looked around, and then he whistled in imitation.

"Who's that?" a voice said. "I pretty near shot you when you didn't whistle back right off."

"Captain Marle, Headquarters. I'm leading a scout."

The sentry came from behind a tree. They could see his silhouette against the glow of the fire. His carbine was carelessly held in the crook of his arm.

"Guerrillas out tonight?"

"Yes," Marle said. "They're out."

The man stiffened, suddenly suspicious. "Did you say you were from headquarters, Captain?"

"You're a dead man if you make a move," Marle said easily. Light gleamed on the upraised barrel of his pistol. "Do it slow, Yank; mighty slow. Lay down that carbine."

Todd Harper dismounted and came forward to pick up the weapon. "This ought to come in handy," he muttered to Sam as he walked back to his mount.

"How many of you here, Yank?"

"Six."

"Where are they?"

"Two more watching the far side. Three at the fire."

Marle pointed with his pistol. "Take us there."

202

As the trooper walked towards the fire, Marle kept the pistol trained on him. It was a gesture in case the man looked back; if Marle used the pistol, it would have to be on an armed man who was an immediate threat to his life. One shot would destroy any chance he might have of accomplishing his purpose. He wondered if any of the company had guessed what he had in mind. Probably not. Tanner was not imaginative enough, and the new men didn't know him that well.

Hodges and Walker would follow as he directed; it didn't matter whether they knew or not. With a little luck tonight, they could get away with the Federal unit's mounts and weapons. McNair had sent word that there were more men available, if he could mount them and arm them. Very well, he'd get the horses, and then there'd be no stopping him. He could stay in the Valley, or ride southwest into Texas, or even head into Mexico. The leader of a trained company could name his own price and enforce payment, too.

The trooper walked into the clearing, where three men were squatting around the fire playing a game of cards.

"Don't move, anybody," Marle said easily. "You're surrounded. Call in your pickets."

A burly red-haired sergeant put down his cards and grinned. "If we're surrounded, how come you didn't surround the pickets?"

With a twinge of doubt, Marle realized that the trooper had guessed that the detachment was not really surrounded. "You're too talkative, Sergeant. Call them in."

The sergeant shrugged his shoulders. "You want to shoot, I can't stop you. But I guess you know they can hear you clear over in the main camp. If you shoot, you'll never make it out of here alive."

"I'll chance that," Marle grinned. "You want to gamble?"

"All right," the sergeant said. "You win. Long! Long and Street! Come on in!"

Sam Dorfer and Todd Harper dismounted and collected the weapons of the group. Each man had an army model Colt .44 and a new Sharps carbine with forty rounds of ammunition. Hodges would be happy, Marle thought; the ammunition would fit his weapon.

"Where are those pickets?" Marle asked.

"Up the mountain a way," the sergeant said. "They'll be right here."

Something was wrong. The sergeant was much too pleased with himself. "Hodges, take the sergeant with you; have him lead in the horses. Walker, you and Tanner get back to where we turned off and listen for trouble."

Marle considered his dispositions for a moment. He and Harper could certainly handle the pickets when they came in; with Walker and Tanner between them and the regimental encampment, there should be no reason to worry. But something was wrong; he could feel it.

Hodges and the Federal sergeant reappeared at the edge of the clearing. "Only four horses," Hodges announced.

His mind cleared: there had been no pickets out. This was no outpost; it was nothing but a well baited trap. When the sergeant had called for the pickets, it had been some sort of signal. Long and Street, he had said; if you added the names you got Longstreet, the name of the Confederate general. Longstreet; come on in. That was what the sergeant had said.

"Mount up, blue belly," he ordered the sergeant. "You're going with us."

The smile faded from the trooper's face. "No, I ain't. You can't make me, neither. You can't shoot me, because they'd hear the shot."

Marle grinned. "A shot won't make any difference, will it? We both know who Longstreet is." He turned to Todd

204

Harper. "Lead one of these horses back to Tanner and start out. It's a trap. Hodges and I will follow you."

In the instant his attention was diverted, the sergeant dove for the bushes. A rifle flashed in the darkness, and Marle plunged spurs to his horse. The frightened gelding charged across the clearing, and then the darkness erupted with flames and the steady roar of a volley.

Tom and Ben Walker reached the shack shortly before dawn. They had heard the pursuit head towards the mountain, and then it died off in the distance. They had stayed near the floor of the Valley, where they had decided it would be safe until daylight. So it had proved.

"We'd better not start a fire," Ben said ruefully. "Somebody might see the smoke. I could eat the north end of a southbound skunk, though. Without salt."

"I've got some hardtack."

"Good enough."

Tom fumbled with the strap of his haversack. "I wonder what happened to Sam?"

"He was with Marle and Hodges." Ben thought about it. "I reckon he got out the same way they did."

"If they did. That was an awful lot of shooting."

Ben grunted. "Don't worry. Old Hodges can get out of anything. Remember that time he swapped with that Yank up on the Rappahannock? If we'd had more time, he'd have got the Yank to come over and fight on our side."

"I remember." It was hard, though, to remember how it had been in that other time. There had been a certain security in the formal structure of the army that was missing now. The company had been battling for mere survival too long for him to be able to recall the comfort of being supported in time of need by other units, to be upheld by the balance of the army.

A glow in the mist outside announced the arrival of

205

dawn. If the others didn't show in the next few minutes, there would be a risk of their being picked off by the Yankees, or worse, followed to the cabin.

"I wish they'd get here!" Tom said fretfully.

"Don't think about it," Ben advised. "You know, your grandpa gave me a whole lot of advice on lawyering last summer. He let me take some of his books, and he taught me some, too."

Ben was trying to divert his attention. "You still figure on being a lawyer after the war?" Tom asked.

"Why, of course. It's something I always wanted, but I never thought I'd make it. It looked for a while like I was aiming a mite high."

"You know what, Ben? I wish we could be partners. We could have an office in Staunton, and I could ride circuit while you took on new work. I only have about a year's study before I can take my examination, and I could help you at the same time I'm preparing."

Ben looked incredulous. "You really mean that, Tom?"

"Of course I do."

"Why! Why, I reckon that's about the best thing I could think of! I was scared of going it alone."

And so was he, truth to tell. What would happen after the war ended was anybody's guess. One thing you had to admit about the present: bad as it was, it was certain. You knew just where you stood.

"You asleep, Tom?"

"No."

"We got to stay awake in case they're followed. We might have to run for it."

"I know." What was Alison doing now? Was she tending her garden, chopping out the early weeds? Cleaning the house? A wave of longing swept over him, leaving him trembling with its intensity.

"What say, Tom?"

"Nothing. I'm all right."

206

Ben opened the breech of his carbine to check the load. The lever snapped back with an oily "cluck."

Then he saw her. She was in the front parlor, dusting the books on the white-painted shelves. She half turned, as though she could see him, too. For a moment she stood holding a book, listening, waiting for him to speak . . .

"Somebody coming," Ben said sharply.

"I'll go look."

Outside the hut, the mist was cool on his face. He crossed the clearing and waited beside a large pine. A hoof clashed on rock, and then he heard the rustle of last year's leaves. Two horses, maybe more. He drew the Yankee pistol from his belt and cocked it. Better safe than sorry, as Hodges would say.

Marle's horse crashed through the underbrush, followed by that of Sam Dorfer. Sam led a third horse. Tom pushed the barrel of the pistol through his belt once more and went out to meet them.

"It was that sergeant," Marle said grimly, as he dismounted. "He fooled me."

"That's the way it goes," Tom said easily.

Sam grunted and slid to the ground. "The sergeant jumped in the bushes, and the others hit the dirt, and then the shooting started."

"Is Harper inside?" Marle said sharply.

"No, sir," Ben Walker said from the doorway. "He hollered to us to run for it, and then he took off. We lost him, so we headed up the Pike for a while before we came here."

Marle nodded. "Well, you got away. That's the main thing."

"Where's Hodges?"

"He was leading one of their horses. I reckon he fell behind."

The sound of a horse on the trail sent them racing to cover, but it was only Todd Harper. His hat was gone, and his face was swollen where it had been lashed by branches on his wild ride.

"I don't know which one of you is worse off," Ben teased. "Offhand, I'd say the horse is better looking."

Todd grinned despite his exhaustion. "He probably feels better, too. Doggone if every blue belly in creation wasn't out last night."

"How come you didn't wait up for Walker and Tanner?" Marle inquired with deceptive calm.

"I figured they was right behind me," Todd said, and Tom remembered with sudden clarity the day the guerrillas had come to Lovatt, and Todd and Mr. Barnes had left the company to take care of their own possessions, despite Will Kinyard's plea.

He glanced at Sam. Sam met his glance and nodded. Sam remembered that day, too.

"You should have made sure," Marle said.

"Wonder where Hodges got to?" Todd asked.

Marle didn't answer, and after a moment he walked off to the cabin.

"Old High-and-Mighty Marle," Todd said.

But no one answered him. Ben unsaddled the horse Sam had led, and Tom tied it to a tree in the rear of the clearing. Two of the new Sharps carbines were jammed in the boot. They and the horse were the sole results of the raid.

Except for one other: Hodges never returned.

Now they were six: Marle, Ben, Todd, Sam, a veteran of Munford's cavalry named Cary, and himself. Yesterday there had been five. Tomorrow? That was anybody's guess. Enough that the weather was warmer, that he was able to shave and bathe and wash his clothes. Tomorrow would take care of itself.

They were all veterans, now; they worked quickly and well together, with a minimum of orders. But it didn't take a veteran to realize that their usefulness had ended, if indeed it had ever existed. They were surviving and no more. Even that would come to an end one day. A larger band would swallow them up in one gulp for their arms and the horses. Some Federal patrol would track them down. Once or twice he awakened in the middle of the night to hear the spatter of shots still echoing in the dream he had just left.

Only Marle retained a confidence in ultimate victory that amounted to insane arrogance. We'll cross the mountains and join up with Hood, he would say, forgetting that McNair had sent word that Hood had lost his army in Tennessee during the winter. Beyond that, he dreamed aloud of going to Mexico with the company.

Cary was in agreement with Marle. He would rather go to Mexico, he said, than live under Yankee rule. A farmer and horse breeder from Rockbridge County, Cary had no reason to return. His house had been burned, and his wife had been dead for several years.

But it was a rare occasion when anyone spoke of returning. For the present, it was enough that they had fire and shelter, and that there was some food, begged or stolen. It was enough that they were alive.

In February they had raided at will; by April the scope of their operations was limited to the ten mile area around the hut. As Ben put it, you seldom saw a Yankee now, but when you did he was too big to handle. The Federal patrols now rode by companies. Eighty or more well fed men armed with new repeating Spencer carbines and mounted on sleek, well fed horses were too many to tackle. The day of the guerrilla in the Valley of Virginia was drawing to a close.

As yet Marle maintained the hut on Massanutten. It provided a certain amount of comfort, and for the present it was safe from the Federals.

"One of these days they're going to follow up the tracks

209

we're making, and that'll be the end of us," Walker said one rainy night, as they huddled around the spitting fire.

"Nonsense," Marle scoffed. "We're careful to approach the hut from different directions. They won't catch us as long as we hang together."

"The six men Custer caught hung together, too," Sam Dorfer retorted. "By the neck, at the end of a rope."

"Mosby hung five of Custer's men in retaliation," Marle replied. "That ought to have taught Custer a lesson."

"I wouldn't want to test it," Sam said.

Cary scratched his head. "It looks to me like we ought to get out of here while we can. Maybe we could head east and join up with Mosby. McNair sent word he was operating over in Fauquier County."

Marle shook his head. "If we go anywhere, it has to be west. Maybe Texas."

"How about Joe Johnston?" Cary suggested. "If he joins forces with Lee, they could get away into the hills and hold out for years."

"Like we're doing," Ben said flatly.

"What's wrong with it?" Marle demanded. "We're the hard core. When we get more recruits, we'll be able to meet the Yankees on even terms. All we have to do is wait."

Tom stood up. "Nobody asked me, but I think we ought to get out of here while we have a chance. We're not doing any good here, and besides, I don't see the recruits flocking in."

The door banged open, and Todd Harper thrust his head inside. "Douse the fire," he ordered curtly. "Somebody's coming."

Marle kicked the logs apart and pushed them into the bed of accumulated ashes until only a glow remained. Now Tom could hear the sound of a horse on the trail below. One horse? Or several? He watched Marle to see if Marle was going to reply to his statement, but the captain was apparently concerned only with his decision.

"All right," Marle said. "Let's go see what the fuss is about."

Outside, Tom began to make out the shapes of objects: the trees nearest the hut, the rain barrel, the edge of the grove where the horses were tethered.

The rider came into the clearing and stopped, a formless blob against the black wall of the trees. Tom loosened the flap of his holster.

"Who's that?" Marle called.

"I'm looking for Captain Marle," a woman's voice said.

"I'm Captain Marle. Come over here."

There was something familiar about the voice, Tom thought. And then he remembered. "It's all right, Captain Marle. The young lady is my fiancée."

Almost reluctantly Marle sheathed the pistol he had drawn; Tom pushed past him to meet Alison.

"Tom?"

He put his arms around her as she dismounted. "I can't believe it's you, Alison," he murmured.

"Oh, it's been so long!"

Marle's voice bit through the darkness. "How did you find us, Miss? This is a dangerous place."

Alison turned to him. "Mr. Hauser told me where you'd be. He said to tell you to move out tonight."

"Why?" Marle snapped.

"The enemy came into Lovatt late this evening looking for you. There was about a regiment of cavalry, and they threw a cordon around the town so that no one could get out. Mr. Hauser said that one of them boasted that he had followed Mr. McNair last time he was up here, and that they were going to close in on you at daylight."

"How did you get out?" Marle asked suspiciously.

"My mother and I are staying at Tom's home for a time.

211

Mr. Hauser slipped away to tell us just before they reached Tom's house. He left his horse in the woods behind the house, and I got out the back door before they guarded it."

"I see," Marle said. "Do they know about the hut?"

Alison hesitated. "I don't think so. I think they just know about the trails coming up, but they weren't guarded when I came through. Part of them went over towards Port Republic, and the other part went down Pike into the woods behind the Barnes place."

"They're guessing, then," Marle said. "They'll surround the area and attack on one side, hoping we'll run into the other band."

"Well, whatever they're planning to do, you can't stay here," Alison said.

"That's right," Marle agreed. "It won't take a regiment long to find us, since they know the trails."

"Mr. Hauser said to get out as soon as you can. He heard that Richmond had fallen to the Yankees, and he said you had best surrender, if you can."

"No," Marle said sharply. "Thank you for the information, Miss. I trust we may meet under more auspicious circumstances."

Alison turned to Tom. "I'll have to get back," she said. "I have to get away from here before it gets light, so that they won't guess where I've come from."

He released her reluctantly. "I wish I could go with you."

"I know."

She turned her face up to him. "Tom? Isn't it time to surrender? Haven't you done enough already?"

"Don't ask me to, Alison. It's hard enough the way it is. I have to see it through."

She nodded as if she had expected his answer. "God bless you, my dear," she said, and then she swung herself back into the saddle. "I'll be waiting for you." She turned the mare and disappeared into the darkness.

Tom stood close to Sam and Ben, holding the reins of his horse. The men presented a somewhat spectral aspect in the gray light of false dawn, with their long, dripping ponchos and their rain-sodden hats.

Marle splashed towards them through a puddle. "All right, you all gather close so you can hear."

The men obligingly moved closer, leading their mounts, while the rain dripped dismally from the sodden branches. It was chilly, and Tom shivered. He thought about the fire Marle had kicked out. If only Marle had waited, they all might have spent another half-hour beside it with warm hands and dry boots. Alison must have been soaked to the skin, despite the old mackintosh she had worn. They might even have followed her out, although she was probably safer alone. But what a joke it would have been on the Yankees, to have rested in Lovatt while the enemy was beating through the wet on a fool's errand!

"They've got maybe two companies out against us," Marle said. "One is going to hit us from the southwest, coming straight up from Lovatt. The other one went down Port Republic way. They'll cross the river there and come at us from the east. If we run north, we'll probably find a third troop up there."

Cary cleared his throat and spat. "Reckon it's time we got out of the Valley."

"That's right," Marle agreed surprisingly. "It's getting too hot to hold us. We'll attack that company coming up from Port Republic. They won't expect us nearly so soon, and if we're lucky, we can hurt them bad and break out at the same time. We can head south and join up with Lee, or we can head west and meet up with the forces in Tennessee."

"What forces?" someone jeered, but Marle gave no sign that he had heard.

They rode out at a trot, in single file, with Marle in the lead and Todd Harper fifty yards in the rear. There

213

were no flank guards out; as Marle said, there would be nothing left to guard if they detached men for that purpose.

Sam dropped back to ride alongside Tom. "That was a mighty brave thing your cousin did. Only she ain't really your cousin."

"That's right." He couldn't think of Alison now. He had to concentrate on what happened next. Now they would head down the mountain, and then they would hit the Yankees. And if they got through the Yankees, they would join another band or General Lee's army. And then? He remembered Alison's words. "Isn't it time to surrender? Haven't you done enough already?" she had said. If you couldn't possibly win, was there still a reason to fight?

Up ahead, Marle raised his right hand and halted. They fanned out to either side of him and peered through a leafy screen into their future.

Below them the ground fell away in a gentle drop that would eventually reach the Shenandoah River. In a natural meadow a group of Union cavalrymen had dismounted. He counted twenty of them, including five who were holding the horses of the unit, and two who were trying to start a fire with damp wood.

Marle grinned happily. "Sunup in fifteen minutes or so. That's what they're waiting for. Harper and Cary, you've got repeating Spencers. Shoot into the horses when I give the word. Drop the men who're holding them if you can. But stampede the horses first. When things get to boiling down there, we'll charge them."

Todd looked dubious. "That's pretty near two hundred yards, Captain," he said. "Far shot for a carbine."

"A good man can do it," Marle said curtly.

"Wouldn't it be better just to charge through them?" Tom asked. "If you wait to shoot up the horses, they'll have too much warning."

214

Marle whirled on him. "What's the matter—afraid some of them'll get hurt? Maybe you want to get the bandages ready so you can tie up some more of your blue-bellied friends."

"That's ridiculous."

"Is it? You let one of them go." He turned to the others. "I'm not trying just to get through them. I'm out to settle a score. If anybody wants out, let him leave now. I've got no room for cowards."

Cary shouldered forward. "I reckon I'm a little old to learn how to live with Yankees. I'm with you."

Tom urged his horse to Marle's side. "If you'll make that remark of yours definite, I'll be pleased to take the proper steps," he said.

Ben Walker spoke just behind him. "I'm sure the Captain didn't intend a slur. Perhaps the Captain will explain?"

"All right," Marle snapped. "Whatever else you are, Tanner, you're not a coward."

"Thank you for the statement, Marle."

"Captain Marle to you."

He shook his head tauntingly, knowing that he was provoking a fight, and knowing that he would regret it; yet still unable to stop. "Captain was my brother's rank once. I'd hate to muddy up the word. You're a disgrace to your rank, to your uniform, and to the army."

Marle's face went livid. "When we get through with those Yankees, I'll settle with you."

"The pleasure'll be mine."

Marle raised his fist, but Cary restrained him. "We ain't got time, Captain."

Marle turned away. "You men with the carbines get set."

Tom knew that he had done his share in promoting the quarrel, and now he cursed himself for a fool. What had the Yankee said last month? "Killing me won't make no

215

difference to the war." And killing Marle wouldn't, either. There was also a good possibility that Marle might kill him; but it didn't scare him unduly. In the next five minutes he would be in as much danger as he ever had been. If he were alive half an hour from now, he'd start to worry about Jonathan Marle.

CHAPTER 17

The End of a Soldier

FOR a moment the tableau in front of them etched itself in Tom's memory: the misty meadow, the horse-holders, the stacked arms, and the men clustered around their cooking fire, which had at last begun to burn; and then Marle slashed his right hand downward.

The reports of the carbines thudded damply in the morning mist. One of the horse-holders fell forward, and the horses under his care broke free. Around the tiny fire, the Federals began to mill, pushing and shoving in their haste to get to their mounts.

Although the other members of the band began to shoot into the milling throng, Tom could see no further casualties. As Todd had said, it was a long range for carbines. Tom took the reins around the stump of his left arm and twisted them to take up the slack. Then he drew his pistol from his belt.

Marle stuck his carbine in his saddle boot and mounted. "Remember what Stuart said!" he yelled. " 'I'd rather die than be whipped!' "

They rode out of the illusory shelter of the woods in a line now, although no order had been given, because a line gave them the best opportunity to make their shots count once they got within pistol range. The mist swirled about them in the high grass, and the hooves thudded

217

with a sodden noise upon the wet turf. Marle drew his saber and waved it erratically as Cary began to yell.

The Federals pulled together to form a more or less regular square. Their carbines boomed in a ragged attempt at volley fire, and Tom could hear an officer chanting the commands. Marle looked back at him and grinned with an unholy joy, and suddenly he realized that Marle had never intended to cut his way through the enemy. Unable to win, he was going to death in the best way he knew.

The Federal line came closer with each stride, and now he could see the snarling faces of the enemy over the gleaming gun barrels. He fired wildly at the square, and then the faces were gone and the woods beyond loomed nearer until they closed behind him.

It was over. He jammed the empty pistol into his belt and pulled up on the reins. The maddened horse stopped, panting and quivering with fear.

"You're hit," Ben said just behind him. "In the leg."

A slug had burned its way across his right thigh. He looked at it intently until his eyes focused. "Only a crease," he said. "How about you?"

"I'm all right, son. Let's ride."

"How about the others?"

"There ain't any. Come on, boy; skedaddle!"

They headed south through the timber. There would be no aid for them in Port Republic, to the east. The only hope they had was to get away from the mountain before the surprised Federals could regain their wits and their mounts and search the area thoroughly.

When they stopped that night, they were well up the flank of North Mountain. Tom helped Walker dismount and unsaddled the horses while Ben gathered twigs for a fire.

218

"Reckon any of them got away?" Tom asked.

"Todd Harper, maybe. He was alongside me, but he turned off and ran away. Marle rode right into them, and they shot him out of the saddle. Cary was hit, and his foot hung up in the stirrup. His horse dragged him. Maybe Sam got away; I couldn't see."

Sam. The lieutenant of the Lovatt company. Suddenly Tom felt a weariness that had nothing to do with the long day's ride ahead or with the sharp fighting of the morning. He was tired of seeing friends killed in a dying cause. He was tired of killing men he didn't know, simply because they wore blue coats. "What do you want to do, Ben?"

Walker's face was cut in ridges by the clear flame of the fire. "I reckon there ain't nothing to do but run. Maybe meet up with some of our men. What do you think?"

"I think we kind of reached the end of something today. The way it looks, the war'll be over pretty soon, no matter what we do."

"Maybe." Ben lay back on his blanket. "Sure glad it ain't raining." He chuckled. "Remember how old Hodges used to say that? If it was snowing or the sun was too hot, he'd always say 'I'm sure glad it ain't raining.' "

"I remember."

"You want to quit, Tom?"

"I reckon so. There's not much point in going on, is there? We can't win any more."

"No, we can't win. Still, maybe we could fight them to a draw. You always feel funny about it; you know? Like the men who held out in the Revolution did the right thing, because in the end they won, no matter how folks said they couldn't. But what if they hadn't?"

"You're saying that the side that wins is right."

Ben chuckled. "Not right, but smart, the way most folks see it. We going to be partners when this is over?"

"Of course we are." If we last that long, he added silently.

"Old Marle didn't figure on coming out of there alive," Ben said abruptly. "You know that?"

"I know."

"He just couldn't stand to get whipped." Ben stared into the fire. "I can understand how he felt, Tom. I ain't saying I'd do the same thing, but I can understand how he felt."

"Maybe if we kept at it long enough, we'd get to feel that way, too," Tom said.

Ben had some captured Yankee hardtack which they shared the following morning. It was a cold breakfast, but as Ben said, it beat no breakfast at all by a wide margin.

They saddled and mounted from habit, and it was only then that Ben asked, "Where are we going, anyhow?"

"I don't know. We'd better see what we can do about rations, though."

Through a gap in the trees below he saw a faint thread of smoke. Somewhere down there was the Valley, with houses and people and books and quiet rooms. How much longer must they continue before they could return?"

"Pretty sight here," Ben offered as he stopped behind a fallen tree. "The woods kind of run together like a stage."

Memory touched him with a gentle hand. Here was where he had come to escape Sandy the day they had killed the deer. So long ago!

"You look like you've been a long ways off," Ben said.

"I was just thinking. I shot a deer from here one day with Sandy. It was his last furlough."

"I wish the deer had a brother," Ben said practically. "I sure could use some fresh meat."

"Lovatt's right down from here. Maybe five miles."

220

"And chock full of Yankees, more than likely."

"I know. I was just saying. There used to be a family lived up around here. Their name was Kinyard."

"Well," Ben said, "what're we waiting for?"

They stopped well outside the clearing to reconnoiter. The house was standing, at least, and the shed that had housed a mangy-looking bull and two or three cows in other days. It seemed to be empty now.

"Looks safe enough," Ben said. A stunted hollyhock, green with April, swayed to and fro beside the door. Other than that, there was no sign of life.

"I'd feel better if I could see somebody." He stared at the dark windows. "Might as well risk it. You cover me with your carbine while I go up and see what's going on."

"All right. Be careful." Ben unsheathed his Sharps and cocked it.

Tom rode out into the open. The house had an air of expectancy, almost as though it knew something was about to happen. He shrugged off the feeling. He had approached too many houses on similar missions during the past six months.

The shed was empty, as he had expected. The cow droppings were old and dry; there had been no cattle here recently. He flicked his horse lightly with the rein ends and circled the house. Something moved in the dim interior. The hair prickled at the base of his neck, and the familiar sweat of fear welled out on his body.

"Hello the house!"

The silence was impenetrable. He rode around to the front, transferring the reins to his mouth and drawing his belt pistol. Suddenly the front door flew open, and a gaunt man with a large and antiquated shotgun appeared. "The gray-backs run off the cow last month," he said bitterly. "There ain't nothing for you here."

221

"Mr. Kinyard, I'm Tom Tanner."

The gaunt man stared in disbelief. "The Tanner boy?" He lowered his shotgun. "Doggone if you ain't. Put away that pistol before you hurt somebody and come in. We ain't got nothing but cornbread, but you're welcome."

"I've got a friend back yonder."

"One friend?" Mr. Kinyard asked meaningfully.

Tom smiled. "One friend." He waved towards the trees, and a moment later Ben rode out into the clear ground.

Mr. Kinyard sat across from them at the bare deal table, while Mrs. Kinyard stood behind him. "Reckon you boys are headed home. We was thinking maybe Martin'd be home before too long." Mrs. Kinyard nodded and smiled nervously.

"No, sir," Ben said. "Fact is, we were looking for a company to join up with."

Mr. Kinyard's eyes narrowed. "There's nobody to join up with except bushwhackers like them cowards that killed poor Will."

"We aren't bushwhackers," Tom said hotly. "We were headed south to see if we could join up with the rest of the army, only we got in a fight yesterday morning, and we had to double back."

"Lee's army?"

Ben nodded. "Any objections?"

Mr. Kinyard rubbed his hand against the stubble of his beard. "No objections, son," he said quietly. "I reckon you ain't heard, is all. We only got the news yesterday ourselves. General Lee surrendered his army the day before yesterday."

If Lee and the proud Army of Northern Virginia had fallen, what was left? Hood had been whipped, and Early. Johnston would not be able to hold out by himself. And the West? No; the West had never been the strong point in the defenses of the Confederacy. Lee had fallen, the symbol of all that was bright and untarnished. The end was here and now.

Tears burned at the corners of Tom's eyes. Angry tears; if they had known this yesterday, Sam might be with them now.

"What do you aim to do, Tom?" Ben asked quietly. "You call the turn."

"I reckon there's only one thing we can do, and that is give up and go home. Maybe we can be of use there."

"How're you going to defend your home against the Yankees by yourself?"

"I can't do it from here. That's certain."

Ben winced. "Going home. That means taking the iron-clad oath, don't it?"

Mr. Kinyard cleared his throat. "Some of the boys was in Staunton yesterday swearing the oath. There's lots would rather take the oath than carry on as outlaws."

"But a Yankee oath!" Ben said.

"Son, it ain't never wrong to admit that you was whipped." Mr. Kinyard rubbed at the stubble on his face. "In fact, it takes quite a man to do that."

It began to rain in the early part of the afternoon. It would be summer before long, though; his stump wouldn't ache so much, once the weather got drier. That was what Ben said, anyhow, and Ben ought to know. Tom looked up into the gray sky, heedless of the drizzle that had awakened him. By tonight it would be over, one way or another.

"How are we going to do it?" Ben asked.

"I don't know. I reckon we could just go home and wait for them to find us."

Ben dissented. "If we're going to do it, let's do it legal and proper."

"All right. We'll find ourselves a Yankee and give up to him." It didn't matter too much one way or the other,

223

he guessed. Ben hadn't said a lot about it, but Tom knew he had given it a good deal of thought. When they had left the Kinyard place, the news was still too fresh for them to fully comprehend its meaning. Now that they had had time to accept the disaster, they could realize what it meant. The end had come at last.

He munched the last of his hard bread and washed it down with water from his canteen. Tomorrow would be different. There would be parched corn coffee, and maybe even meat and potatoes.

"We better not go in there with all the guns," Ben said. "They might shoot us first and parole us after."

"All right."

They concealed Ben's carbine and the gunbelt Tom had taken from the bushwhacker in a hollow tree, wrapped in Ben's oilcloth. Then they rode down to the Pike and headed north, towards Harrisonburg. Half a mile from town they saw the Federals; three videttes standing to horse beside the Pike.

"Here goes nothing," Ben said grimly. "You got something white to wave at them?"

"No. I never thought of that."

"They're watching us mighty close. I'm going to take off my shirt and wave it. It ain't white, but about six months ago it used to be."

Tom gripped the reins in his teeth and held Ben's gun belt while Ben stripped off his jacket and shirt. The drizzle gleamed on Ben's naked torso like oil.

"All right," Ben said as he replaced his jacket. "Let's move in closer and see what happens." He held the shirt up in the air with his right hand and guided his mount with his left.

Light winked on the shining barrels of the troopers' carbines. He felt his mouth turn to cotton. No matter how many times you saw the face of death, you got scared. He looked at Ben. Ben was scared, too. Somehow it made him feel better.

"Hold it, Johnny!" one of the troopers called. "Get off them horses and keep your hands up."

Obediently they dismounted and led their mounts towards the carbine muzzles. Fifty feet from the Federals they were halted again.

"Hold it, Johnny. You Rebs coming to surrender?"

"We sure ain't coming to enlist!" Ben called.

"Lay your guns down in the road and come ahead." The Federal with the corporal's stripes grinned as he watched them dismount. "Ain't but a whole man between the two of you."

"You're getting your money's worth," Tom said tersely.

"Darn slim pickings," the corporal retorted. "Gordon, mount up and take them on into town to the compound. Then come back here. There'll be more of them."

This then was surrender. Not a formal, gentleman's agreement to lay down their arms and return to peace in clean uniforms, with badges of rank and honor upon their tunics. Only a meeting between two groups of shabby soldiers in the rain, in the middle of a muddy road, with a cold wind cutting down from the mountain. Two groups of soldiers who, but for the accident of geography which resulted in their being born in different regions, might have been one group of civilians, with a full complement of arms and legs.

The corporal permitted them to remount, and one of the troopers escorted them into town. Their horses were taken from them by a second man and led into a barn. Another man herded them into an open place where five or six others were under guard. The rain was still falling, and Tom shared his oilcloth poncho with Ben.

They were guarded by two youthful-seeming troopers in rubber waterproofs, armed with Spencer repeaters. It

225

was somewhat superfluous, Tom thought wryly, since not one of the men under guard had been captured in the technical sense of the word. All had come to give themselves up and ask for parole, yet they were guarded as carefully as though they had been formally captured and might attempt to escape at any time.

Late in the afternoon, they were herded into an empty granary, where a Federal major, a sergeant, and an American flag awaited them.

"Is there anyone here who does not desire to take the oath of allegiance to the United States of America?" the major asked.

No one answered. Outside the rain tapped with inquisitive fingers upon the shakes, and someone bawled an order.

"You men have fought against your flag and your country. You have been traitors to the land of your birth. Now you have been humbled by the strength of the armies of the Union you sought to destroy . . ."

"By God Almighty and nobody else," the man next to Tom growled.

"Who said that?" the major asked.

No one answered, and after a moment the major called out "Sergeant!" It was already an old ritual to him. He didn't care what they said or what they felt, so long as they allowed him to recite his piece.

The sergeant Tom had noticed earlier walked among the prisoners handing each one a small, cloth-bound Bible. The Bibles were well worn; it was an old ritual to them as well.

"Raise your right hands and repeat after me . . ."

The tired voice droned on.

From the back of the granary came the mouth-watering aroma of beans and coffee. A trooper in a waterproof swung a big ladle from side to side. "All right, Johnnies!" he called cheerfully. "Come and get it!"

226

They joined the line and received tin cups and plates. Ben stepped out spryly enough, tapping along on his peg without recourse to his cane. Tom balanced the tin cup on his plate and held it out to be filled.

"Kind of at a disadvantage, ain't you, Johnny?" the Federal grinned.

"Reckon so."

"Set your cup down here and take your plate over to your friend there to hold for you. Then you can get your coffee and you won't have to wait out the line."

"That's an idea. Thanks."

As he took his place beside Ben, the trooper waved his ladle cheerfully at them. He smiled at the man. "He seems like a right nice fellow for a Yankee, Ben."

"Maybe there's some of them are all right."

"I wonder what they did with our horses?"

Ben shrugged his shoulders. "Your guess is as good as mine. You about done?"

"Pretty near. I could put away about ten more platefuls of those beans, but so could everybody else."

"Let's go, then."

They rinsed their plates in a kettle of hot water, and then they walked out into the chilly rain. The enclosure where they had been held was empty now, and the trampled area was a sea of mud.

"You got your parole, Ben?"

Ben grinned mirthlessly and tapped the pocket of his jacket. "Sure do. I'm not apt to leave it behind; it was too hard to come by."

At the barn where they had left their horses, a truculent sergeant and two troopers held court. "What do you want?" he demanded.

"We left our horses here this morning. We came to get them," Tom answered.

"Oh, you've come for them?"

"That's right," Walker said sharply. "They told us inside that we could keep our horses, the same like General Lee's men."

One of the troopers snickered.

"Them horses was branded U.S. That means they belong to the United States Government. They don't belong to a couple of ragged rebels."

"Those horses were captured fair and square," Ben fired up. "They're ours."

"In my books, a rebel's got the right to six feet of dirt and that's all," the sergeant said. "Now I'd advise the pair of you to get out of here while you're still in shape to."

"We're thirty miles from home," Tom said evenly, holding his temper in check. "Are you going to ask a man with one leg to walk thirty miles?"

The sergeant spat at the toe of Tom's boot. "I wish it was sixty," he said. "This is the last time I'm telling you, Reb! Get out of here!"

Over Ben's protest, Tom urged him back to the barn where they had received their paroles. "You were the one who wanted to do it the legal way," he reminded Ben.

The major was still there, arranging his papers. "Yes?" he said testily. "I'm busy, so be brief."

"I intend to, Major. My friend and I were mounted when we surrendered. When we went to recover our horses just now, the sergeant refused to give them to us. I understood that we were extended the same terms as the men who surrendered with General Lee."

The major nodded. His ill fitting tunic bloused over his belt in front. He looked more like a country doctor than a soldier. "Were they your horses? Or horses stolen from the government?"

"They were horses we captured, Major."

"Son, I want to give you some advice. We're not as hard to get along with as you may think, but we don't like to

228

be told we're wrong. Maybe nobody does. Did anybody give you a receipt for those horses this morning?"

"No, sir. They said we wouldn't need one."

"All right," the major said. "Sergeant Neely? Go tell Sergeant Barton that I require two saddled horses in good condition—immediately. You will select them."

As the sergeant went off on his errand, the major turned back toward Tom and Ben. "I lost a boy at Chancellorsville," he said quietly. "I bear no love towards Rebels or ex-Rebels. But if there is ever to be a Union of all the states, it has to be based on a firm foundation that doesn't depend upon human emotions. Can either of you name it?"

"Charity?" Ben jeered.

"No, sir," the major said triumphantly. "And not faith or hope, either. Plain, simple justice, wisely administered and impartially dispensed. That's your only hope—and ours, as well."

CHAPTER 18

An End and a Beginning

THE houses of Lovatt shone dimly in the darkness. There were no lights, although it must still have been early. It was as if the town was waiting for something that lurked in the further corners of the night.

Here was Grandpa Hauser's house, here Will Kinyard had been shot. There was McNair's tavern. It was all the same, but somewhat out of focus, like a daguerreotype on which the subject had moved.

In the cemetery beyond Hunnicutt's timber yard Will and Sandy rested.

Past Ryan's now, and the dark road that led to Dorfer's branching off: How would he tell Sam's mother that he was dead, shot down in a stupid, unnecessary action? What good was valor when it could no longer be negotiated in terms of victory?

"Much further, Tom?"

"Half a mile, Ben; that's all."

Half a mile to the end of the journey. The end of the long and bitter road that led from Lovatt to Pennsylvania, to the outskirts of Washington, that twisted back on itself, that wound through two years and a lifetime besides. The names of obscure and never-to-be-forgotten places flashed in his brain like the muzzle blasts of a battery firing in darkness. Mine Run. Spotsylvania Courthouse. Cold Harbor. Winchester. Fisher's Hill.

Half a mile further.

230

The house came up out of the darkness like a fortress, solid and tangible. Although the shutters were barred, a faint light came through the slats that shielded Pa's office windows.

"We're home, Ben," he said gently.

He held himself steady with an effort as Ben dismounted. Home! The familiar hollows in the steps proclaimed it. The very odor of damp whitewash was familiar. He knocked on the door.

He could hear a quickly taken breath beyond the door and then Pa's voice, a cautious murmur. "Who's there?"

"It's me, Pa. Tom."

The door swung open. A sandy stubble covered Pa's face. He seemed smaller now: shrunken and tired and old.

"Thank God you're safe! Hurry; get inside!"

"I have a friend, Pa. And our horses."

"It's right pleasant to see you again, sir," Ben said.

Pa nodded hastily. "Come in, boys; come in. I'll see to your horses. But hurry!"

"It's all right, Pa. We surrendered today. The war's over."

"Surrendered?" Pa asked. "You mean you were captured and paroled, don't you?"

Suddenly he realized what it meant to Pa. In Pa's war you didn't quit. If there were a gun at your head, you might lay down your arms with honor. But you couldn't quit, because to Pa that meant that you had been wrong, and that you could never fight again.

It would be easy for him to lie about it, to tell Pa what he wanted to hear, but there had been too much lying already. "No, Pa," he said. "Ben and I surrendered and took the oath of allegiance."

Pa looked at him as if he had been a stranger. "You took an oath to the government that killed your brothers? You swore not to avenge their deaths?"

Anger grew in him, overcoming fatigue and the habits of a lifetime. "Are you saying this as a father teaching his son, Pa? Or as a doctor, sworn to preserve life?"

"I say it as a man of honor."

"There's no more war, Pa, and there's no more cause. I've killed two men that I know of, probably more. And I'm through with it. I've tried to be what you wanted, you and Mama and Sandy, but there's a limit to the amount of hate and anger that one man can have, and I've reached that limit. Once General Lee surrendered, the war was over. Any killing after that time was murder."

This was the end of something. It was like the day he had gone hunting with Sandy and killed the deer. It was like the day he had killed the bushwhacker; it was like the day he had discovered that his arm was gone. It was the death of a part of him. Time would go on and he would go on, but nothing would ever be quite the same again.

"If those are your sentiments," Pa said formally, "I suggest that you find a more congenial place to stay."

It had come as he had known all along it would, the time when he must once and for all decide what manner of man he would be, the point at which his decision would necessitate a break with everything he had known. But it was an easy decision to make.

He turned to Ben. "I'll be riding with you," he said.

When Tom and his friend had ridden off, the doctor walked out into the damp spring night. It was his custom to take a look around before retiring. Even old Brutus might be stolen, the way things were now. You didn't have to worry about the Yankees any more; they had plenty of horses. But the country was full of ex-soldiers trying to get home and all sorts of lawless people who didn't care from whom they stole. If anyone really wanted to break

232

into the stable, of course, the lock wouldn't stop him; but it pleased Doctor Tanner to go through the motions of protecting his property.

The kitchen door opened a wedge of yellow light in the gloom. "You out there, Doctor?" Betsy called anxiously.

"Yes, Betsy. I'll be in directly."

He walked in out of the night with conscious reluctance. It was good to smell the burgeoning odors of coming summer, to reaffirm the inevitability of the cycle of the seasons. It was also good to be away from the charged atmosphere of the house, where a careless word might bring on an outburst of tears or a dark, brooding stare and a lapse into that silent, spectral world to which Mary returned with increasing frequency.

"I thought I heard Mister Tom," Betsy said.

"He stopped by for a moment. He won't be coming back."

Betsy nodded. "I figured he wouldn't. Mister Tom's a man, now, and he's got his own life to make. Everybody's got to get one chance."

"I've just lost my last son, Betsy."

Betsy looked at him scornfully. "Mister Tom has lost everything you've lost, Doctor, and an arm besides. If he's lost his father, now, it wasn't his fault."

His anger at Tom evaporated as quickly as it had arisen. Of course Betsy was right. Tom had a right to make a decision, just as the rest of them had an obligation to respect that decision. Betsy had overheard the conversation; there was precious little that Betsy didn't know about.

"I reckon I didn't think about it when I was taking offense at the boy's surrender. You're right, Betsy."

Betsy smiled good-naturedly. "It's a big man who can say he's made a mistake."

If he went into their bedroom, Mary would waken. He didn't want to talk to her just now. He needed some time in which to think things out and decide what to do. He mounted the stairs and went into Will's room.

The ambrotype taken of Will just before the war was on the mantel; Mary's doing, he'd be bound. Here were Will's notebooks and writing stand upon the desk. It was a room that belonged not only to Will, but to his time as well, to the sentimental fifties with their extravagant valentines and their enviable innocence of the coming cataclysm that would destroy them. It was a room with a door that would be forever closed, no matter how many times you entered it. If Mary could find Will here, then the room served a purpose. To him it was only a room frozen in time, in which a beloved son had lived, but in which no one lived any more.

The doctor crossed the hall to Sandy's room, where Sandy's weapons glinted in the dim light of his candle. On the wall hung the white ensign of the Confederacy that had covered Sandy's coffin. In the upper left corner the star-studded St. Andrew's cross was a remote blue against the dull crimson field. He closed his eyes, and for a moment the war unfolded in his mind's eye. The pageantry and the colors came first, gray uniforms and scarlet guidons snapping in the breeze. And then the sounds returned, the slap-clap of poorly shod feet on the Pike, the clatter and jingle of horses and guns, the raucous voices: "We-all don't wear our Sunday clothes to go hog-killing . . . this here's fighting music, Mister! . . . close up, men."

And the music. Play the music on a dusty harp, Lorena; play the song that bears your name and play the one that mourns the vacant chair. Sing how quiet it is along the Potomac tonight.

Now let there be a brass band, a little out of tune; let them trumpet before the world the desirability of the

234

yellow rose of the sovereign state of Texas. Let them blare the great desire to be in the land of cotton. Let them skip along that lovely quickstep: We are a band of brothers . . .

He opened his eyes.

The music was gone, and the voices. The scarlet dulled again to a shadowy crimson splotch upon the wall, and the gleam of weapons was the candlelight on Sandy's saber and pistol.

The inevitable ambrotype of Sandy in uniform stared at him across the years. Forever young, forever beloved. The doctor would grow old, and Tom would grow old in his turn; but Sandy would be forever young, forever gallant. He was beyond the hand of any enemy; he was even beyond the hand of Time, the worst enemy of all.

Joseph Tanner turned away with unshed tears burning at his eyelids and closed the door gently behind him. It was time to go to Mary, now. In the morning he'd find Tom and make it right with him.

"I knew your Pa would take that stand last night," Grandpa Hauser said reflectively between mouthfuls of bacon and eggs. "He worked harder than any of us setting up the guerrilla recruiting center. He just can't seem to realize that the war is over."

They were sitting in Grandpa's kitchen. Mrs. Ryan had already gone back to her house across the road, and they were alone. The morning sun was streaming in the windows, and a willow branch in the wind made shadow-magic on the table.

"What are you going to do now?" Grandpa asked.

"First of all, I want to go down to Scottsburg and see Alison. We have plans to make. And then I'm riding on to Staunton. Ben and I are going into law as partners, as soon as we can."

"Where are you going to stay?"

"Probably at Ben's. We're going to read law under Judge Carter, if he'll have us. Ben rode on ahead after Pa chased us out. He's going to speak to the judge."

Grandpa Hauser nodded. "Sounds like a good idea, if you can manage to make a living while you're doing it. Have you thought of that?"

"Yes, sir. I don't know what it'll be, but I'll figure something out. I don't reckon anybody wants a cavalryman, just now, so it'll have to be clerking."

"I can help you out, Tom."

He smiled. "Mighty nice of you, sir. But I think I'll try it on my own, first."

Someone knocked on the front door. It was a hesitant sort of knock, as if the knocker were not quite sure what he was going to say if anyone answered.

"Pour some coffee, Tom. I'll go see who it is."

How many times he had poured coffee from a tin pot heated over an open fire! In all probability he would never again have coffee that way. That, too, was part of the past.

"Get out another cup," Grandpa said from the doorway. "We've got company."

Pa was standing beside Grandpa, looking a little sheepish. "I thought you'd be here, Tom," he said. "I wanted to apologize for last night."

"That's all right, Pa."

"Well, Joe," Grandpa said. "Sit down, will you? If you don't, I can't; and I'd like to get my coffee while it's hot."

"What changed your mind, sir?" Tom asked.

"It started with Betsy. She said you had a right to make up your own mind, and she told me I was wrong. And then I went up to Will's room and Sandy's. I got to thinking about how they died for the cause, and then I saw that their dying hadn't changed it a bit. The cause was lost anyway, and nothing you could do would make any difference. There's nothing left for us, now."

"Stuff and nonsense, Joe," Grandpa said. "There's as

much of a future for us as there ever was. All we have to do is go out and fight for it. Tom's going to read law and go partners with his friend. He's not quitting. Not by a jugful!"

"Now, Andrew. What is there for a poor boy with one arm and no money?"

Tom put down his cup. It was the old story, in a way. He was being compared with Sandy and found wanting. It was time to set the record straight.

"What's left for me, Pa? The rest of my life and a chance to make the most of it. Ever since I can remember, you and Mama wanted me to be like Sandy. He was everything a man could want his son to be, I reckon. Good looking, well mannered, brave—and to top that, he was a real hero. But a long time ago when I went hunting with Sandy, I wondered just what would happen to him when the war was over. He wasn't suited for anything but being an artillery officer. Not any more. And what was worse, he didn't even want to be anything else."

Grandpa winked at him across the table.

"When I went in the army, I went because it was a part of what a man had to do. But I never figured it as anything more than a means to an end. The end of the war hasn't changed the fact that I have to make a living. I fought for something I believe in, and that's the right of a man to make up his own mind about things. I'm still going to fight for that. But not with a gun."

"Sandy was a brave man," Pa said slowly. "But you might be right about him, at that."

"I reckon I was tired of being measured up against him. He was a better man in a lot of ways than I'll ever be, but I'm tired of being compared with him every time I turn around. I'm tired of living in the past, too. We may have lost the war, but there's still a future for us, if we have the guts to build it."

Grandpa went over to the stove and lit his pipe with a

237

pine splinter. "There's two sides to almost everything, Joe," he said. "You remember how the newspapers always said Sandy did something or other and showed valor? Well, he did. He wasn't afraid of anything, or, if he was, he didn't let on that he was. When it came to war and fighting, he was the first one every time. But it doesn't go far enough."

Pa looked up with an expression of uncertainty. "What do you mean by that?"

"Well, Joe. Sandy had the kind of valor most of us can see. I can see him fighting to the last cartridge, dying before he'd quit, just so long as he could take some of the enemy with him. But it takes a special kind of courage not to kill any more. You see, the second face of valor is hope. It's hope that there's going to be a future to live for, and it's the courage to live. A lot of people have the courge to die, but you'd be surprised at how much more courage it takes to live. That's the kind we're going to need from now on."

"I don't know if I qualify," Pa said. "It seems as if everything I had is gone."

Grandpa snorted. "Stuff. You've got a son who's a fighter. You've got Mary. And you're not an old man. You've got a future, if you want to have it."

"My country is dead," Pa said quietly.

Tom broke in. "It's not dead, Pa. It's right where it always was. It's the whole Confederacy and the Union rolled into one."

"You mean you'd deal with Yankees? With the people who killed your brothers?"

"Pa, when we surrendered yesterday, we took the oath from a major whose son was killed by our people. He said that the only hope for us or them was to learn to live together, and he said that the only thing that could make it work was justice. Plain and simple justice. The protection of everybody's rights. If the major can overlook his

238

son, I reckon I can overlook my brothers, if that's what it takes."

Pa stood up. "I don't agree with you, Tom. But you've got a right to your own opinion. I didn't see that last night, but I've learned a little since then. You come on home when you want."

"Thank you, sir."

Pa managed the wraith of a smile. "Like your grandpa says, I've got a son who's a fighter. I'd be a pretty big fool if I couldn't be proud of him."

When Pa had gone, Grandpa went over to the parlor door. "It's time to wind Amy's clock. It's been going pretty well since the surrender. I wouldn't wonder if the peace doesn't agree with it, too."

"I have a hunch the peace is going to agree with a lot of us, Grandpa."

Grandpa turned to him. "Speaking of peace, what are you doing around here? If I were an ex-soldier in your boots, I'd be halfway to Scottsburg by this time."

He grinned. "That's a fine idea, sir. I reckon I'll act on it."

Grandpa held out his hand. "God bless you, boy. And give my love to Anne and to Alison."

He released Grandpa's hand, and then he remembered something. He unbuckled the pistol belt he and Ben had retrieved after their pardon and handed it to Grandpa. "You keep this, sir. I won't need it."

A faded hat, a ragged butternut jacket, and boots with holes in them weren't the ideal costume in which to call on one's intended, Tom reflected. Still, there was nothing else he could have worn without alteration, and he had had no time. He had stopped briefly at the house to see Mama, and she had offered to find something for him; but he didn't want to wait.

He rode the gelding the Yankees had given him at an

239

easy canter up the Pike, across the Centre Creek bridge, and then up the road towards Staunton. It was a different road this morning; the sun was shining, and everything was clean and newly washed from the rain yesterday. He held his head up to smell the fresh odors of spring, and he listened to the sound of the larks in the meadows alongside the road.

There was something different about this morning, and it took him a while to realize just what it was. It was the first time he had ridden along the Pike in over four years without having to worry about whom he might meet. There was no carbine strapped to his saddle; there was no pistol girded around his waist. In their place was a piece of paper in his breast pocket stating that he had been granted a pardon for his part in the rebellion and that he was entitled to the rights of a free man, so long as he did not bear arms against his country.

That was what it really meant: he was free. He was free of the necessity of killing, of hiding and running to keep from being killed.

The road to Scottsburg branched off into a tunnel of overhanging branches. It was cool and shady, and the sunlight filtered through the leaves in a haze of gold and green. How long had it been since he had ridden this road with Alison and Aunt Anne? The gelding's hooves echoed in the deceptive twilight of the lane, just as Brutus' hooves had echoed in that past time.

In a curious way, the land brought back the past. It reflected the ride with Alison and Aunt Anne, and it also reflected the ride back home that day when he had driven Mama from her visit and he had first known that he loved Alison. And when they reached home, they had found the strange, tortured Jonathan Marle waiting to tell them of Sandy's death.

He had ridden down the lane with Hodges just after the

240

battery had reached Staunton on its way down the Valley to join the rest of the second corps, and he had asked Aunt Anne's permission to marry Alison.

The next time he had ridden down this lane, the second corps had been all but wiped out and the battery with it. And he had been in the buggy, holding the stump of his left arm to try to quiet the throbbing.

The lane had marked the ends and the beginnings of the important parts of his life, just as Grandpa Hauser's gilt clock measured spaces in eternity with its soft chime. It had marked the end of innocence and the beginning of manhood for him, as surely as if it had had signposts announcing the fact.

For innocence had gone from him. He had fought in a war, and he had killed men like himself, men who had believed in their country as fervently as he had believed in his, with one exception. He would remember the war and the killing for the rest of his life. Perhaps that was the price he had to pay for the loss of innocence.

Ahead of him, the shadows broke apart as the trees thinned. He was riding into Scottsburg now, and the sun was gilding the edges of the leaves. In a sense, leaving the road to enter the town was like leaving the savagery and the gloom of the war for the warmth and brightness and civilization that peace might hold. Would he bring some of that gloom with him?

To a great extent, that would depend upon him. If he brooded about what he had done, it would doubtless appease his conscience, but at the expense of everyone else. If he put it behind him and concentrated upon the task of being a man of peace, he might in some way atone for the lives that he had expended.

A good man can do evil through necessity, he thought, but that need not make him evil unless he wills it so. I may not be guiltless, but I'm not a criminal. I did what I

241

had to do when the time came to do it, but it's over now. I'll never have to do it again.

He reined in the gelding at the house and dismounted and hitched the reins to the iron post. The front door was open to the breeze and he knocked on the post. There was no answer, but he could hear Alison singing, somewhere in the rear of the house.

He went into the hallway and looked in the parlor. The sun was tinting the books with a spurious gilt. It was the sort of room that one would want to share with books and with the one who mattered most to you. It was the room he had wanted to come home to all along.

He turned around. Alison was standing in the doorway smiling, and he knew that he was home at last.

Author's Note

The villages of Scottsburg and Lovatt and their inhabitants are imaginary, and are intended to bear no resem-
blance to any places past or present, or to any persons
living or dead.

While the battery to which Sandy and Tom Tanner
belonged is fictitious, its actions generally conform to
actual operations performed by the artillery attached to
Lieutenant General Early's Second Corps. Marle's guerrilla band is likewise fictitious, but its movements are not
intended to create an exaggerated view of the Valley Campaign of 1864-65. The operations of guerrilla units and
Federal cavalry during this period are a matter of record,
and the record is a bloody one.

All references to "the Valley" or to "the Valley of
Virginia" are understood to mean the Shenandoah Valley,
since the terms were used interchangeably. Since the
Valley's lower end is to the North, "up the Valley" indicates a southerly direction, while "down the Valley"
indicates a northerly one.

Sources

DeForest, John W. *Volunteer's Adventures.* New Haven, 1946.

Freeman, Douglas Southall. *R. E. Lee.* 4 vols. New York, 1934.

——. *Lee's Lieutenants.* 3 vols. New York, 1944.

Henderson, Col. G. F. R. *Stonewall Jackson and the American Civil War.* New York, 1949.

Miller, Francis Trevelyan, editor-in-chief. *The Photographic History of the Civil War.* 10 vols. New York, 1912.

Wiley, Bell Irvin. *They Who Fought Here.* New York, 1959.

Wise, Jennings C. *The Long Arm of Lee.* 2 vols. Lynchburg, Va., 1915.

RAY GRANT TOEPFER

Born in Hays, Kansas, Ray Grant Toepfer attended the University of Wisconsin where he received a Master's Degree in English Literature in 1943.

The Army then took the prospective author far from his Midwest origins. For a year he served in Greenland as librarian and as editor of the base newspaper.

Upon his discharge from the Army, Mr. Toepfer worked as an advertising copywriter and encyclopedia editor before enrolling, in 1963, in the Ph.D. program of the City University of New York, Hunter College. He is currently working on his doctorate, teaching English and creative writing at Brooklyn College.

Mr. Toepfer's previous work, *The White Cockade*, was based upon events in New York State during the American Revolution. *The Scarlet Guidon*, the author's first novel, was described by *The Library Journal* as "a vivid and readable portrayal of the War on the Southern side." *The Second Face of Valor* is in the same fine tradition.